Calm Sparkle

Deluxe Edition

KIMBERLY D.L. PITTMAN

Copyright © 2017 Kimberly D.L. Pittman

All rights reserved.

ISBN: **9781549529702**
ISBN-13: 978-1549529702

This is a work of fiction. Names, characters, businesses, places, events and incidents are either the products of the author's imagination or used in a fictitious manner. Any resemblance to actual persons, living or dead, or actual events is purely coincidental.

Calm Sparkle Deluxe Edition is dedicated to my besties. We have certainly had our share of novel-worthy adventures—stories that I will take with me to the grave! We have been thick as thieves since the Stone Age, and you ladies continually inspire, encourage and love me unconditionally.

Thank you Reva Goffigan, Katrina Perry, Melissa (Missy) Smith, Shinetta Robinson (Becky w/the good hair), Cherieta Early, Toosdai Gipson, Melva Jones-Singleton, and my very first BFF, Angelica Garland-Stevens.
BFFs4LIFE

Contents

	Acknowledgments	i
	Prelude	1
1	Price Check on the Act Right Juice	3
2	By Any Means Necessary	15
3	Death by Ringtone	27
4	Hypocritic Oath	56
5	Timing is Everything	68
6	Real Eyes Realize Real Lies	95
7	When the Funk Hits the Fan	132
8	Siri, Call Mom	148
9	Sunset Wishes	174
10	Better to Have Loved	198

Acknowledgements

The greatest love to my parents, Clarence and Mackie Pittman; my siblings, KDLP II and MCP IV; my sons Kendrick Anthony and Michael Alekzander. Sparkly blue blood runs forever.

A special thank you to my friends who continually inspire me: Pamela Morris-Bolden & Lynett Bowens.

May this book be a source of escape, entertainment and encouragement for women everywhere—in Jesus' name. Amen.

Prelude

    I have got to figure out my life. I can't even remember the last time I've been truly happy. The best I can recall would have been about six years ago right after I accepted Christ and "got saved," as my grandmother would call it. Of course, since then I've fallen into the rut of working on the weekdays, sleeping in on Saturdays and being plain lazy and staying home on Sundays. My excuse for no longer going to church was that I needed to mentally prepare myself for Mondays. I may sound like a self-proclaimed heathen right now, but there actually was a time when I would genuinely enjoy going to church. My praise time was all the high I needed. Spending quality time with God was my primary focus and it gave me such a rush—connecting with the Holy Spirit and feeling that love in the core of my being. The peace and comfort I felt while in my war closet was a far cry from the misery and confusion that surrounded me once I said "amen," opened my eyes, and left His presence. The real world was an emotional battlefield.

I can still remember the day I got "saved." I was ecstatic because I'd never felt such love and joy. Anyone who has truly experienced the love of God fill them from the inside out can understand the inexplicable feeling. Arnold, however, was not pleased, and I would dare to say even disgusted at my newfound spirituality. "What does this mean for us?" was his response when I came home bursting through the door excitedly blurting out my good news of receiving the Lord. I didn't care. I kept smiling and feeling the lingering warmth the spirit left with me.

Arnold continued to express his disdain, saying, "Don't think I'm going to change just because you decided to get all saved and shit." He grabbed his keys and cigarettes and headed out the door. I didn't bother to ask where he was going. You would think that moment would have been a breaking point for us, but as any good Christian knows, you have to pray for the unsaved and the unequally yoked. You have to shower them with the love that God bestows upon us. I was a newbie, so I had to at least try. I should—you know—fix him. Besides, the bible says the only way out of marriage is adultery, and while he is far from innocent, I didn't have any concrete proof at that point.

So, how's it working out for me? Well, here we are, six years later, and I'm sitting here talking about this rut called my life. In other words, our marriage has been downhill ever since. Not that it was a picnic to begin with.

Chapter One
Price Check on the Act Right Juice

I think I have finally arrived at that pivotal point in time that R. Kelly used to sing about, "When a woman's fed up, there ain't nothing you can do about it." The funny thing is—now that I'm at this point, Arnold has finally converted himself into the husband that I used to pray for—the man that I used to beg him to become. Now that I, literally and figuratively "frankly, my dear, don't give a damn" about what or whom he does, or when or where he goes, he stopped going and doing. Go figure. No more hanging out with his friends every weekend, he's cut down on drinking, and he even decreased his weed intake. Then, to top it all off, he has even started to spend more quality time with Andre, our son. I guess the joke's on me, huh, Lord?

Yup, for the past six months, Arnold has been on pretty good behavior. So, what's the problem? The problem is that even though the last six months have been consistent and smooth, I ran out of love for that husband of mine about a year and two chicks ago. Before his miraculous turn around, Arnold spent his weekends on the party scene as if he didn't have a wife and child at home. And so, on weekends we argued. That was back when I cared. I remember, during one of our episodes, I was in tears when he came strolling in at 6 a.m. supposedly after partying with his boys—only this time my crying eyes held tears of anger instead of heartache. I told him that I was starting to go numb and explained to him that each time he hurt me, it chipped away at the love I had for him and that eventually there would be nothing left.

In his drunken haze, he just kissed me on the cheek, climbed into bed and passed out. Such was the case on many occasions before and after that incident. Since that time, there have been many more drama-filled arguments with various starring and supporting actors. All with mostly me doing the arguing and him doing the passing out. Now, at this point in life, I no longer care. So much dirt has been done that I am just numb. Each late night and each argument over the eight-year marriage has taken its toll. The love slowly dissolved until there was nothing left. I'm operating on auto-pilot just to keep my son in a two-parent home and to keep the church mothers from dousing me with olive oil and bottled water—praying for me to stay until God saw fit to save the man.

Eventually, my prediction came to fruition. Today there is nothing left in my heart for our relationship. Where a night out until 3 a.m. would make me angry and feel disrespected, now I couldn't care less if he even came home at all. I am tired. I'm tired of arguing. Tired of explaining why I pay tithes, or why, as the church secretary, I am the one that has to answer the pastor's mail. Oy vey (and I'm not even Jewish)! Life was much better in our household when I stopped caring. I was able to enjoy reading novels on quiet nights after Andre went to sleep. Arnold and I had really good conversations when we did see each other. There was no more arguing, no more tears. It was all a peaceful existence, predictable routines and G rated family outings. I thought I was happy. What more could I ask?

Well, there was one thing that I could ask for. No more sex! What was the point? It was just an added chore—nothing enjoyable about it. I think my vagina checked out of the relationship long before my heart did. Other than having to muster up tolerance for sex a few times each week, our plateau was good. I thought this was the norm for all couples. You get married, have a family, the end. Right? That was my perception until a life-altering conversation with my cousin. She helped me realize the cold, hard truth. She inadvertently helped me come to the realization that I am actually supposed to want to be with my husband. Sexually. I know! I know! Hard to believe, isn't it?

It became crystal clear to me that I was obviously missing this important lesson from marriage 101 when I revealed to her a routine that I had been following for years. I actually prayed to God to make me wet so that sex with Arnold would be bearable. I never thought of it as out of ordinary. I thought everyone did it, until I shared this tidbit of news with Katherine—we call her Kat for short. She looked at me in disbelief when I casually mentioned that I need to make sure that I pray tonight for moistness so that we could have a peaceful week since he constantly complained about our sex life, or lack thereof.

"How do you PRAY for something like that?" she asked, almost choking on her blueberry muffin. We were in my kitchen having snacks and hot tea while Arnold took Andre to basketball practice one Saturday morning.

"Easy. I just very humbly say, 'Lord, thank you for giving me a husband who desires me. Please fill my loins with the desire for him as well. Please make me moist--.'"

A very loud snort, followed by a series of coughs, interrupted my sample prayer. Kat was on her knees in hysterical laughter with tears and all.

"What?" I asked innocently. I was dead serious. That really was my prayer and I didn't see the humor in it.

"Girl! Please do NOT tell anyone else on planet earth that you send that prayer up to heaven every time your man wants to do the deed." She laughed even harder before finally calming down.

That's when the lightbulb appeared. *Ting!* Is it possible that I might not be in love with my husband? From that point on, I started to pay attention to other couples, not just on the television, but in real life. The couples that I observed seemed to actually enjoy each other. They even appeared to *want* to kiss each other and hold hands. I, on the other hand, could not stand kissing my husband because his kisses were wet and sloppy. His hands are always dirty and greasy from working on cars all day as the owner of a mechanic shop. They always smelled like oil and gas no matter how often he scrubbed them. Needless to say, I don't find handholding to be an enjoyable experience either. It could very well be the years of arguing and settling that added to my severe case of physical unattraction to the man that other women seemed to find irresistible, so don't take my word for it.

After my conversation with Kat, I began to wonder if other wives looked forward to sex with their spouse or did they dread it as much as I did? I would often read about women having lustful urges for men, but I always chalked it up to some fantasy editing that was done by a male publisher. The way I see it, there is no way the heroine of a romance novel could really "ache for the throbbing manhood" of some male character.

My state of mind at the time was if I never had sex again, I'd be the happiest woman on Earth. As hard as it may be to believe, I was at a place of contentment in my life. I believed that I didn't need the romance or the passion, let alone the sex. I was at peace coasting along and doing my day-to-day routines. Don't worry, I still made sure to give in to Arnold at least twice a week to help minimize the drama factor.

My way of thinking, coping, and living worked for us. Well, at least it worked for me. Things were smooth until, let me pause here for a sweet sigh of remembrance—deep sigh—until I ran into Alex's mom a few months ago.

Alex is an ex-boyfriend from college. We met in our

freshman year but we were both still attached to significant others back home. We hit it off immediately after learning that we were from the same hometown. We were blown away by the fact that we attended rival schools and were at the same games, but never ran into each other. We even had mutual friends and hung out at the same spots. By midterms, we decided that we were fated to be together and officially cheated on our high school sweeties with each other.

By the end of summer, we both knew that it was time to break up with the high school sweeties and jump into an official side-chick-guy turned main-chick-guy relationship. We dated throughout Sophomore and Junior years, but as the old saying goes, "how you get him is how you lose him."

Senior status, along with becoming the starting quarterback of our school's football team, brought out the groupies. How could any young man resist? He enjoyed the attention and felt it was his duty to please his "fans." He was heavily courted by NFL scouts, and even hired an attorney to help with the offers. Unfortunately, a bad hit followed by an intense pile up during a blindsiding sack ended his football career at our homecoming game. He left school and returned home. He never returned my calls, texts or emails and completely shut me out. His mom, however, kept me posted on his progress and how he was doing, but eventually we lost touch. When I saw Mrs. Weston at a local book store, all of the memories and emotions came flooding back. She immediately came over to me and gave me her infamous "mama, I can't breathe" hug.

"Sparkle! It's sooooooo good to see you! How are you, Dear?" she said, giving me an extra squeeze. I really could not breathe. If she added in a few more "o's" on that "so," I would have been smothered to death.

"Oh wow! Mrs. Weston, I can't believe it's you!" We released our embrace and I could reward my lungs with much needed air, and to thank them for not collapsing under the pressure of Ms. Weston's love. Finally able to get a good look at her, it appeared that she has not aged, with the exception of a tiny pair of crow's feet at the crinkle of her eyes, and her hair was now a lovely salt and pepper mix thanks to the sparkle of gray marrying her off-black strands. She wore it in long, neatly kept locks that were up in a bun and held together with chopsticks. Yes, chopsticks.

She was always fashionably eccentric, and this day was no exception as she sported gypsy attire—a white, pirate-style blouse with puffy, loose sleeves, a long, pleated and wrinkled red skirt, and a belly dancer's turquoise scarf complete with bells tied around her waist. Her accessories of both silver and gold included necklaces of various lengths, bangles and chandelier earrings. I know it sounds like a crazy mix, but she wore it beautifully, and the sight of this pudgy, old lady with the dimples and caramel skin was a sight for sore eyes.

We walked over to the reading couches and took a seat to play catch up. She wasted no time telling me all about Alex and how he was doing. She was very proud of her only son who served as a pilot in the Air Force, and who now owns fleet of luxury private jets. I learned that he is married with a beautiful blended family of three children. She also suggested that I check out his website if I ever needed to charter a private flight. (Wink, wink.)

Just the mere mention of Alex's name sent my heart into a rapid-fire pitter patter. It was at that moment that I wanted to break down and cry; it was when I finally realized that I wasn't numb after all. I could still feel things that a woman should feel. It was amazing to feel that irregular heartbeat and the butterflies in my belly. In that brief moment, I actually felt alive. I wanted to tell Mrs. Weston what an impact she'd made and how she's just reminded me that I haven't been living at all these past years. I've merely been existing.

Since that chance meeting with Mrs. Weston, I checked out his website. There were no pictures of Alex, and no personal tidbits, but being on the site made me feel that much closer to him. I began visiting the website daily—just to get a dose of excitement and to feel alive again. Each day, I would look at the contact information. Once, I even picked up the phone and dialed 9 of the 10 numbers to his office, and then chickened out and hung up.

This went on for about a month. One day, while doing lunch with an old classmate, she mentioned that Corey, a fellow alum who just happens to be Alex's best friend, was having a cookout the next day. When she invited me to come along, I couldn't resist.

The morning of the cookout, I went straight to the salon for an emergency hook up and then to the mall for a pair jeans—and not "mommy jeans." I had plenty of those, and I wanted MILF jeans. I knew Alex wouldn't be there, but Corey would be sure to give him the report on my appearance. I had to represent! For the actual event, I settled on a classic look of a white embellished tank top to show off my cleavage, a fitted, black blazer to protect against our cool island night breeze and to not appear that I wanted to show off my cleavage, my new, dark washed jeans, and black, open-toed stilettos. I was going for less "mommy mode" and more inner-Kardashian.

My off-black hair had light brown highlights and was usually pulled back into a ponytail or in a bun, but that night I decided to let my layered wrap fall, and it reached right below my shoulders—all natural, but straight and bouncy thanks to my blow out. After squeezing into my girdle, I was ready. Unfortunately, the girdle was a necessity and not an option thanks to an emergency vertical cesarean. The unplanned incision that formed from the belly button to the pubic hairline completely obliterated my stomach muscles, which are now non-existent. So, although I am "sistah-fine" at 5'6," and wear a size 12 for a loose fit (or a size 10 for the painted-on look), thanks to stretch marks and surgical scarring, my bare belly looks like a Rand McNally rough draft, centerfold crease included. Trust me, it leaves much to be desired.

I called my friend for directions, and she insisted on picking me up and driving. I insisted that she not. I have a rule. If I know you, but don't know you - know you, then I drive my own ride so I don't get stuck somewhere trying to figure out how I'm going to get home. Besides, in high school she was known for hooking up with the fellas, and I was not trying to get stuck sitting on the porch waiting for her to finish getting her freak on. She finally gave up the directions and we arrived at Corey's at the same time. Once there, I saw a lot of old classmates. It was like a high school reunion, but more fun. Corey immediately zoomed in on me,

"Oh my stars! Sparkle, is that you!!?"

I guess by now you've figured out that my name is Sparkle. Weird, I know! My mom is a huge fan of the seventies flick and she named me after Irene Cara's character. You would think the name would fit being a PK, a preacher's kid, and all, but unfortunately, growing up, I was more like Lonette McKee's character, Sister. Don't tell my mom. Back to my story, Corey came over and gave me a hug.

"COREY! How nice to see you!" I shrieked in response being genuinely happy to see my old friend.

"Girl, when did you get back in town?"

"Oh, I've been back about 6 months now."

"Boy, look-a-here. I can't believe I'm seeing you, man! How long has been it been?" He stepped back, giving me the once over with his eyes while a toothpick hung loosely from the left side of his mouth.

"Oh, about 15 years or so," I answered, shuddering at the thought of just how long it really had been.

"Well, come on let me show you around my humble abode!" He grabbed me by my hand and guided me through the crowd to meet various co-workers, neighbors and his fiancé' before reaching the kitchen where there was a restaurant style buffet. This is where he dropped me off and instructed me to fix a plate.

I hung out in the kitchen for the rest of the night as this seemed to be the revolving door and the best seat in the house to see everyone. I filled in on a game of spades, but my partner was lousy. She couldn't even shuffle a deck of cards, let alone tell the big joker from the little joker to save her life. After about an hour I'd had enough. That was all the time I needed to set my trap.

I made my entrance, played catch-up with everyone, and I had gotten the once over that would be reported to Alex, so I was ready to go. My friend that I'd come to the party with had cozied up with her old high school flame who just so happened to be going through a nasty divorce. She was more than happy to be his shoulder to cry on. I went over to tell her that I was leaving, all while thanking my blessed stars that I stuck to my rule about driving my own car so that I didn't get stuck anywhere.

Working my way out to my car, which was parked about three houses down due to the crowd the party had drawn, Corey yelled out and stopped me. Doing a light jog, he quickly caught up to me.

"Hey, hold up, Sparkle. Let me walk you to your car." Once we made it to my driver's side door, he whipped out his cell phone. My heart stops at the mere thought that he was about to call Alex.

"Hey, what's your number? I can't let an old friend get away and not be able to keep in touch." He grinned.

"Oh!" I said, half relieved and half disappointed that he was not calling Alex after all. I rattled off my number and he plugged it into his cell.

"Alright, man. It was good seeing you. Don't be a stranger." He hugged me again. Then his phone rang.

I laughed, "Your girl is telling you to get your butt back in there to help her entertain your peeps."

He smiled, put the phone to his ear, and said, "What's up man?" There was a pause while a grin stretch across his face. "Yeah, she still here." He handed me the phone. I knew who it was without having to ask. The smug look on Corey's face let me know that it was his plan all along.

"Hello," I said in the sexiest, but innocent, voice I could muster—a delicate balance between Beyonce' and Michele Le. That was always my niche with Alex. I was his sexy kitten, innocent in the day and a tigress at night.

"Hey, you. Long time no see." His voice was like Crown Royal on ice—heavy, smooth and intoxicating. My knees became weak, my heartbeat sped up and my hands started to tremble. Yes, all of this from a simple "hello."

This was another clue for me that life as I had known it with my husband was not living, and there was no way on God's green earth that I could go back to just settling for the norm. I looked up at Corey to see if he could tell that I was about to lose all composure. His snicker and the shaking of his head as he walked away, told me that he could. Ok, Sparkle, get a grip! It's just a freaking phone call!

"Well, hey yourself, Mr. Weston! How are you?" I managed to sound like I was chatting with an old friend that I'd just seen a couple of days before. I bit my bottom lip, trying to control my breathing, and wondered if he was as nervous as I was.

"I'm doing pretty good. It's nice to hear your voice. How's life treating you?"

I wanted to say that life was treating me well, but it was my husband that I couldn't stand. I didn't want to drag him into my drama. "That's a loaded question. How's yours?" was my response instead.

He laughed. Man, I missed that laugh. Have you ever known someone that knew how to enjoy life and didn't care what other people thought? You could tell by their laugh. It was loud and joyful and unapologetic. It was free, and made you want to chime in and laugh with him. That was the laugh of Alex Weston. And he only released it when something truly tickled his funny bone, which made it not only unapologetic, but genuine as well.

"A loaded question, huh? Well maybe one of these days we can sit down and talk about it. As for mine, I can't complain. Things are hectic, but you know me. I like to keep busy, so it's all good."

I was spellbound by hearing his voice again; there was nothing else in the world that mattered to me at that moment than what was being said between the two of us—two past lovers who had drifted away from each other. Alex was the only man that I felt free to be myself around. Even after all these years. Underneath the initial nervousness of hearing his voice again, there was a familiar comfort and security. My breathing returned to normal.

"Alex?" I said gingerly as I wrestled with whether to ask my next question while fighting back tears of joy for hearing his voice again, the pain of possibly not having him again, and the fear of losing him again, I decided to ask him. No more existing; it was time to live.

"Yeah, Sweetie?"

"What happened to us?" A single, defiant tear slid down my cheek. I inhaled deeply and held it as I awaited his response. Although I knew the answer, I just had to hear him say it.

"Life, baby. Life happened." He paused. "Shit happens. Life happens," he spoke in a whisper, "and love happens."

My heart shattered into a million pieces all over again. I'm sure he's referring to his love for his wife and he probably thinks that I love my husband. We were both silent—lost in memories. He finally broke the silence.

"I'm coming to see you. I don't know when yet, but I'm going to work something out. How can I reach you?" We exchanged contact information, and before hanging up he said my two favorite words. "Miss you."

My heart leapt and I allowed the tears to fall freely. With each tear, I shed the old Sparkle that had emerged through last 11 years of drama and heartache, and rebirthed the Sparkle that I had lost touch with over a decade ago—

the confident Sparkle who knew what she wanted and how to get it, the Sparkle who loved herself and cared about making a difference in the world. Alex didn't know it, but he had just awakened me emotionally, intellectually and, of course, sexually. I felt revived. I felt—wanted. And that was a very empowering feeling. Look out world! Sparkle is back!

I wiped away any trace of tears and sashayed—yes, sashayed—back into Corey's to give him his phone. I found him at the dominoes table and handed it to him. He looked up at me and grinned ear to ear. "So, when's my boy coming to town?" he asked.

"Corey, please! What makes you think he's coming back to Moonbow?"

"Because, I know him. And I know if anybody can get him to come back home it's you. So, I'll ask again, when is he coming?"

I blushed but didn't give him an answer. "Good night, Corey! And happy birthday!" I gave him a hug and a kiss on the cheek, and walked away.

I heard him yell behind me, "You're welcome!"

"Thank youuuu!" I answered and continued towards my car. On the way home, I played the conversation over and over in my mind. I was cheesing like a schoolgirl before I quickly got a dose of reality as I turned into my driveway and was reminded that I was a wife with a kid.

Chapter Two

By Any Means Necessary

Lisa

Hmmm. In the words of Keith Sweat, "something, something…just ain't right." My husband of 3 years has been taking an awful lot of trips to his hometown to see his mother recently. Why does that raise a red flag? Because in the three years we've been married, I can count on one hand the number of times we've been to Moonbow, Florida. It's only a 2 and half hour drive from us, so there's really no excuse. But lately, he's been making the road trip at least once a month. What's up with that? My Spidey senses are tingling and I'm trying not go all out Inspector Gadget on his ass. This is precisely why I need to get my butt out of the house and meet up with my girl.

"Yes, Huntee! It's girls' day out!" I squeal as I hug my best friend, Dorinda. "It's been a long time, girlie! What is going on out there in the land of single ho's?" I asked jokingly as she joined me at the table. It was what used to be our bi-weekly hang out spot at a local coffee shop. Sadly, I've had to cancel on her the past couple of times while trying to be a good wifey and all. It was a hard adjustment to being a mom again and to married life.

"Girrrl, I can't believe Alex let you out the house!" Dori

taunted. I had to quickly remind her that I am a grown ass woman and nobody *lets* me do anything. "Mmm-hmm," was her only response. "So how is married life treating you?"

An ear to ear grin spread across my face, "Faaabuuulousss!" I sang. "Look at my 3-year anniversary gift." I stuck out my right arm and swirled my wrists around to show her my new, 5-carat tennis bracelet.

"Gorgeous!" she gasps.

We continue our afternoon meal, cocktails and gossip—getting caught up on the 411 of who drop-kicked who, who's doing who, and who's been added to the DL listing. I couldn't believe the dirt that I had missed by not meeting up with by BFF.

"Dori, girl, that damn single life. I don't miss it in the least little bit! But when Alex goes to Moonbow next week, let's get together and hit that new jazz spot just to see if I still have what it takes," I said with a wink.

Dori stopped laughing. "Alex is going to his momma's house *again*? Didn't he just go a couple of weeks ago? Girl, you better check that!"

"Check what? What's wrong with a man going to see his momma? That's sweet! I want my boys to come see me when I get old!"

"Whatever, Lisa. I know the man took your heart, but did he take your brain too? He's been up there three times in just as many months, and all without *you*. All I'm saying is, you may want to go with him to visit his momma and see what's really going on."

"Please! I'm not going to no country ass Moonbow, Florida. Home of dirt roads and plantation tours. No, thank you. You know how bored I am when I go. His momma is nice and all, but I know she's still disappointed that he married me. Alex Jr. seems to make her happy enough, but before that—."

"I know, I know!" Dori interrupted, throwing her right-testifying-hand up. "Girl, I've heard the drama all before, and I know the story by heart. But that's exactly what your fast tail get for seducing that woman's baby boy, and then running off to the courthouse to get married—knowing full well that your man's mother is a professional wedding coordinator. Hell, she lives for that kind of shit and you snatched him right from under her feet when she was looking the other way. And he's an only child. You evil bitch!" We both laughed. Dori was right on the money with that one.

"And you know the fact that I'm 10 years his senior didn't help matters."

"You cougar!" Dori lashed out.

We laughed some more and slapped high fives before I responded with "Girl, that man was just too foine to let go!" I'm sure we looked like a pair of hyenas but I was with my girl, and we were having a blast.

When we finally calmed down from a fit of laughter, hysteria, and random mocking of my mother-in-law, Dori circled back around to the topic at hand. "Well, Lisa, you're not the only one that may be thinking he's fine cause something back in his hometown has his attention, and if I were you, I'd find out, not what, but *who*."

"Girl, stop tripping. I've got that good-good and I put it on him almost every night. So, even if there was another someone, she gets nothing. And you know I track the finances. There isn't any money that's not accounted for."

"Mmm hmph! What about the cellie?" Dori asked as she took a bite of her honey-BBQ chicken wing.

"What about it? You know I don't go through his cell. I'm too old for that shit. If he's gonna cheat, he's gonna cheat. But believe you me, he ain't cheatin'." Dori could tell I was getting agitated and left that subject alone.

We switched to talking about old office gossip and her latest beau, but I only half-listened. Could Dorinda be right? Was I so confident that I fell off my game? I decided right then and there to go home and put it on him double time—just in case.

Before picking up the baby from daycare, I went home to get things ready for the night. As I walked through the den, I stopped to admire the family portrait we had taken the month prior. I hadn't had time to get it custom-framed so it sat on the couch waiting to be admired. There we were—the five of us. Alex and myself smiling our Colgate smiles, and Junior sleeping comfortably in my arms as I sat in a throne-like chair. Marvin, my 23-year-old son from a previous relationship, and Nicole, Alex's twelve-year-old daughter from his last long-term girlfriend. My perfect little blended family.

I reflected on my conversation with Dori. Hmmmm. I thought Junior would be enough to keep Alex's mind on me for a while, but obviously, I'd better do some investigating into these "momma trips."

I remember when Alex and I first met. We were at happy hour at a local sports bar one Friday after work. He was with his boys and I was with my girls. He immediately caught my attention the moment he walked in the door—tall, brown and handsome. I wanted to lick the chocolate off him right then and there. He strutted in dressed in a custom-fitted, black Armani suit, crisp white shirt with the top five buttons undone. His tie hung loosely around his neck and his Dolce shades were tucked into his shirt pocket.

He strolled in and greeted his friends. My supersonic hearing (you may call it eavesdropping) heard him order a Corona. A quick check of the hands showed no signs of a ring. Game on! I got up to go to the ladies room to give him a chance to notice me, making sure to walk slowly and deliberately. I gently put my hand on his back to squeeze by him with a shy "excuse me," made eye contact, and continued on my way.

Once in the restroom, I stalled by freshening up my makeup, checking my hair, adding some gloss, and popping a mint before going back out to the scene. One last glance in the mirror told me I was indeed fine and sexy. My mocha skin was glowing; my makeup was applied to look as if I weren't wearing any; my gloss had just enough shine to scream *lick-able*; my hair was laid in a short, Rihanna-style bob, and no one would ever guess that my 5'8", 140-pound frame was the home of a 46-year-old woman. I could easily pass for a thirty-something—early thirties at that. and I worked hard to keep it that way!

I straightened my camel-colored pencil skirt and unbuttoned an extra notch on my white, long-sleeved collared blouse. My nude stockings and leopard Louboutins finished off my office attire. Not the most alluring outfit, but it would have to do. By that point, he should've been watching the door and waiting for me to come back out so that he could offer to buy me a drink. I'd done this many times before. And it never failed—until then, that is.

When I strutted out of the bathroom, preparing to act surprised to see that he noticed me, he was deeply engaged in a game of pool with some young trick that had her boobs practically spilling out of her shirt and onto the billiard table whenever she tried to take a shot. I looked over at my girls and Dori gave me a look that said, "Yeah, girl. I see it." I strolled back over to my table and took a sip of my cosmo.

"Hmph. Another fine brother falling prey to the young vixens," Dori snorted as if she were truly insulted and disgusted at the young thot. She knew full well that had we not been in our work clothes, that young thot would have been us acting like cats in heat and spilling cleavage all over the place.

"Dori, please—this game has just begun." I answered back. "That is my next husband over there, so get used to seeing his fine ass."

Stacy's annoying voice joined the conversation. "Whatever, Lisa! What makes you think that PYT is going to pay any attention an old huzzie like you? Especially when hot little miss black Barbies like that one over there is also vying for his attention. Girl, a man that fine will keep you on your toes and at the spa for the rest of your days. You'll be going to a plastic surgeon for facelifts right along with your annual mammogram." This was coming from my cousin. Family. Gotta love them.

"Okay, Stace. Watch and learn." I headed to the bar even though I didn't need a drink. This was my way of putting plan B into motion. I ordered a Corona and hand-delivered it to my mystery man.

"Excuse me," I purred. "I noticed you were running low and I'd hate for you to have to interrupt your game for a refill. Enjoy this one on me." I handed him the beer

He responded with a gorgeous smile that showed a beautiful set of pearly whites accompanied by a simple "'preciate it." He tilted the bottle in my direction before lifting it to his LL Cool J lips to take a sip.

"Mmph, mmph, mmph—that is one lucky bottle," I thought to myself. I walked away knowing that I was in full view and made sure to stop by a table with some random guys to give one of them hug on the way back over to my table.

"Girl, who the hell were you just hugging on?" Stacy asked.

Dori just laughed and said "Ahh, grasshopper. You have so much to learn."

"Okay, ladies, are we ready to go?" I suggested as I started gathering my purse and jacket. Dori was on cue considering she damn near invented this game of cat and mouse. We named it "The Hook, Line and Sinker." The Hook was to get his attention with something he liked (the Corona); The Line was showing that other men would love to have me (the random hug); and The Sinker was leaving right after the Hook and Line were thrown so that the subject would have to come chase you. You see, guys know the hook and line part and figure you are doing it for the benefit of their attention and acknowledgement. Then they naturally assume that you will sit around and wait for them to approach you, so they take their time to make you sweat it out. After all, a guy can't be too anxious, right? But once you pull the sinker and he sees you packing up to leave (and believe me, he is keeping an eye on you) then he feels like he must hurry and make a move because you really couldn't care less if he follows up or not. Hook. Line. Sinker. You've got him.

As I started to put on my jacket, I felt a pair of strong, warm hands on my shoulders. I turned around and it was Mr. Fine himself.

"I'm going to get the car, c'mon Stacey, help me remember where we parked." Dori and Stacey left me alone with my future husband.

"Leaving so soon?" His voice was smooth and confident. His eyes told me I wasn't going anywhere, but I couldn't let him know that.

"Yes." I smiled hard to make sure he could see my dimples in the dimly lit area. "It's been a long day and I just came out with the girls to unwind. I don't normally hang out too late at this kind of scene," I lied. We were here, there and everywhere so much that most owners knew us by name.

"Really now? So where do you and your girls normally like to hang out when it's late?"

"Who says I hang out with my girls when it's late?" I asked with a raised eyebrow.

"I do," he said. "Because from this day forward, if you're not with your girls, you'll be with me." Sssssinker!

And he was right. From that day forward, if I wasn't with the girls, I was with him. He's the first guy I never cheated on. And six years later, with the last three being spent in marital bliss, I still can't fathom being with any other man. But I am constantly reminded of our age difference every time I look in the mirror.

Oh! I still look good thanks to a healthy diet and a vigorous workout routine, but there are small tell-tale signs beginning to appear: crow's feet, the occasional gray strands of hair—downstairs! And the sagging breasts. I refuse to make love to him with the light on unless I blindfold him. I don't want him to ever be reminded of my age. Don't get me wrong, I know you are as young as you feel, and 46 is still pretty young since they came up with "40 is the new 30" phrase. But when your husband really is in his 30's, it makes you work twice as hard to make sure a 20-something doesn't snatch him away.

He's never given me any reason to doubt him, but I wanted to nip whatever it was in the bud. I fixed all of his favorites for dinner and arranged for my mom to keep the baby, which meant Alex and I would have the house to ourselves.

I called Alex to see where he was, and he said he had to work late and it would be around 9 before he made it home. It was only 6:30. This gave me plenty of time to do some snooping. I poured myself a glass of wine, grabbed my Jazmin Sullivan CD, and went to the room in the house that was affectionately dubbed "the office." This is where Alex did most of his work from home. I very rarely entered. My mom always said to let a man have a sanctuary in his own home so he doesn't feel so crowded. Because of her wise words, I made sure not to invade his privacy. What was in the office, stayed in the office, but it was time to pay it a visit.

I popped an old CD into the player to give me some mood music and glanced around the room—trying to figure out where to start. My eyes rested on the stack of mail sitting on his desk. I sifted through it, and nothing unusual jumped out at me. There were a couple of unopened credit card bills. If I opened them, he would know I had been in there, so I decided to leave those pieces alone.

"I bust the windows out yo carrrr," I sang along with Jazmin. As I grooved, sipped, and snooped, I came across the cell phone bill which was already opened. I interpreted that as an invitation to read it. I took a gander at the contents. At first glance, there was nothing unusual, tons of local calls, which was to be expected. He uses the cell as his business phone.

I began to look for numbers with a 786 area code, and

Calm Sparkle

then tried to narrow it down to numbers I didn't recognize. No luck there, because I didn't know *any* of the numbers except Corey's and his mom's. The other numbers may as well have been written in Greek. I knew it was useless. I tried to log into his computer, but didn't know any of his passwords. It was pointless. I felt too much of a buzz and enjoyed the music too much to even let it concern me after a while. I reminded myself that he married *me*. I had his child, the house—him. Dori had me tripping for nothing.

Alex made it home a little after 9, as promised. We enjoyed a quiet, romantic evening at home. Then the witching hour began and my glass dream house of innocence was shattered. I went through Alex's cell phone as he slept. I know! I know! I said I would never do that, but curiosity got the best of me. And sure enough, it killed the cat.

There were text messages between him and someone named Sparkle. I didn't know who Sparkle was, but her number had a Moonbow area code. The message from Alex to her said, "looking forward to seeing you soon." Her response was "ditto." Who the hell uses "ditto?" I committed her number to memory so that I could easily recognize it when I had another opportunity to check his phone bill.

Since that night, I began checking the caller ID religiously, but nothing out of the ordinary ever popped up. It had been a week since I found the first text message. My initial instinct upon seeing those texts was to yank Alex by his bald head and rip him a new one, but I worked too hard and too long to get him that I wasn't about to lose him over some minor flirtation. I hoped that's all it was. I kept my eyes and ears peeled to see what was really going on.

To test my theory of minor flirtation, I told Alex that I wanted to go home with him to see his mother on his next trip since she hadn't seen the baby in a while. The look of horror that danced across his face told me that he was indeed planning that trip to see Sparkle and not his mother.

"Baby, are you sure you want to come? You know how bored you get, and I won't be able to give you much attention because I'm going there to help mom close the deal on her new property." He tried to look genuinely concerned. Negro please!

"Yes, shuga! I want to go see your mom, I haven't seen her since she came down here for Junior's birth, and that was six months ago. I'm sure she's ready to see her grandson again. And besides, we need to spend some quality time with Nicole as well." She's a sweet little girl, a bundle of energy, but a true daddy's girl. I knew that mentioning her would leave Alex no choice. Nicole and Alex's mom are two peas in a pod. Those two act like best friends forever when they are together.

"You're right," he gave in, "it can be a nice family trip."

"Try not to sound so excited," I thought, but kept it to myself. I was ready to get to the bottom of this "Sparkle" thing.

The day went on as it normally does from there. I was my usual loving self, making sure to give him extra attention in the bedroom. After all, my momma told me a long time ago, "Baby, all men cheat, but you don't have to hand him over on a silver platter. Keep your man satisfied at home, and he won't have nothing left to give the other woman, and he won't have a reason to leave what he's got. If you do your job, the most that huzzy can get from your man is a sorry lay!"

I resigned myself to making sure that every night I would either ride him like there was no tomorrow or suck him dry. I wanted to make sure that there was *nothing* left for him to share with any other woman.

Calm Sparkle

Calm Sparkle Discussion Questions:

Chapters 1-2

1. What do you think of the "hook, line & sinker"? Do you think it will work realistically?
2. What "signature move" did you or your girls use when going out?
3. Sparkle mentions that she feels she has to stay with her husband to "fix him". Have you ever experienced this urge in past (or current) relationships?
4. How do you feel about Arnold's initial reaction to Sparkle announcing her spiritual rebirth? What would have been your reaction to Arnold's words?
5. Sparkle confesses to her cousin about a moisturizing prayer. What was your reaction to reading about that? Do you feel it is an appropriate thing to pray for?
6. Sparkle's view of marriage was mundane. You get married, have kids and live on autopilot. What is your expectation of a fulfilling marriage?
7. Lisa's intuition is telling her that something isn't right. Have you ever experienced "women's intuition"? Were you right?
8. Lisa found text messages between her husband and Sparkle yet she didn't confront him about it. What would you have done?

Chapter Three
Death by Ringtone

Sparkle

Dear Diary,

I'm not in love with my husband anymore. I confessed to myself and to God. I don't know if I ever was. Is it fair for me to keep hanging on and pretending there's a chance for us when I know that I have no desire to be with this man? I mean, he is a good security blanket (emotional security, that is). I know that he'll be here on the cold nights when I want to snuggle. I know that he'll be here on the date nights when I want to go out. But that also means that I'd have to sleep with him and kiss him and make him feel all warm and fuzzy, and that is the part I am just NOT feeling for this man. Maybe I should write a Strawberry Letter to Steve Harvey's Morning Show. He always gives good advice on these matters. I know, I KNOW!! I need to just pray!

Sparkle
3 am

No—not now! I silently cursed as I was rudely awakened out of my sleep. "Don't move. Pretend to still be asleep," I told myself. The intrusion that invaded my dream that night is the same intrusion that aggravates me almost every other night—my husband trying to slide it in with the hopes that I'll miraculously be in the mood, roll over and screw him to oblivion. Give it up—it ain't happenin'.

"ZZZZZZ," I tried to fake a loud snore. He stopped for a few seconds and then starts rubbing the tip of his penis on my lower back. I shifted my body with a loud snort and smacked my lips as if I was just rolling over in my sleep. And then I let out another loud, "Zzzzzz."

Again, his hesitation was only temporary. I flopped on my belly so that he no longer had any access to my goodies and continued to snore so hard that my throat became scratchy. He got the hint.

I heard him taking matters into his own hands—literally. When he's done pleasing himself, he scoots toward me. "Ughhh, please don't touch me!" I silently screamed in my infuriated mind. I feel the slimy, wet tip of his shaft sliding back and forth, and up and down, my back. At that point, I could no longer take it. I jumped up with the attitude that any sistah girl would have.

"Are you writing your name on me?" I screamed at him in disgust. He grinned sheepishly as if I should actually be complimented by the fact that he laid next to me, masturbated, and then was using his cum-covered penis to spell out his name on the side of my body.

"What gave it away?" he responded. "Was it the exclamation point?"

"Negro please! That is not cute!" I replied while simultaneously trying to wipe the wet spots from my body. "What is this? Some kind of Arkansas voodoo?"

Is that why I stayed with him for so long—because he's been "marking" me? "Calm down," I told myself. "This is not the Christian way to act. He is your husband, and biblically, you should've just given him some. Oh, but, Lord, can I please just have one night of peace?"

I'm so glad Valentine's Day was the following weekend. Now, don't get all sentimental. Valentine's Day just happened to be his mother's birthday, so every year at that time he went home to Arkansas and took our son with him, which meant that I'd have five glorious days of solitary bliss. It was the next best thing to Christmas for me, but that year would be extra special because Alex was coming to visit.

Just the thought of reigniting with my old flame made me grin from ear to ear and, dare I say, there is a tingle going on in the vajayjay area? Lord, you are going to have to give me strength.

Twenty minutes or so passed and I was able to calm down. I felt halfway cleaned up from Arnold's self-imposed autograph signing session, and thankfully the sandman was calling me back to sleep. I glanced at the clock, which blared 3:27am.

"Hmph! That didn't take long, glad I didn't bother to get up." I climbed back into bed and eventually dozed off.

2 pm

The sound of my cell phone buzzing on my desk seemed magnified in my groggy state. Who the heck is calling me now? Don't they know I'm at work?

I'd already had a bad start to the day with Arnold waking me up, and then I overslept because I hit the "off" button instead of the snooze button on the alarm clock; the shower was out of hot water; and I got stuck in traffic. By the time I got to work, it was 9 am—thirty minutes after my designated arrival time. I had a report due to my VP by 3 pm, which I hadn't even started working on. Now was not the time for idle chit-chat. I glanced down at the cell phone's glowing light. My right eyebrow raised a bit and then the edge of my lips began to curve.

"Oooohhh!" I accidently said out loud as the Kool-Aid smile continued to grow and spread across my face. The caller ID silently announced that it was Alex. I guess it wouldn't hurt to take a quick break.

I let the phone ring one more time because I didn't want to seem too anxious. How silly and old school is that? Then I answered using my professional voice because I work with some nosey heifers that are always eavesdropping.

"Hello, this is Sparkle."

The cheerful voice on the other end replied, "Sparkle Timmons! How you doing, Sweetie?"

Mind you, Timmons is my maiden name. Alex refused to call me by any other name. I got up to close my office door. "Well hello, Mr. Weston!" I sing as if I'm surprised to hear his voice. "I'm doing well, how about yourself?" trying to maintain a bit of platonic resonance in my voice as the door closes and I am out of earshot of anyone wandering in the halls.

"I'm hanging in there," he began his reply. "Listen, I just wanted to call and let you know that I can't wait to see you. I'm really looking forward to spending some time with you."

"The feeling is mutual, Alex. So, when do you think you'll be getting into town?"

The conversation continued innocently in this manner for the next couple of minutes, and then he drops a bombshell on me.

"I need to tell you something," he paused and I waited with baited breath. "She's decided to come with me."

"What do you mean? Are you telling me she's coming here—to Moonbow—with you?"

"Yeah, baby. Looks like she wants to bring the kids for my mom to spend some time with them."

I sank back in my chair. Kool-Aid grin shape-shifted itself into a pout. "Well, there goes that."

"This doesn't change anything," Alex tried to reassure me. "I still want to see you. Even if only for a few minutes—just whatever you can spare."

How did he go from "can't wait to see you" to "spare a few minutes?" That was some fragerknacklebull if I ever heard it. But how could I be upset? After all, he was still married. I finally found some words to respond to the news.

"I dunno, Alex. Maybe this is God's way of keeping us

on the straight and narrow, ya know?"

There was no response. I could hear him breathing, but he didn't say anything.

I broke the silence with, "Well, I guess I can see what I can work out. Just give me a call as time gets closer and let me know what the final plans are."

In my mind, the deal was sealed. I had no intentions on seeing Alex. In a weird way, I was grateful because I knew that we would do something that neither of us had any business doing.

"Aight, Sweetie. I'll keep in contact. Take care." Then I heard a dial tone.

Well, wasn't that the feces from a dying maggot on top of my trash heaped day. I mean, I know I had absolutely no right to be upset, but damn! Oops! Sorry, Lord.

Lisa

It was 3 in the morning. Alex was sound asleep but I heard his phone buzzing. "Now who could be calling him at this time of night?" I thought.

I got out of the bed and tip toed around to his side. His cell phone was on his night stand next to his watch, wallet and some coins. The phone blinked "1 missed call." I peeked over at Alex who was still sound asleep. I picked up the phone and pushed a few buttons. The caller ID obediently displayed the caller was Sparkle. Siri is a damn snitch, and thanks to her, anger arose up from the tip of my toes to the top of my head. No that bitch did not call my husband this time of night! Without thinking, I shoved Alex and demanded him to get up. He rolled over and looked at me as if my hair were on fire.

"What's the matter? The baby alright?"

"Sparkle just called you!" I spat the words out and threw the phone at him—barely missing his head. "It's 3 am, Alex! Why is Sparkle calling you at this time of night? And who the hell is this Sparkle?" My neck rolled, my hand tightly clenched my hip, and my voice was harsh but not loud enough to wake the baby. Nicole had stayed over and Alex Jr. was sound asleep in his room right across from ours.

Before he could say anything, the phone rang again. Alex casually picked it up, glanced at the caller ID, and then laid the phone on the nightstand. I cleared my throat with an angry "ahem" and shot him the "no the hell you didn't just ignore me" look.

"Aren't you going to answer that?" I was damn near hysterical.

Alex nonchalantly reached out to me and said, "Come back to bed, baby." I slapped his hand out of the way and snatch the phone off the night stand. Sure enough, the missed call again came from Sparkle.

"Why didn't you answer it?"

"I'm sure it was a misdial. C'mon back to bed," he said as he yawned. He always yawns when he's nervous.

"Who is she?"

"Look, can't we do this in the morning? I'm sure she didn't mean to call me this late."

Well, *who* is she?"

He finally sat up, realizing that there was no way on God's green earth that I was going to let it drop.

Alex

"Damn, damn, damn!" was all I could think. "What the hell could I say to calm her down? That couldn't have been Sparkle calling me at that time of night. She wouldn't do that. Her husband must've gotten wind. Shit!

"Baby, come back to bed." I tried to coax my wife into bringing it down a notch while controlling my own woody. Lisa stood there mad as hell, which is sexy as all get out. Make up sex is the best sex and my penis stood at attention as soon as she threw the phone at me. She wouldn't budge though. I sat up to give her my undivided attention and to try to camouflage the fact that I was excited. I couldn't let her know that yet. I had to calm her down first.

"Sweetie, look, Sparkle is an old friend from college. My mom is doing her sister's wedding and I ran into her the last time I was at home. We exchanged numbers and that's all there is to it." I lied, but at that point I had nothing to lose.

I watched her chest and could see that her breathing was beginning to slow down. She wore a sky blue, silk camisole with matching panties that I'd bought for her weeks earlier. I loved how the material hugged her body, and I could see the outline of her breasts. "Not long now," I thought, "just keep it soothing."

I reached out for her hand again to try to pull her back into bed. This time she accepted. She sat on the edge of the bed and I began to massage the nape of her neck. She sighed and I seized the opportunity to say, "Look at how you've gotten yourself all worked up. Sweetie, I married *you*. Not anyone else. Come on back to bed and we'll—." I was interrupted by the phone going off again. Lisa glared at me. Shit!

Lisa

"Aren't you going to answer that?" I hissed through clenched teeth. My mind raced.

Should I answer it? Should I make him answer it? Did I really want to know? I decided to allow him to stall because I wasn't sure if I was ready to deal with having him know that I know. That would mean I would have to act on it. Nope. I couldn't let that happen so soon.

The name of this game is "Hold on to Your Man by Any Means Necessary." And at that point the necessary thing to do was buy some time.

I continued to stare him down. "Well?" I asked after I counted the fourth ring.

I knew the voicemail would pick up by then and it would be another missed call. He reached over for the phone, knowing full well that there was no longer someone on the other end. He handed the phone to me. "Oh, shit! I don't want the phone!" I thought.

"Call her back," he said as he tossed the phone in my direction. "To be honest with you, Sparkle is just an old friend," he continued. "Call her back. Talk to her, and she'll tell you."

I knew he was lying. Anytime he started a sentence with "to be honest with you" he was lying. I pulled a stall tactic by asking more questions. "Well, how did your mom get to be the one doing her sister's wedding?"

"Baby, like I said, we go way back. Besides, it's Moonbow. You know my mom does half the weddings for everyone in that town. Call her, she'll tell you," he repeated. I could tell he was calling my bluff, so I couldn't back down.

I picked up the phone, and holding up my act, I called the number back. Don't get it twisted—I wasn't scared to call her. I was just afraid of having confirmation for what I knew to be true. Once he knew that I knew, I would have to act on it, and that is what I was not ready for. I don't want to have to kick him out. I don't want to have to threaten to take the kids and leave. And God knows I don't want to pull out the dreaded 'D' word. As Beyonce' would say "*She* gon' be rockin' chinchilla coats if I let you go. I can't let you go! Damn, if I let you go!"

Hell naw—ain't no other chick about to get my life. For that reason, I need to continue with my naïve act until I can reel him back in to loving only me. Like I said, I worked too hard to get this man, and I was not ready to let all of that hard work go with just one phone call.

The phone began to ring, and I prayed she wouldn't answer.

Sparkle

"Saving all my love for youuuuuu." The sound of Whitney Houston's perfect melodic voice filled our dark, otherwise quiet, room. Normally, I welcomed the sound. One, because I absolutely love Whitney Houston. Two, because it was the special ring tone that I assigned Alex so that I would immediately recognize his call. "Yes I'm saving all my lovin'—" Bobby Brown's ex-wife continued to cut

Calm Sparkle

the silence of the night, but this time, all I could do was say, "Ooooohhhhhh shit!"

Thirty-five minutes prior to that call was pure torture. Arnold had decided to get up in the night and go through my cell phone numbers. Apparently, he was suspicious of my new-found confidence. Although Alex and I had not done anything physical, an emotional affair was just as bad, if not worse. Once Arnold saw a name he didn't recognize in my phone, he called it. Arnold always made it his business to know each of my friends, but he never heard me mention an Alexa Westington, yet there were several calls in my log history to and from this Alexa.

Nosiness and suspicion got the best of him and he called the number. The voicemail on the other end announced that he had reached the phone of Alex Weston—not Alexa Westington. I was completely and totally busted.

Arnold was on fire, snorting like a bull with bloodshot eyes. He knew exactly who Alex Weston was. Alex was the ex-boyfriend from my college days that seemed to haunt him to no end. When Arnold and I were first married, my parents hosted a celebratory dinner for the family. Everyone was there chatting, drinking and having a merry old time. Once we were all seated at the table, one of my elderly aunts finally asked Arnold, "Well, who are you?"

The room became quiet. "Lula!" my mom exclaimed, breaking the silence. "This is Arnold! Sparkle's new husband!"

"Whaaaaat? Sparkle's husband?" Well, what happened to Alex?"

"Who's Alex?" Arnold spoke up, sticking his chest out.

My aunt didn't hesitate, "Alex is Mrs. Weston's son. We all thought that she would always marry Alex. Where did you come from?"

Was that a smile dancing across Mrs. Weston's face? I was so embarrassed.

"Auntie, Alex and I haven't been together for a while

now," I answered in Arnold's defense.

"Well, we liked him! He was there for us even when we had to build my Habitat house. He stood right next to me and helped me put up my walls and lay my foundation. Hmph! That's who you *should have* married. We don't know this boy!"

It was all downhill from there. Aunt Lula called Arnold by Alex's name for the rest of the night—accidently on purpose of course. I had to hear about that for the two weeks following the situation. Arnold would not let it rest. As time passed, I helped him realize that I married him—Arnold, and not Alex.

Since then, Alex's name would come up here and there. And the fact that Mrs. Weston was hired to organize all of our family events didn't help. It seemed as if Arnold could not escape the Alex shadow. And obviously, neither could I.

"Saving all of my love for youuuuuu—." Whitney was still singing to me—and Arnold. Poor Arnold. He was visibly hurt when he heard that ring tone and saw the name "Alexa Westington" flashing on the caller ID. I took advantage of the moment and snatched the phone out of his hand. I couldn't let Arnold start a bunch of drama with Alex. This was between husband and wife—leave out the middle man.

I quickly pressed the talk button and said, "Hey." I listened for a response, but didn't hear anything. I thought it was strange, but I continued because I didn't want Arnold to get the phone. "Hey, it's not me." I hung up the phone.

Arnold lunged for the phone and snatched it out of my hands. He immediately dialed the number back. No answer. He glared at me, and from the look in his eyes, I knew he wasn't himself. He wrapped his hands around my neck and began to squeeze.

"Arnold!" I panicked. "Arnold, get off! Leave me alone!" He got up with one final push and grabbed a suitcase.

"You want to be alone? Fine. I'll give you alone." He began throwing things into the bag. Tears streamed down his face. He was genuinely hurt. And I felt like dirt.

Lisa

I sat there stunned. I heard her voice. That officially made her real. A pain shot through my heart. I wasn't expecting that. The only good thing is that she hung up. All she said was, "Hey, it's not me." Then there was silence. I knew exactly what that meant. Her husband must have been having the same suspicions that I knew to be true. He must've been the one calling—trying to get answers to this newfound intrusion on their marriage. Although I was experiencing the same intrusion, it's not answers that I needed—it was a diversion. A diversion away from her and back to me.

"Baby, are you alright?" Alex asked out of concern for his own fate more than for me and my broken heart. Little did he know, it would take a hell of a lot more than that to get rid of me, but what he didn't know, made me stronger.

"Yes. I'm fine. She answered, she said it wasn't her doing the calling and then hung up. There must be some real drama going on over there." I responded.

Concern swept over his face. His fingers flinched as if he were reaching for the phone and then realized he shouldn't. He looked in my eyes. "Are you sure you're okay?" he asked again. Only this time, he and I both knew that was really meant for Sparkle. I knew I had to take his mind off her quickly.

I softened my voice and leaned into him. "Oh, baby," I crooned, "I'm so sorry I doubted you." I kissed him on the nose. "I should have known better," I continued and kissed his lips. "You know how jealous I get. I just still cannot believe that a man as wonderful as you chose me to be his wife." I kissed him passionately and placed his hands on my breast. He gave in as usual. Men are so easy.

Sparkle

Arnold packed his bags, threw his wedding ring at me and stormed out of the house. That was the last that I'd heard from him for three days. I would hear Andre on the phone talking to him so I knew that he had not stopped communicating with our son, but he wouldn't return any of my calls or text messages.

I just wanted to explain to him that there was nothing physical between Alex and I. It was just crazy old emotions mixed with being in a marital rut that sparked it all. At least that's how I felt some of the time. The other half of the time, I felt a strange sense of freedom since Arnold was gone. I felt wildly invigorated and excited at the possibilities life had to offer with my newfound independence. I just wished that it hadn't come in such a way that I could practically feel Arnold's heart breaking.

When I talked to Kat about it, she gave me the "Girl, whateverrrrrr" speech. Actually, her exact words were: "Girl, What the fuck everrr! Be glad he's gone! After all the shit that man put you through—hell, we need to be throwing a party. Fuck that mother-fucker!"

And thus, began my initiation into the life of being single again.

As for Alex, I was so embarrassed at the fact that Arnold was blowing up his phone that I sent him a text apologizing for the confusion as soon as Arnold was out of the area. He replied with "I'll call you when I can talk." I guessed that meant he was also busted, and I wondered if she'd be mad enough to leave him? Naaah. I know from experience that one incident does not make a woman leave. Not that I would want her to—well, I would, but not like that. I don't want to be the reason a family dissipates. I couldn't live with that guilt. So, no matter how bad I would love to rehash an old flame, he has got to live out his commitment to his wife, and I had to find my true soulmate.

Alex called back later that evening. We exchanged our varying stories of the early morning events that shook up both of our households. That was when I first found out that she is the one that I was speaking with and not him. I was like, "damn!" If she hadn't called back, we would all be in the clear right now! It was the freaking ring tone that set Arnold off. Ironic, isn't it? Oh, well, what's done is done.

Alex

"What's up, Corey?" My homeboy called me as I was driving.

"What's going on, Al? Still headed this way this weekend?" Corey, sounded as if he were ready to party as usual.

"Yeah, man. I'll be heading out tomorrow evening. Why? What you got going on?"

"Ahh, you know me. Just putting together a little fish fry and crab boil for my boy! The word is out and erreybody will be here in your honor, man."

"Really now?" I laugh. "And who is 'erreybody'?" I know my boy, and his term "erreybody" means a couple of honeys, and I had to make sure he wasn't planning to get me into trouble.

"Awww, man, you know how I do. Wait, are you trying to say you can't party this go round?"

"Naw man. I can't hang with you this time. Lisa is talking about making it a family getaway. You know she's had her radar on ever since the late night phone call incident. She's been real leery of every move I make."

Corey let out a hearty laugh. "Yeah, man, that was a trip. When you told me about that I was trying not to laugh at your ass, but that shit was funny!" He laughed some more, as if he were hearing it all over again for the first time. Then he added, "But hey! I thought you had smooth talked her out of that situation."

"Yeah, I did, but then I slipped up again. I called Sparkle last night, but she didn't answer. She sent me back a text asking me to call her back when I could talk. And guess who sees the text before I do?"

"Damn! Not Lisa!"

"Yup, wifey saw it first."

"Aww, bro, sorry to hear that. But damn, you gots to be mo careful. How the hell do you just *keep* getting busted? You used to be the master playa. What the hell happened, dawg?"

"I dunno. When I finally did marry, I meant that shit. I wasn't planning on being with any other woman til death do us part and the whole nine. I packed all those playa moves up and settled down for real. It's been 3 years since I even entertained the thought of being with any other woman." I left it at that because I didn't want to say out loud what I was thinking. And that was, although it had been three years since I had entertained the idea of being with any other woman, now all I thought about was being with another woman—Sparkle.

Well, then just bring the fam by and we'll do it rated G style. You know I got plenty for everybody."

"Ok, dude, I might just take you up on that. I'll give you a call when we get in town and get settled. I'll see what my mom has planned and take it from there."

"Aight, man, hit me up. Peace."

"Peace." I hung up and immediately the phone rang again. It was Lisa.

"Hey, baby!" I had to test the waters to see if she was still mad about last night's text, but I wasn't concerned about her doing anything drastic. The make-up sex was too great. Hell, all our sex was great, and she kept me well fed. All reasons why I hadn't even considered tipping out on her—until now.

"Babe?" she sounded a little worried. "Would you be terribly disappointed if the kids and I sat this one out?"

Is she serious? My smile stretched a mile wide across my face, but I couldn't reflect this of course.

"Why, baby? What's wrong? You feeling alright?"

"I'm fine," she sighed "but mom just reminded me that my cousins from New Orleans would be in town this

Calm Sparkle

weekend and I haven't seen them in ages. I kinda' would like the time to hang out with them if it's okay with you."

My suspicions raised. Is she trying to play "get back?"

"What cousins?"

"My aunt Neicey's kids. You know Stacey's sister. They haven't been here since right before we were married."

My gut told me she was lying. My need to see Sparkle said, "fuck it."

"Yeah, baby, that's cool. You ladies have fun." I know it was a half-hearted response, but it was all I could get out.

I didn't immediately call Sparkle, because I needed to process this recent change of heart. Please understand that I love my wife. She was there for me at a time when I needed someone the most. She brought me through a dark patch. My senior year of college I was riding high. I was starting quarterback. Our team was undefeated. NFL teams were salivating over signing me. And it all ended with a "crack." That was the sound I heard that changed my life.

I thought I had out maneuvered the linebacker from the opposing team and was just about to release the ball to Mario who was wide open near the end zone, when suddenly the wind was literally knocked out of me. I didn't even see him coming as he dove head first into my left ribcage—sending me inches from the ground and then slamming me down onto the field. I had taken hits before, so this was nothing new, but I landed one way and my leg landed the other before I could think about fighting my way into a protective position. It felt like the entire team had pounced on top of me. One by one, I grunted as the pile-up became unbearable. I blacked out from the pain. Not only did I have cracked ribs from the impact of the hit, but I also had a broken knee cap, torn ACL, and a completely fractured fibula in my left leg. My right hand had a broken thumb. And add to that a minor concussion. That was the end of my chance to be an NFL player.

While recovering in the hospital, Lisa was one of the nurses on my floor. She doesn't remember it though. Back then, I was just some kid with a bunch of broken bones. Even in my morphine-induced haze, I could see how fine she was. I was embarrassed by all my bandages. I didn't realize how horrible I must have looked until Sparkle came to see me and she immediately burst into tears when she entered the room. I told my mom not to allow her to come back. I never wanted her to see me in a weakened condition. I was supposed to be her superman.

Lisa never looked at me with sympathy. Never shed a tear. I was just human. Sometimes I would tell them to leave the door to my room open. I could see the nurses' station from my bed. I would watch Lisa as she flirted with the doctors, took personal calls when she thought no one was looking. To her, I was just another patient. After a week in the hospital, I was able to go back home to Moonbow to continue my healing and then start physical therapy. I didn't see Lisa again until a night at happy hour. She had no idea who I was. I told her how I'd had a patient-caretaker crush on her for an entire week over ten years before, and she thought it was hilarious. I told her how she gave me hope because she didn't have the pity in her eyes that I noticed coming from everyone else including Sparkle and my mom.

Of course, I didn't tell her about Sparkle. At the time, it was irrelevant. For some reason, Lisa treating me like a normal person who wasn't battered, bandaged and bruised kept me from feeling sorry for myself. Otherwise, I would have rotted in that hospital. Once I fully healed, I went back to school and finished my remaining credits. Sparkle was gone by then. I was glad. I had hurt her enough. First with the lies and the cheating, and then with having to watch me get knocked out by another dude. I was sure she thought I was weak and less of a man. I don't want to see that sympathy in her eyes ever again. It was best to just cut my losses and keep it moving.

Lisa

Calm Sparkle

I sure hoped my mom was right. I stopped by her house to see if she needed anything before I headed to Moonbow with Alex. I was sitting at the kitchen table sipping her fresh brewed coffee while she kneaded biscuit dough.

"Chile, don't go runnin to Moonbow trying to keep tabs on that man. You let him be!" she said as she sifted more flour into the dough to cut down on the stickiness.

"But Mom! You're the one who said not to hand over a man on a silver platter. And that's what I'd be doing if I don't go."

"Baby, I also said that if a man's going to cheat, ain't nothing you can do to stop it. You can just limit the frequency and the pleasure of the cheating until eventually, he loses his appetite for it. Pass me one of them smooth drinking glasses out the cabinet. Now what's really going on? Why are you all in Alex's crack all of a sudden?"

I did as I was told and passed momma the glass so she could roll out her dough, and returned to my seat. "Oh, no reason, mama." I lied. "I just thought it would be a good opportunity to visit with his mom. That's all."

"Chile, how can you fix your mouth to lie to your mama like that? You just said you would be handing him over on a silver platter not more than 5 minutes ago. Now, what's *really* going on?"

I had to laugh. I never could lie to momma. I always got my stories mixed up and my versions would vary. Lying to everyone else was easy, but I couldn't get it right with her. I don't know why I kept trying, but it was kind of embarrassing to tell momma that after all the strategizing I did to marry Alex, I could feel him slipping through my hands.

"I think he's hooked up with an old flame, momma." I confessed.

"Well, baby, that would be a powerful force for you to be up against. You know old flames never die. Look at how sprung you were on Jesse from the time you laid eyes on him. And I'd bet you ten to one that if he were still alive today, God rest his soul, that you would still run back to him with open arms."

Momma was right. Jesse was my first love. He lived next door to us when I was growing up, and we were inseparable. We were the actual version of *Love and Basketball*—without the basketball. Jesse was into golf. It may sound nerdy, but he was all about finding his own beat, which made him even more intriguing. He died in a car accident on his way home to his wife after he and I had an uncensored rendezvous. The guilt ate me up inside for years afterward. During that time, I was married to my first husband, John.

Knowing for myself how deep a first love could go, I had to find out more about this whole "Sparkle" thing. Maybe she was just an old girlfriend that didn't mean anything, or maybe she was just a nobody in school that blossomed after graduation and has piqued Alex's interest. Whatever the case, I had to know so that I could counter-attack.

"Lisa Renee Weston! Are you listening to me?" Momma interrupted my thoughts. By now the biscuits were rolled, cut and placed into a pan.

"I'm sorry, momma. What did you say?" She looked right at me, but before she said another word she placed the biscuits in the oven, wiped her hand on her apron and then sat down at the table across from me.

Arms folded, she returned her gaze to my eyes and said, "Okay, now that I have your undivided attention, let me tell you something. If you want to send Alex running over to his clean up woman, which in this case you think is also an old flame, then go right ahead and start tripping like a ghetto, drama queen. Now, if you go down to Moonbow, then what? You hate being there. You'll complain of being bored, you'll complain that he's spending too much time at his friend's house and use the kids as an excuse to leave and go back to the hotel because you know you don't want to stay at his momma's house. All of that will lead to Alex being miserable and feeling like he's being chained down. He likes to go to Moonbow to relax, to see his old buddies, kick around and have some beers without the constraints of a time clock, spend time with his momma without feeling tension between her and his wife. You go there with him and mess all of that up, and he'll resent you for it. What you need to do is not give him any the night before, and then just before he leaves, while he's packing his bags, you suck him real good. Don't give him any. Just please him without intercourse and let him know that the episode will be finished when he gets home."

"Momma!" I blushed. "That's nasty coming from you! I don't want to hear my momma talking like that!"

"Chile please, I ain't held on to your daddy all these years by not knowing a trick or two!"

"Eeww! Momma! Stop! Please!"

"Okay, but mark my words. You go to Moonbow and ruin his plans, and it will be the beginning of the end. Just sit back and know that *you* are the wife. There's a lot of power in that."

I thought about what momma said. She may be right. I didn't tell her about the late night phone calls and how I began cross referencing the phone numbers with the phone bills, or how I was snooping through his office. One thing I did know—I was going to do a thorough rundown of that space once Alex was gone and on the road to his hometown. I just needed to figure out how to get his password.

I left momma's house with a full belly, a little wiser and with a new plan. After calling Alex with my lame excuse of seeing some long-lost cousins and not being able to go on the trip with him, I headed for the house.

I knew Alex was off-site scoping out some commercial properties. He was looking to expand his corporate office. I took advantage of this time to snoop around for the password. I pulled down a box from the top shelf in the closet and knocked over an old wrinkled, brown lunch bag.

I opened it and immediately recognized the old bag of birth control pills. I laughed out loud as I thought back to the day that I hid them so Alex wouldn't know that I had stopped taking them. We were in the middle of a heated, lunchtime sex session when his daughter called and needed to be picked up from school early. Later that night, I asked him if he wanted anymore children, and learned that he didn't. He said that he was happy with our family as it was.

I, however, decided otherwise. I figured I'd better lock him totally and completely—hook, line and sinker as they say. I haven't taken the pill since. It took six months, but I finally became pregnant and blamed it on a faulty batch and the idea that it must have been God's will to give us a child. And he believed me. Hell, why shouldn't he? After all, I am his wife.

I took the pills and buried them in the bottom of our kitchen trash and returned to the closet to go through the box I'd been eager to rummage through. It was the box where we kept our important papers: marriage certificate, tax returns, insurance policies, etc. If my memory served me correctly, we also listed our passwords on a sheet of paper and placed it in the box.

Sparkle

Arnold finally stopped giving me the silent treatment. It had been three months since he moved out and things calmed down. After a stretch of not speaking to me, he began to call me repeatedly. Sometimes he yelled about how I had fucked him over—how he had given me everything he had to give and yet it still wasn't enough. Other times he would text me saying "selfish bitch." Then he started being extra nice to me. His erratic behavior was alarming to say the least. I understood his hurt and it was my fault, but come on now. He had a single night of circumstantial evidence compared to my many years of putting up with his shit. The late nights, the *all* nights, the going to spring break weekends knowing he was too damn old to be anywhere near college parties.

I was beyond over it and made an appointment with an attorney to start the divorce proceedings. My absolute last straw was when he used his key to come into the house one weekend. When I stepped out of the shower, he was in the bathroom. Darn near gave me a heart attack. Out of instinct, I immediately grabbed my bath sheet sized dry towel to cover up. He snatched the towel from me and said that I'd better not cover up seeing as how I am still his wife. I snatched the towel back from him and proceeded to dry off while asking what the hell he wanted. On the inside I was terrified, but there was no way that I would show it. My mind immediately flashed back to the night he wrapped his hands around my throat, and I did not want a repeat of that.

In response to my question, Arnold just chuckled and grabbed the remainder of his stuff from the medicine cabinet. I continued to dry off and get dressed as if he weren't even there. He eventually left thinking that he had made his point. That afternoon, I called the attorney's office, and the locksmith.

Since that visit, he was nice when he called. No more cussing me out, but tried to act as if we were best friends. I spoke to him cautiously—using one-word answers. If he got off the subject of our son, I would end the conversation. It was time for he and Andre to go visit his family in Arkansas, and he came over to the house to pick Andre up.

When he arrived, he was in a very good mood (thank goodness). I found myself tip-toeing around him so to not set him off. I didn't want anything to upset him before they left. I've seen him flip on and off like a light switch. I tried to keep the switch on 'off' so that I could enjoy my weekend. This tip-toeing thing was different and felt out of character for me. I used to think that I was the one that controlled our relationship. Funny what a hand around your throat will do to your perspective. I knew that hell had no fury like a woman scorned, but over past months, I learned that a woman scorned has no fury like a man who thinks his wife has cheated on him.

So, I was having not-so-innocent conversations with an old boyfriend. I admit that I got carried away in the reminiscing, but hell, that is all it was. And yes, I know I shouldn't have assigned that ringtone on the phone. What they say is true: hindsight is 20/20. Do I regret any of it? No. I was at a crossroads before the whole getting 'busted' incident occurred, and if it was my way out, so be it. I gave up the comfort and security of a family for the trials and tribulations of single-motherhood—the church mothers were sure to point it out to me—but happiness was worth it. Wasn't it?

As I gave Andre goodbye hugs and went over the contents of his packed bags one last time, Arnold went outside and came back a few moments later with bags of his own. He parked his luggage at the kitchen door. He loaded Andre's suitcases into the car and prepared to leave. On his way out, he kissed me on the cheek and said, "When we get back from this trip, I'm coming back home." Then he left with Andre as if he were the happiest man on earth. I am sure the look of confusion on my face added to his amusement.

I poured myself a glass of wine and tried to process the news Arnold unloaded on me. The church wanted me to make things right with my husband. Yet these were the same women who kept a steady stock of Mary Kay and MAC to cover up the bruises from they received from their deacon board husbands. The women who had what they called foster children, yet these children were the spitting image of their spouse.

As the pastor's secretary, I knew everyone's business in that congregation. They all knew that I was never one to gossip, and their secrets were safe with me. What they didn't know was that I had no respect for any of them. I loved them as a sister in Christ should, but you know what they say about living in glass houses. Yet all of them kept pebbles in their pocketbooks. Even so, with all of that non-

Christian-like drama, I loved my church. My pastor and his wife were phenomenal. Our first lady was not like the rest of the flock, and I admired her tremendously. She is the reason that I stayed and helped as much as I could, but that was until I decided that I had to live for myself.

I'd had many talks with God about the situation. My prayer was no longer to "make me moist for Arnold." My prayers became "give Arnold a good woman that will love him the way he deserves to be loved—someone that understands him and will keep him happy." I was so over the marriage.

I ran myself a nice warm bath. After loading the water with lavender scented bath salts, I turned on the radio to listen to "The Sweat Hotel." As the tub began to fill, I turned on the jet stream to give it the Jacuzzi effect. Right before I stepped in to completely immerse myself in a Calgon moment, my cell phone rang. I glanced at the caller ID. It was Alex. I had long before removed the Whitney Houston ring tone.

"Hello?" I answered.

"Hey you."

"Hey yourself. To what do I owe the pleasure of this unexpected call?"

"Well, just wanted to let you know that I am on the road; I should make it to the bridge in about forty-five minutes." Moonbow is one of the islands located in the keys of Florida. Too small for an airport but accessible by the seven-mile bridge or by boat. Our island town was the second largest key located southwest of Duck Key. What made our town different was, unlike the rest of the keys, the minorities are the majority. It was our own island oasis and "Black Wall Street" all rolled into one.

"That's nice to hear. I hope you're traveling safely. Wait. Did you stop for a bathroom break or something? I know you're not calling me with your wife in the car."

There's that laugh again. "No, Sweetie. She decided not to come after all." My jaw hit the floor and a flurry of mixed emotions ran through me.

"What? Say that again," was my verbal response. I had to make sure I heard him correctly.

"I'm on the road," he said slowly and deliberately before adding "and I'm coming alone." He reiterated.

"How the heck did you swing that?"

There's that laugh again. "Well, you know. God is good."

"Don't put God in this because you are up to *no* good, Mr. Weston." I'm sure he could practically hear me smiling.

"Yeah, well, you just make sure you make some time for me."

"I don't know. It's kind of short notice. I wasn't planning to see you since our last conversation, and I've already made plans for tonight. I might be able to see you tomorrow." Who was I kidding? If that man asked me to drop everything and step outside right now, I would—butt ass naked with nothing but the cell phone.

"Oh, really. Well how about I call you once I get settled and see where you are, then we'll just go from there." It did not sound like he believed a word that I'd just said. Neither did I.

"Sounds like a plan. Talk with you then." His disregard for me telling him that I had plans left me motivated to find something to get into. I sent Kat a text telling her to include me in whatever it was she was doing. Kat always had something fun going on, and besides, I needed to remember what it was like to be a single woman out on the town.

It seemed as though making plans to be out for the evening played right into fate's playbook. By midnight, I'd already had a shot of Patron and was halfway done with my drink of Patron and pineapple on ice when Alex strolled in and stepped up to the VIP section where we were sitting. He and his boys apparently had the table next to us. He was right in front of me as he stood waiting for the club crew to remove the reserved sign and situate the bottles and glasses. He didn't even realize that I was only a heartbeat away. He was looking to the right and Corey was scanning the area to the left. I don't know when I actually got up and walked over to him, but the next thing I knew, my arms were around him and he was holding me tight. How could something so wrong feel so right?

We danced to a couple of songs and he poured me another drink. I was already past my limit, but what the hell. I wasn't driving and I didn't have to go home and play mommy. I was going to let go and let live! When Alex came back to my table with a freshly poured drink, another Patron and pineapple, one of my favorite side B tracks came on: "Insane" by Eric Benet. That is one sexy song and was made for grinding. I was already feeling frisky and full of myself. From where I was sitting, I looked up at him and he was already looking at me. No words were needed. He pulled me up and wrapped his arms around my waist while we made our way to the dance floor.

As we moved to the music, I laid my head on his chest and could hear his heartbeat. It matched mine. I shuddered at the memory of him touching me in forbidden places. I glanced up at him and he lowered his head to kiss me. Slowly—passionately— as if he had memorized every curve of my lips. His tongue returned home to mine and the two danced like reunited lovers. My knees grew weak. Thank God he was holding me up. We were both intoxicated with alcohol and each other, and it showed in his eyes, and I'm sure mine reflected it as well.

"Let's get out of here," was all he said, and it was all I wanted to hear. I allowed him to lead me through the crowd and out to the parking lot. He was leading me right into the bed of adultery—something I swore I would never do, and I followed—willingly and without protest. I begged God for forgiveness for what I was about to do, and The Lord's Prayer came into mind. "Lead me not into temptation," I thought, but I quickly dismissed it. If Alex was my apple, I wanted a bite. I wanted a bite more than I've wanted anything in a long, long time.

We didn't speak much in the car ride to his hotel. While stopped at a red light, he leaned over and kissed me again. "Mmmm. Delicious," he moaned as he pulled away, giving my bottom lip an extra lick. From that point on, he drove with his left hand on the wheel and his right hand holding my left. Kris Kross's "Jump" came on the radio. We both laughed and Alex cranked up the volume. That was our song when we were in college. It was the first song that we danced to as a couple. That was also the first night we had sex. We were both 19-year-old virgins. Neither of us knew what we were doing. I just laid there, he pumped away like a jack rabbit, and we called it love-making.

That was many, many moons ago and I could barely contain myself trying to imagine what kind of lover Alex had grown into. He'd always had a thing for older women, and I knew that he married someone 10 years our senior, so he *must* know how to put it down. His rapping jolted me out of my revelry. Our hands were no longer clasped together. His right hand was now in the air, palm side down, going up and down in a vertical motion along with the rhythm of the song as he chanted along with the chorus "jump—jump! The mack Dad will make you, jump jump."

I had to join in. It was a 90's classic and one of the best party songs of our day. "Cause I'm the miggida miggida miggida miggida Mac Daddy."

We grooved just as we did all those years before when we used to cruise down the strip in his Honda CRX. When the song was over, Alex told me that I still got it. We pulled into the hotel parking lot when it dawned on me. Why the hell did he get a hotel? Was this his plan all along?

As if reading my mind, he said, "I have a confession."

"What's that?" I asked.

"I almost didn't meet up with you tonight. Right after I hung up with you the first time, my wife called. She went through my emails and saw some of the things we've written to each other."

That sobered me up quick. "She what?"

"She saw where we were planning to meet up while I'm down here. Needless to say, she was not happy. She called and cussed me out from A to Z."

I was speechless. I really did not want to be a homewrecker and the gravity of what we had been doing finally hit me. The flirty conversations, the memory jolting emails, the kinky text messages were all with someone else's husband. In my mind, I justified everything by believing that he was still mine and would always be mine, but the ton of bricks that landed in my lap reminded me that he hadn't been mine in over 15 years. He belonged to her. And I was trespassing. Damn.

"Sparkle, you know that you and I haven't really done anything. We've had inappropriate conversations, but that's about it. Yet, she's already tried and convicted me."

"Well, Alex, I can't say that I blame her. I've been in her position and it's no fun." I turned away from him and looked out the car window. Ironically, it was starting to rain. I had a million things running through my mind—like how I had let myself get so wrapped up. How hurt his wife must be. I even thought about Arnold. Maybe I should have tried a little harder to ignite some passion into our lackluster—oh, who am I kidding—our non-existent sex life. Maybe if I had been open to him like I was with Alex, things would have turned out differently. Maybe.

"You can't make yourself happy by bringing misery to other people." I recited the line from a character named Alice in an old Tyler Perry film. Although we had yet to cross the road of no turning back, in the eyes of God, I had already become the other woman.

"Hey." Alex began to stroke the back of my hair. "I couldn't be here and *not* see you. We've come too far."

"So, what are you suggesting?" I asked, "that we become fuck partners?" Alex looked shocked at my vulgarity and use of the word "fuck."

"You know we go deeper than that. We have history. We both know that if our situations were different, we would be together. But it is what it is. We're both married and have families that depend on us."

"Excuse me, *you're* married," I interjected

"No, we're *both* married. You may be separated, but you're still married." I couldn't argue with that. Especially with that bomb Arnold dropped on me before he left with Andre. "Look," he continued, "I miss you. Truly. But life won't allow us to be together right now. Only time will tell where we'll end up in the future. But for the here and now, I'm asking that we give each other what we can and then go from there."

In my heart, his words meant that we were still in love with each other and we would patiently wait for Father Time to grant us another chance to be together. My head was telling me that he was asking for a one night stand. A romp in the sheets for old time's sake and a way for us to finally say goodbye—closure.

I decided to go with my heart's interpretation of Alex's speech. It was easier. I leaned over and kissed him, giving him the green light to proceed with our dive into deeper depths of sin. He got out and came around to open my door. We ran into the hotel just as the rain was really starting to pour. We managed to contain ourselves as we walked through the lobby and got onto the elevator. He put in the key for the concierge floor. I leaned against the back wall and took in the sight of him. I wanted every inch etched into my memory because deep down I knew that it would probably be the last time I would see him. He felt me watching him and turned to match my gaze. He knew it too.

When the elevator doors opened, he took my hand and raised it to his lips for light peck as he guided me down the hall to our room. I felt the gentle kiss on my knuckles and it sent tingles through every nerve of my body. Once in the room he fixed us a drink. The lust between us was undeniable as he positioned to give me a warm bear hug.

"Mmmm. You are so soft," he mumbled. We took our drinks over to the couch.

Calm Sparkle

He sat at the end, and I kicked off my shoes and laid down with my head in his lap. I sat my drink down and closed my eyes. He stroked my hair with one hand and massaged my breast with the other. "I can't believe how soft your breasts are." He was starting to get that husky growl in his voice that men get when they are aroused.

I opened my eyes and he was studying my face. "Kiss me," I commanded. A smirk crossed his face and he leaned down. He kissed my hair, my eyelashes, my nose and finally my lips. It started out slow and gentle then grew into a heated frenzy. His tongue thrust its way into my mouth as if it hid his life's supply of oxygen—hungrily and forcefully giving me its all.

When he finally came up for air, the yearning was all over his face. He lifted my shirt and slid my right breast out of the bra cup and began to gently lick my nipple. It was a drastic difference from the aggressive kiss we had just shared. I, in return, lifted his shirt and sucked his nipple. He unbuttoned my jeans and began to softly massage my lips until he found the clitoris. His touch was so sensual I immediately gasped. The sound seemed to turn him on even more, so he began tugging at my jeans to get them off. I decided to help him.

I stood up and removed my clothing. When I turned to face him, he was still in his same spot on the couch, but miraculously he was naked as well. "How the hell did you do that so fast?" I chuckled. I stood in front of him and he just looked up at me with undeniable desire in his eyes. I knew that I had rendered him speechless.

I straddled his lap and poised myself right above the tip of his penis and kissed him one last time before we took the plunge into an unforgiveable sin. He reached over for his condoms and quickly placed it on, then I slid down his shaft and welcomed him home. We made love for the rest of the night. Does God forgive us even when we don't' try to fight temptation?

Chapter Four
Hypocritic Oath

Alex

"Do you hear how crazy that sounds?" The anguish in Sparkle's voice immediately brought me out of my comatose-like sleep. I opened my eyes and saw that she was talking on the phone. I glanced at the clock. It was 5:30 in the morning. "That's ridiculous! And none of that even matters anymore! Arnold! Get over it!"

She hung up the phone and tossed it onto the night stand. I was about to move closer and hold her when the phone rang again. She quickly snatched it up. "What?" I heard her say through gritted teeth. There was a pause and then, "No! I am not doing that! That's insane! Go to sleep, Arnold!"

This time when she hung up the phone, she turned it off and threw it across the room. She sighed heavily.

"Is everything alright?" I asked.

"Yes. Arnold's just tripping."

"What did he want?" I asked as if I didn't already know.

"He wants to know who I'm with and where I am since

Calm Sparkle

I'm not answering the house phone. He wants me to get up and text a picture of the bathroom to prove that I am not at a hotel. How crazy does that sound?"

"Sounds like a man that loves his wife and wants to make sure no one else is dipping in his goods" was my response. I wanted to ask her more, but could tell that she was completely frustrated. I rolled over and massaged her shoulders, and not before long she was sleeping again.

As her breathing slowed and she returned to a REM state, I couldn't help but wonder how I would feel if Lisa was creeping like I was at that very moment. I fought the urge to call her, not because I was missing her, but because no man likes the idea of someone else tapping his wife. Call me hypocritical, but it is what it is.

I watched Sparkle sleep and my heart began to ache at the gravity of what had happened between us. For the first time, I realized that while I love my wife, I couldn't help that I was madly, deeply, undeniably in love with Sparkle. She just did it for me. Always had from the first day I laid eyes on her when we were freshmen at Albany State University. She had her boyfriend back home and I had my girl, but it really didn't matter if she had a boyfriend or not. She was mine from the time she walked past me in the square that day. She didn't even see me—which is a good thing because at that age it was an instant erection at the mere sight of her.

I had seen many hunnies walk by during freshman orientation, but something about Sparkle made me stop and take notice. I never did get up the nerve to ask her out. Lucky for me, she loved to dance. She was at the freshman welcome party learning to do the electric slide when I managed to boogie woogie my way to the space next to her and volunteer to teach her the infamous line dance. She was a quick learner and rhythmically we moved well together.

Fifteen years had passed, and I still couldn't get enough of her. I ran my fingers through her hair as she slept. My hands found themselves massaging her scalp and then letting the long strands run through my fingers. She'd recently had it cut, but it was still soft and silky. Eventually, I drifted back to sleep. My arms embraced her warmth. My mind replayed the memories and my heart prepared itself for life without her—again.

The next time I awoke, the sun was shining. Sparkle had just come out of the bathroom and I called her to come back in the bed. Her hair was a mess and I could see the evidence of child bearing on her belly, but she never looked more beautiful. Just like many times back at ASU, I was at attention. As soon as she was comfortable, I moved closer to her to give my version of a "good morning" greeting. I just had to have her one more time.

The night before was feverish and insatiable, but I wanted to take it slow, memorize the moment, watch her facial expressions. I loved the way her body felt against mine. I couldn't get enough of the enveloping softness that laid beside me. I had to have it one more time and she happily obliged.

When I was completely spent, I collapsed on top of her and kissed her shoulders. Not having the energy to remove myself from inside of her, I whispered, "Good morning." She hugged me tightly and I felt her vaginal walls tightening around my limpness. This made me get hard again. What is she doing to me?

When our lovemaking was finally at an end, it was 11:30 and I had 4 missed calls from Lisa. Shit. Back to reality.

I got up and went into the living area to look for my clothes from the night before. "Hey, Sparkle," I called to her from the kitchenette. She was still lying on the bed. "I'm going to run downstairs and get my shaving kit out of the car so I can shower. I'll be right back."

Once outside, I sat in the car and called Lisa. When I heard her answering the line, I feigned a yawn and tried to sound groggy as if I had just awakened.

"Good morning, baby." I yawned.

"Good morning, my ass! Where the hell are you?" she

hissed.

"Huh?" I tried to buy some time. "What are you talking about, babe? You know I'm here in Moonbow"

"Don't play dumb. You heard me! Where—the—fuck—are—you? You're with that girl, aren't you?"

"Lisa, what is wrong with you? I told you I was not meeting up with Sparkle. Yes, we initially tried to plan it, but I cancelled when I saw how it upset you. Damn, Lisa! We talked on the phone until well past eleven last night. I damn near fell asleep while talking to you! I call you first thing when I wake up to hear my *wife* tell me good morning, and you come at me with this shit? Is this what you're going to do for the rest of our lives? Huh? Keep accusing me because you found out I was planning to meet up with a friend?" I knew I was reaching, but I had to flip the script on her.

"You Gott-damn right! I'mma keep bringing up this shit! I know you fucked her! I can smell her on you from here! Damn, Alex! How could you do this to me? To *us*?"

"Baby, listen," I toned it down. I could see that flipping the script was not going to work, so I had to go for the "you're imagining things" routine. "I did not *fuck* her. Okay?" This was a true statement. I could never fuck Sparkle. I loved her. "I talked to you until I could no longer keep my eyes open, baby. After we got off the phone I went to bed. That's it." I held my breath to see if she bought it.

"Where?"

"Say what?" I was confused.

"Where did you go to bed?" This was starting to sound like the same conversation that Sparkle had with her husband a few hours earlier.

"My mom's house. Where else?" I always stayed with my mom when I would come to town. Lisa never called the house; she always called my cell phone, so this was completely believable.

"Mm-hmph. So, why doesn't your mom know that you're in town?" The venom in her voice was undeniable. She wasn't trying to fish for information. She had actually called my mom's house. Damn! The one time I didn't cover my bases. I usually go straight to Corey's, call my mom and let her know that I'm in town, and then go to her house after a night of hanging with the fellas. I veered off course. My mind was on Sparkle. I got into town, checked into a hotel, and then sat and talked to Lisa on the phone until she felt comfortable enough to think I was going to sleep. I didn't get to meet up with Corey to hit the club until a quarter to midnight.

I know Lisa was getting sick of Sparkle's name popping up all over the place. First, the late night phone calls from Sparkle's husband, then the text message she intercepted, and the day before she found the emails, and then this situation was staring us in the face. I just had to man up on this one.

"Alright, baby, listen. Yesterday when I got into town, I went straight to Corey's. I was all wound up after our conversation about the emails. I went over there to unwind. I had too much and Corey wouldn't let me drive. And like I said, I went to bed."

"Then why did you lie about being at your mom's, Alex? "

"Because I didn't think you would believe me. It's been so rocky between us lately."

"Don't give me that bullshit, Alex. Matter of fact, I don't want to hear another word from your lying ass lips. Go ahead, Alex. Live it up, but I hope you are using protection. On second thought, I hope you're *not*."

Her words stung and my heart ached. Another reason why Sparkle and I could never be together.

"Did you tell her, Alex? Or is she like us? Huh, Alex? Is she HIV positive like we are?" She hung up the phone. I sat stunned as I listened to the dial tone. I couldn't believe she took it there.

It was the first time either of us had brought it up since the baby was born. Once the baby tested negative, we moved on with our lives—business as usual.

Calm Sparkle

I remember when we got tested. It was 6 months before we got married. Lisa insisted that if we were going to continue to be together that we get tested. I wasn't feeling it. Shit like that didn't happen to me. I was always careful and used protection, but I figured what the hell. It would get her off my back and then we could start skinny dipping without a rubber. It had been so long that I'd forgotten what it was like without a second skin. As a matter of fact, the last girl I'd skinny dipped with was Sparkle, and that was when we were teenagers.

I told Lisa I wasn't going to a public clinic where everybody and their momma was sitting around with some sort of sexually transmitted disease. "Find somewhere clean and discreet, and let's get this shit over with," were my exact words.

The next day, she took me to see her girl, Dori. I had forgotten that Dori was a nurse practitioner as well as volunteered as the clinical manager over the county's AIDS and HIV prevention program. Dori was a loud mouth gossip, but she had her good qualities. She drew the blood and had it sent in to the lab with the other tests she had that day. A couple of weeks later, the news came in—positive—both of us. I was pissed off. I figured she knew she had it all along and I got it from eating her coochie.

It was a week before I talked to Lisa again, and she convinced me that she had no idea and she was just as devastated as I was. She even pulled out her negative test results from the previous year, which meant it had to be me that gave it to her. I was shattered. Then guilt came over me after realizing that my years of indulging in downtown dining was responsible for passing this death sentence on to Lisa. She seemed far more accepting with the diagnosis than I was. As I saw it, she loved me enough to stick with me and wasn't even mad about it. She said that since we were both positive, we may as well stick this out together. This way, no one else would get infected and we could keep our status in the shadows. So, there we were—stuck together for life.

I just had to figure out how to tell Sparkle.

Lisa

I slammed the phone down. I'm sure my last comment brought his ass back to reality. He is *mine*! 'Til death do us part—end of story. The HIV card was my last joker in the deck. It had to work.

After dating for two and half years with no ring in sight, I decided to take matters into my own hands. I started volunteering to do clerical work at Dori's office. Hell, her office was mess, and she needed the help. Then I convinced Alex to come and get tested. The rest was easy. The results came in, and they were negative, but I regenerated fake letters using Dori's computer saying we were both positive.

I figured then he would have no choice but to marry me. After all, who else would marry an HIV positive man? It was a rocky road at first, and I almost lost him, but I convinced him to come back to me and let's "get through this together." After that, I knew his pride would take over, so I told him that Dori would prescribe us the necessary drug regimen and he wouldn't have to see his family doctor right away. Thank God, he didn't know the real testing, poking, prodding with a genuine HIV positive diagnosis before actually determining which prescriptions fit a particular strain. I bought a variety of vitamins and put them in prescription bottles, and again said that Dori hooked us up. No one knew about this little trickery--not my mom, not Dori, not anyone. But I'll be damned if it hadn't been my most clever trick!

The emotional affair had gone too damn far and I needed to figure out how to erase this girl from my husband's heart, mind and soul. I'd have to play the wounded "woe is me" wife role for a minute until I figured something out.

Sparkle

I showered again while Alex went to the car to get his bags. I was pretty sure he was calling the Mrs. to check in.

Calm Sparkle

"Oh, God! What have I done?" A pang of guilt shot through my heart and rested deep in my spirit. I'd always been a strong advocate of "thou shalt not commit adultery." Yet, I was washing off the scent of another woman's husband. I may as well have booked a first class, non-stop ticket to hell.

The water felt extremely good on my exhausted body, but I bathed quickly to avoid a shower scene with Alex. Guilt or no guilt, that is one man that I crave. Having him inside of me after all these years only increased my desire for him. I could have him morning, noon and night and never get enough. Insatiable.

I stepped out of the shower and wrapped myself in a towel. I was on the bed applying lotion to my legs when Alex came in. He looked drained. Go me! I smiled to myself.

"Hey you." He spoke with the sexiest of smiles.

"Hey yourself." I smiled back, and I'm certain he could see the lingering signs of desire in my eyes. He walked over and kissed me. Tracing my lips with his tongue then delicately joining it with my own tongue, slowly they entwined and danced together—rhythmically and sensuously as if we had all the time in the world to enjoy each other.

When he finally released my mouth, I could barely see straight. I wanted more. I stood up and allowed my towel to fall from my body and pulled him close to me. I hoped he had enough stamina for just one more time. I allowed my hand to rub his chest and move towards his six-pack. I stopped at his downstairs hair line and toyed with hairs there while my tongue softly flickered his right nipple, making it hard and alert. I then tongue-kissed his entire nipple area, slowly moved my hand further south, and grabbed his testicles, giving them a slight squeeze and gentle massages.

His breathing became labored and he rested his knees on the bed behind me for support. I pulled his mouth to mine and began to stroke his shaft, which was already hard and ready for entrance. He hungrily took my mouth into his and let out a moan. A drop of semen escaped. I used the tiny bit of moisture to lubricate his shaft as my hand continued to move up and down, simulating the feeling of sex. I began to pull his pants down and he gladly obliged me the rest of the way by completely removing them.

I patted the bed, motioning for him to sit down. He obeyed. I straddled him, allowing his penis to barely skim the skin of my vagina and held it there. I wanted to enjoy the anticipation. He seemed to read my mind as he did not plunge into me, but instead began using his mouth to make love to my breasts. I moaned in pleasure as his tongue brushed against my nipples. I looked at him and he returned my gaze—one last kiss. He reached over and grabbed a condom from where he'd left them earlier. He seemed to hesitate when putting it on.

"You okay, baby?" I asked.

In response, he looked at me. It was a look I couldn't read. Was it sympathy or was it pain? The desire was still there in the darkness of his eyes, but there was a hint of something else that I hadn't seen on him before. Sadness. That's what it was. But why? Before I could ponder it anymore, I felt him entering me. He filled me as if we were a perfect fit.

"Hold it right there, baby," I whispered. "Let me remember this." I kissed his ear.

He couldn't take it anymore and began to thrust. We made love for the third time in less than 12 hours. And this time when we came, it was in unison; it was explosive and it was beautiful.

We sat and held each other for moments afterward. Both of us knew that once we let go, it was back to the real world—him back to his wife, and me back to dealing with my divorce. We would not be together.

Calm Sparkle Discussion Questions:

Chapters 3-4

1. Arnold found a unique way to "mark his territory". How would you have reacted to this?
2. Lisa experiences late night phone calls from an unwanted presence but chooses not to answer. Would you have the same restraint?
3. Lisa explains her reasoning for not wanting Alex to know that she knows something is going on. Have you ever been in a situation where you dismissed the truth because living the lie was easier / better?
4. Lisa's mom seems to have her own set of rules on how to keep a man. What do you think about the advice that she is giving Lisa?
5. How do you think Sparkle feels about her church family? Does she feel supported by them? Does she trust them?
6. What do you think she means when she says "..They all keep pebbles in their pocketbooks"?
7. Do you think it's possible to have a strong bond with God when you have lost respect for the church?
8. Sparkle noticed a hint of sadness in Alex's eyes, what do you think were his thoughts at that exact moment?

9. Lisa's true colors are revealed in Chapters 3 and 4. What was your reaction when reading the big secret?
10. We're almost halfway through the book. Are you Team Sparkle or Team Lisa?

Chapter Five
Timing is Everything

Lisa

It had been well over a month since the Moonbow fiasco with that Sparkle chick. The first night he came home was thunderous and filled with arguing. I pulled out all of the stops and made sure he felt like dirt, but he didn't go down so easy. He put up a good fight and tried to flip the script and declare his innocence. In the end, it was a draw. I played mad for a night and then initiated make-up sex. That's when I knew for sure that he had definitely slept with her. Our love making wasn't the same. He didn't seem to be into it and the tricks that usually drove him to toe-curling excitement only seemed to bore him. He may have ejaculated that night, but a true orgasm was not reached. Just as I had feared, I lost a piece of him during that trip he took to his hometown.

Fortunately for me, however, Sparkle does not live in Orlando. I run shit in this neck of the woods. I won his heart one time and I'll do it again. Besides, I'm the bitch with the ring.

Sparkle

"Girl, I haven't heard from him in about two weeks."

Calm Sparkle

I was chatting with Kat on my way home from work.

"You mean he *still* hasn't called you?? "

"Nope. I've only spoken to him twice since we shared what I thought was a magical night."

"That's some bullshizzle! His wife must have him on some serious lockdown."

"Whatever. I'm so over it." I lied.

"Stop lying! Girl, you know you want to go down there and whack him up side the head for trying to make you a one night ho." Kat laughed as she said this. I laughed too, but deep down her words cut. I quickly ended the conversation, saying that I was about to pull over and get some gas. Lying again—it was becoming a habit. I guess the old folks were right; if you'll cheat, you'll lie and if you'll lie, you'll steal. I had already committed two of the three in less than a thirty-day time span. I thought about attempting to commit the third one when I plotted that I could take Alex away from his wife so that he could be with me. I quickly dismissed that idea when I realized I was beginning to think like a homewrecker.

And even if I had continued to consider becoming a husband stealer, Alex dashed those dreams by pulling a disappearing act. The two conversations that I had with him were friendly, but not nearly as flirty and steamy as they were before our night together. He mentioned we should cool it a little bit, but he completely stopped the train. My pride quickly took over from that point. I was not about to take a second seat to anyone, and I was definitely not about to let anyone, not even Alex, toss me aside like a used rag. And after hearing Kat's comment about being a "one night ho," that sealed the deal for me. After hanging up with Kat, I went through my phone and deleted Alex's number.

Alex

I looked at Sparkle's profile picture on Facebook for a fifth time. "Beautiful," I whispered to the image as I did every time I caught a glimpse of her. A quick click of the mouse and the image disappeared—fading back into the virtual world from which I'd summoned it. And just in time since Lisa was heard entering the house.

I loved Lisa. We had been through a lot in our short marriage. I knew that Lisa would hold me down no matter what. As the kids would say, she was my "ride or die chick." Literally. Thinking back to when we first found out we were HIV positive, Lisa was the one who urged me to get tested in the first place, so if it weren't for her, I would have lived with HIV and may never have known it. I would have passed it on to Sparkle. Sparkle—the thought of her made my heart ache. It just made me more grateful for Lisa. She handled my maintenance medications discreetly with Dori so I didn't have to deal with the embarrassment. Lisa was my rock. The only one who knew my secret. Who else could I trust with it? Who else could handle it? What will happen to Jr if we didn't make it? My son. Grief filled my heart. If Lisa and I had a death sentence, who would take care of my kids? For the first time, I came face to face with reality. "I'm dying."

Right then and there, I decided that it was time for Lisa and I to come clean. We needed to set up a plan—to let our families know the situation so that they can be prepared. I picked up some paper and a pen from my desk drawer to jot down a list of things that needed to be done and people to contact. I didn't even hear Lisa come in until her voice broke through the thoughts in my head.

"What's this?" she asked as she peered at the list that had engulfed my attention.

"Lisa, do you realize that we need to make plans? How irresponsible it has been of us to know that we have AIDS and not plan for Jr's future?"

"Slow down, Al, we don't have AIDS."

I cut her off with a very curt, *"Yet!"*

"Ok, *yet*," she continued. "We don't have to worry about that right now. Let's just keep taking our meds, eating right, and just enjoying each other and our family. We will have plenty of time, and will have plenty of notice before we need to start planning our doom." She giggled.

I know that she was trying to make me feel better. She tried to take my mind off things as she always does when I mentioned our health status. Why wasn't she more concerned about this? The thought had crossed my mind several times. I rationalized it with the fact that she volunteered at Dori's AIDS clinic, and she would know when it was time to hit the panic button. For some reason, I couldn't shake the feeling that we needed to get our affairs in order. More importantly, I needed to ensure that Lisa's mom wouldn't walk away with all of my assets if we checked out before she did. I got along very well with my mother-in-law, but she was no doubt an old school gold digger—an OG of the female type.

Lisa took my list, read over it then balled it up and tossed it in the trash. "Honey, please don't worry yourself about this. Trust me, I'll know when we need to get things in order. Besides, keep a little faith. They may find a cure before we—*if* we—get the full blown AIDS virus. Just look at Magic Johnson." She straddled my lap and then leaned in and kissed me.

I knew she hoped that her sudden urge to do a tongue exploration would remove any desire for me to move forward with outing us and preparing for the future. I gave in and kissed her back, just to let her think that I agreed. Once she felt satisfied that she had skillfully played her roll, she ended the kiss and used her thumb to wipe the lipstick from my lips.

She eased herself off of me and planted one final peck on the top of my head before she went back into the kitchen to resume cooking dinner. I turned my attention back towards the computer and began typing out my bucket list. I wanted to give Lisa one more chance to realize the importance of getting our affairs in order. If she wouldn't get on board, I was willing to take care of everything myself.

First things first, I needed to tell someone else of my

status. Who could I tell? Not my mom; I didn't want her to worry herself into an early grave. And definitely not Sparkle. It would have to be Corey. We had been friends since pre-school. I trusted him with everything else. I planned to tell him the next time I went to Moonbow. That would give me chance to lay out a plan and convince Lisa to redo our will.

Lisa

Things had been calm for a couple of months. Alex stopped running to Moonbow every chance he had, and there were no more calls to Sparkle on the cell phone bill, and most importantly, no more text messages. Hallelujah! I wasn't sure why the complete 180 all of a sudden, but I was not going to complain about it. After all the scheming, plotting, and planning, I could finally just relax and enjoy being Mrs. Weston.

Sparkle

Summer, spring and fall had come and gone. It was Valentine's Day and I was officially single again. The freedom was, for lack of a better term, liberating. I felt alive for the first time in years. The sun was brighter, the air was crisper, and the color of life never felt so vibrant.

Oddly enough, I couldn't help but wonder why I hadn't left Arnold sooner. I definitely was not a stereotypical, bitter divorcee. I hadn't heard from Alex since he said we needed to cool it after that fateful night we shared with each other. Aww who am I kidding? That night we damned each other to hell in a handbasket wearing gasoline drawers is more like it. I'm sure God is tired of hearing my promises to never do that again. My mantra for the first few weeks afterwards was "Thou shalt not covet thy neighbor's husband." The guilt was not even worth it. Okay, maybe a little. No! No, Sparkle! It was *not* worth it. Sheesh.

We were at a karaoke bar chomping on some wings and waiting for Corey to get drunk enough to sing his rendition of Bruno Mars' "Uptown Funk." It was my divorce party and girls' night out. Our plan was to start slow and finish hard.

"Girl what are you over there thinking about?" Kat asked.

"Nothing. Nothing at all." I took a sip of my sweet tea.

"Sweet Tea? Is that all you're drinking tonight, Sparkle?" Corey came back from the bar and took a seat at our table where few of our other friends congregated. He thought he was being inconspicuous, but I knew that he was taking this opportunity to study everyone to feel out which one he could take home.

"How's everyone doing tonight?" he addressed the table. "You all sure look lovely. Sparkle, you uhhh--," he paused to stroke his beard and lick his lips, "you gonna introduce me to your friends?"

Corey looked like Sylvester the cat right before he'd pounce on poor little Tweety bird. Ever since he broke up with his fiancé' the year before, he had been trying to prove to himself that he was better off being a Hugh Heffner type of guy. He wanted a harem of women in a sister-wives style agreement. He believed in the Michael Baisden philosophy of "choice based on truth." No more sneaking around, just being open and honest. If the lady can handle his truth, then it is her choice to stay or leave. I had to respect him for that. There's no drama when all motives are laid out on the table.

"Yes, Corey. Sweet Tea is it for me for right now. At least until I can get some food in my stomach." I introduced him to the ladies at the table and Corey ordered a round of shots for everyone.

"Come on now, Sparkle! You know the tradition. Every night starts with a shot. Let's get it; let's go!" He raised his glass and my friends quickly obliged.

"Hell, why not?" I thought to myself. It's Valentine's Day, my divorce finally came through, and I was a free woman.

"Okay, Corey. Let's do it!" I raised my glass and said, "here's to happily ever after."

"To happily ever after!" everyone chimed in, clinked glasses and simultaneously bottoms up. We all did the stank face and a vigorous shaking of heads, a few gags and coughs and hitting of the chests as the tequila oozed fire down our throats.

"Whooooo!" escaped my lips involuntarily, but I wasn't alone in that sentiment.

Corey jumped up as a group of very nice looking gentlemen entered the bar. They threw a nod and began heading our way as Corey waved them towards us and started pulling more chairs around the table. The ladies started sitting up a little straighter, pouting their lips a tad bit more and did a quick check of the teeth with their tongues to make sure there were no remnants of the wings they had just devoured.

The fellas were handsome; I can't deny that. However, being that I was with 'big brother' Corey, the ultimate cockblocker, I knew he would never allow me to holla at any of them. Somewhere along the line, he told himself that no one could have me except Alex, and he would make damn sure to protect that at every opportunity. I wasn't up for the debate or the hassle. I just wanted to have a great night out with my girls, get a wee bit tipsy and then go home and sleep until lunchtime.

The fellas made their introductions and squeezed in seats at the table so we were sitting in boy-girl-boy-girl fashion. Corey was on one side of me and Alex's cousin was on the other. How convenient. As the heat from the tequila shot began to settle and I was dipping a fry into some ketchup, I saw a vision of testosterone perfection walk through the door. "Is it the tequila or is it getting hot in here?"

"Huh? What was that?" Kat and Corey both responded.

Dang, did I say that out loud? Gots to be more careful. "Oh nothing. Pass me the wings!" I hoped that would change the subject, but Kat knew me all too well. She raised

Calm Sparkle

an eyebrow, and I pointed with a roll of my eyeballs towards the vision of masculine beauty that had just walked in.

Kat, who was already sipping on a mudslide before the tequila shot, let out a very loud "DAAYYUUMMM!" and quickly drew the attention of the others at the table.

"Really, Kat? Really?" All I could do was shake my head at her. Kat quickly recovered by reaching over and feeling the biceps of the guy sitting next to her and saying, "look at those guns! Do you work out?" Poor little fella blushed so hard he could barely catch his breath. He eventually managed to find a little bass for his voice as he responded to Kat's unexpected admiration.

Corey leaned over and whispered to me, "Y'all ain't fooling nobody."

"Damn, Corey. Mind your business," I whispered back. Managing to maintain my composure, I excused myself from the table. I needed to shake off the buzz from the shot and to also maneuver my way over to get a closer look at Shemar Moore meets Morris Chestnut meets golden mountain of fineness. I stepped outside to catch a breath of fresh air. It was warm out with a cool, gentle breeze blowing. That is the beauty of living in Florida—warm winters. I pulled out my compact mirror to check my hair, popped a mint, and applied a little more gloss to my lips. I returned my thoughts to the mystery man that had just graced the building with his presence. What exactly am I supposed to say to him?

The single life was still new to me and I was not quite sure what the etiquette should be. Do I approach him? Do I wait for him to come to me? Did he even see me? I may have looked cool, calm and collected on the outside, but on the inside I was frazzled. Butterflies were being birthed by the second. As I worked myself into an unnecessary nervous breakdown over the mere thought of approaching a guy, my phone rang and interrupted my thoughts. Saved by the bell. I glanced at the number and it was an out of town area code that I knew all too well. It figures that he would call tonight.

Ain't nobody got time for that foolishness. I quickly silenced the ringer and placed the phone back in my pocket.

Annoyed and anxious to tell Kat about my missed call, I turned to go back into the bar and ran smack into the chest of "Shemar Chestnut." He literally had to catch me from falling as my bosom bounced off his body and I stumbled backwards. How embarrassing.

"I'm so sorry. I didn't see you there." My words trailed off as my eyes locked with his honey brown irises, thick long lashes and perfect, more than perfect, teeth. It was definitely the work of a very skillful orthodontist, but that was when I felt it. That "it" feeling that you hear about from other people or in movies. I'm sure we only locked eyes for a couple of seconds, but for the first time ever, I looked into someone's eyes and I saw their soul. Not only did I see his soul, but I recognized it as my own.

He loosened his grip on me, and with a shy smile he responded, "It's my fault. I wasn't paying attention. Are you okay?"

My feminine wiles kicked in and I tilted my head slightly and matched his coyness, "Yes, I'm fine. Thank you for catching me."

"Anytime, pretty lady. Anytime."

And just like that he was gone. Did I imagine that magical moment? My violin orchestra quickly interrupted like the sound of a scratched record. I couldn't even hide my discombobulation. I stood dumbfounded for at least a good 5 seconds. I did a breath check. Yep, minty fresh. I quick glanced down and my zipper was intact—no wardrobe malfunctions. I'll never understand men.

My cellphone rang again as I walked back to the table. Alex. Again. Get the freak outta here Mr. Missing in Action for the past four months. I shook my head in disgust and disappointment as I rejected the call and tossed the phone onto the table. There would be no drama that night. I was free. Free! I ordered another round of shots for my girls. It was a time for celebration.

As soon as I sat down to enjoy the music and conversation, Kat pounced on me, "Woman, where were you? That golden hottie was here at the table sitting in your very seat! And might I add, he is even *finer* up close and personal! I'm talking FOINNE!"

"I knoooow! I know!" I squealed like a teenager. Not sure if it was the lingering effect of the mystery man or the shots that I'd taken. I told Kat the story of how I literally ran into him and he had to stop me from falling. I left out the part about how I felt our souls connected and somehow reunited even though we'd never met. I'll just chalk that up to temporary effects of tequila.

Dr. Adonis

"Damn! What was that?" I spoke more to the air and no one in particular. I shook my head in disbelief as I walked away from *whoever* that was. Damn again! Why didn't I get her number, or name for that matter?

Once inside my car, I was tempted to go back into the bar. But naaahh—it's not that serious. Ladies are a dime a dozen. I glanced through the windshield trying to get a glimpse inside the bar as people were going in and out. Hunnies may be a dime a dozen, yet for some reason, she rocked me to my core. When we locked eyes, it felt like something I've never experienced. My phone vibrated and reminded me of why I had to leave this spot so soon. Ahhh yes, Keilani, the exotic Hawaiian cutie that was the most recent of my match ups according to LinkingUp.com. She was eager to meet up with me—as they all were. Amazing how easy it was to get laid. If a brother was ever in a drought then it's *his* fault. I sent a quick text to my stress relief for the night to let her know I was on my way. I cranked up my music and headed towards the meet up spot, but I was two blocks down the road and still couldn't shake the feeling from that encounter with…with…who *was* she?

I made a U-turn and headed back to the bar. I just needed her name and number, then I could meet up with

Keilani and follow up on the mystery lady later in the week. Something about her was different and I was going to find out what it was.

Back at the bar, she was easier to find than I thought. She was a vision on stage doing a pretty good rendition of "Tyrone" by Erykah Badu. Every woman in the club was singing along with her, hands up in the air, shouts of encouragement coming from various spots in the room. "Go on, gurrrl!" "Sang that thang, sistah!" "That's right! Call him!" were just a few of the choice banshee screeches heard from the audience.

My buddy Corey was still in the same spot as he was when I'd left minutes earlier, and the seat was still vacant right next to him, so I saddled up and watched this lovely vision sing her heart out. Obviously enjoying her sisterhood's "amen choir," she easily moved around the stage and engaged her onlookers—giving attitude as needed with the roll of the neck or hand on the hip. I must admit, I was quite amused. She was beautiful, well poised and great vocalist. If she could cook and had intelligent conversation, she could be the one.

"Yo, Don! You back so soon?" Corey interrupted my thoughts as he leaned in and yelled to be heard over the women all singing back up "call him" in unison.

"Yeah, man. Spotted this hunnie outside and came back in to see if I could catch that number before I head back out."

"Who? Where is she? Maybe I can help you out. I know a lot of people in here. Perks of being the owner," Corey chuckled. He was right; he did know a lot of people.

"That one right there." The lady in front of me who was obviously listening whipped her head around to see who I was pointing at. When she realized I was talking about the one stage, she completely turned around in her seat and joined the conversation.

"The one on stage?" she chimed in as if invited, and took a sip of her drink. I was annoyed, but never one to be unnecessarily rude, so I gave her a quick nod.

Corey, in a surprised voice said, "Sparkle?"

"Is that her name? So, you *do* know her? Hook me up, man!"

"Naw, dude. Can't do it. You're on your own with that one."

The nosey lady across from us giggled, and then said, "you most certainly can have her number. She's my cousin and I think I can arrange an introduction." I caught Corey cutting her a stern look like your mama gives you when you're about to blurt out a family secret while in public. You know—the "don't you dare" look that makes kids immediately stop talking. Watching this silent transaction piqued my interest.

"Really now?" I egged on the nosey cousin. I turned my attention to Corey, "So what's the deal bro? Is she your ex or something? You know I respect bro-code."

Corey quickly denied that. "Naaaw, man. Not *my* ex. She's like a sister to me. She dated my boy for years, so I just look out for her is all."

"Good. Well, no bro-code broken on my part." I clasped my hands then started to rub them together like an evil scientist thinking of a master plan.

"Yo, dude. I said she's like a sister to me. You can, try to hook up but if you dog her, I'm on you." Corey was serious. I hadn't seen him respect any woman up until that point. My interest was really piqued, and just then my mystery woman came to the table and stood right behind me.

"Well, looks like someone has taken your seat, cousin," the nosey one spoke and looked directly at me with a mischievous grin. "I guess you'll have to sit in his lap," she continued.

Corey stood to make the introduction as I stood to offer her a seat. "Sparkle, this is my boy, Don. He's the doctor that cared for my dad the last few years before he passed."

She glanced at me bashfully, a far cry from the woman that was just on stage leading the women in a Badu chant to call Tyrone. I wanted to call her out for it, but thought better of it. Instead, I just offered her my hand in the formality of a shake and offered the overused "please to meet you." My intent was to get in, get her number, and get out so I could resume my original plans for the night, but the conversation flowed easily; the group that was with her was fun and carefree. We all ended up dancing the night away, laughing at karaoke performers and even singing a few more songs amongst ourselves. I managed to get Sparkle alone for a few minutes, which felt like only a few seconds. I got her number and we agreed to meet up soon for a one on one date.

Alex

Was she ignoring me? I'd called twice and no answer. I knew she was with Corey because he filled me in on the party plans for the night. Maybe she just couldn't hear the phone. I shot her a quick text, "Hey you. What's good?" I knew I shouldn't have reached out to her with all that I had going on; I just needed to hear her voice and explain why I pulled away. My timing sucked to shit, I know, but it was for the best. As I sat back in my recliner and lit my cigar, Lisa came into the den wearing nothing but my favorite pair of heels and a smile. All those years and she still tried to keep the spice alive. I loved her for that. My other buddies complain that they had to beg their wives for sex. I never had that problem, but while the sex was plentiful, it got a bit dry. Literally. We used KY or Eros or whatever lubricant was close but it had gotten monotonous. Lisa could suck and buck all night, but I wanted a little variety.

I never thought I'd see the day that I would think sex could be boring. I loved Lisa though. She held me down. She gave me a son. She broke her back to make sure that I always knew that I was king of the castle. They don't come any better than that. My phone vibrated, notifying that a text had come through. Ahhh shit—was it Sparkle replying back? We finally had some peace in the house and I was not about to reignite the drama.

"Heey, babe! Look at all this sexiness." I jumped up to greet Lisa before she could focus on the lit-up phone screen previewing an unread text message.

"Showtime," I whispered in her ear as I pinned her against the wall. I guess if I wanted variety, I'd have to lead by example.

Lisa

Damn. I could still feel the effects of the pounding from Alex the night before. I wonder what got into him.

"Hello?" I waited for the 3rd ring to answer the call. It was Corey. Surely, he'd dialed me by mistake. Corey is cool and all but we really had nothing to talk about and I was sick of his player wanna be ass always acting like Alex was still free to do single man shit.

"Whaddup, sis?" Corey chimed on the other end. I managed to fake a cheery disposition.

"Hiii, Corey! What's going on?" I needed him to get to the point—no idle chit chat was needed. No love lost; just spit it out. I rolled my eyes toward the ceiling as my inner thoughts said what I didn't dare say out loud.

"You know our boy has a birthday coming up. What you got planned?" Shoot, I forgot!

I blurted out, "Nothing." I responded to his question before realizing it.

"Cool! What do you think about all of us flying over to Kingston to celebrate?"

"Sure, Corey! That sounds like a blast and I'm sure Alex would love to see you. And ummm—which lady will be accompanying you this time? I don't want to get the name wrong like I did last date night!" I smiled so hard my cheeks hurt. It was genuine as I recalled the last evening when Corey came to visit and I accidently called his date by his ex-wife's name.

"Aww see. You got jokes," Corey chuckled. "Actually, I don't know yet, but I'll be sure to get her name tattooed across my forehead so you don't mess it up!"

I had to giggle at that. He was a playa, and I didn't like him hanging out with my husband, but he was always a funny guy. Besides, I could use this trip to my advantage. I hadn't been off of mommy duty in a few months and I could use the down time.

"Great! We'll be there the Friday before his birthday and we can all fly out together." Corey wrapped up the call and surprisingly, I was quite excited about the new plans. "Get your sitter lined up; it's going to be a weekend to remember!"

"Sounds, good. We'll be ready!"

The weeks flew by. It was hard to not let the cat out of the bag about Alex's birthday trip to Jamaica. All he knew was that Corey was coming with his latest Jet beauty of the week and we were going to celebrate the entire weekend. When the day finally came for Corey's visit, Alex was hyped. He was like a kid at Christmas. Those two greeted each other as if they hadn't seen each other in years. There was stomping and frat calls throughout the house. Remind me again of why I married a younger man. Oh yeah, because I can.

Once all the celebratory hoopla died down, we piled into a sleek black stretch limo to head out for dinner. Little did Alex know, that the limo was also packed with our luggage for the island getaway on a red eye flight to paradise. The next thing I remember is the bright glare of the sunlight coming through the windows and blinding me. I don't know how much I drank that night, but none of it prepared me for what was coming. I awoke our first morning at the Kingston resort to find Alex frantically going through the luggage.

"What's wrong, bae?"

"Lisa, where did you put the meds?"

For a hot minute, I was puzzled. Meds? What meds? Ahhhh shiiiit. I smacked my palm against my hungover forehead. How could I forget to pack his damn Flintstone vitamins? They were really just multi-vitamins, iron, calcium, b-12, whatever was on sale. I would explain the different pills by saying the doctor was trying different cocktails to keep the strain from getting immune to any one therapy regime. I almost laughed out loud when I realized that was what was giving him a panic attack. If only he knew but he never would.

"Awwww, hunnie. I completely forgot our meds. Come on back to bed, and we'll double up when we get back." I laid back down and pulled the covers over my head. Before I could close my eyes good, I felt a sudden breeze. Alex had snatched the blankets not only off me, but off the entire bed. The pure white comforter and sheets flew in waves through the air like Superman's cape before listlessly falling into a pile in the corner of the room.

"You did what?" the boom in Alex's voice made me jolt straight up. Hangover or not, I needed to get my wits about me fast.

"Babe, calm down." I cooed.

"CALM DOWN! CALM DOWN! What the FUCK you mean 'calm down'?" he barked.

I wasn't prepared for his blowup. I had never seen him that angry. I almost let it slip that it was just some damn vitamins, but I knew better than to do that. I had worked way too hard to get there. He was standing at the end of the bed, so I crawled over to him and wrapped my arms around his neck while nuzzling on him. Very gently and lovingly I said, "Please calm down, hunnie. I promise it will be ok if we just skip a couple of days. We can double up when we get back home. I'll call Dori and I know she will say that it's ok."

"Call her now." He growled. His response caught me off guard, as had the entire morning. That was not how I envisioned spending my grown-folk's getaway. He walked over to the dresser and grabbed my phone then tossed it to me on the bed. "Call her," he repeated. "Make sure it's okay." His voice was softer. It was filled with concern and fear rather than anger. I got out of the bed to hug him as a way to bide some time, knowing damn well that I couldn't call Dori. She still had no idea that I forged her stationary and signature to write a fake HIV test result.

"Okay, hun," I soothed. "Can you get me some ice? I'll need a bloody Mary for this headache and I'll call Dori. You'll see. Everything will be just fine." Alex grabbed the ice bucket and headed out of the room.

I fell back on the bed exhausted and kicking myself for not remembering the damn vitamins.

Sparkle

"And remember, for every blessing, be a blessing. Thank you for coming out to support! Live! Love!" I concluded my speech at the closing ceremony of my first annual "Single Ladies Expo" to thunderous applause. It was good to know that my journey gave me the ability to help so many women. Since the divorce party, I'd made several life changes. I quit my VP job and obtained certification as a life coach. I mentored a handful of high end, very private clientele due to connections made during my executive years in the corporate world, and then kicked off my very first national event, which catered to single women from all walks of life. Things were good and I was finally happy—mentally, physically and emotionally.

I actually enjoyed being single. The dating scene was a source of entertainment while others found it frustrating. I'm not sure if it was because marriage was the absolute last thing on my mind, or because I truly enjoyed studying the male creature and his thought patterns.

When my phone chimed a calendar reminder, I glanced at it. "ALEX WESTON'S BIRTHDAY" it visibly announced. Alex and I had spoken on several occasions over that last couple of months. We were comfortable being friends. Correction, *I* was comfortable being *just friends*. After our last physical encounter, it was a wrap for me. I wanted no more romantic delusions.

Calm Sparkle

Alex came to visit the weekend after my divorce party. I'm sure part of that had something to do with Corey telling him that I was entertaining conversation with an eligible bachelor. At the time, I was playing hard, yet holding on to a sliver of hope that we were indeed the fairytale couple that our classmates thought we were destined to be. I allowed him to come over once Andre was asleep. My intentions were for us to talk it out and find out where to go from there.

As soon as I opened the door and looked into his eyes, I knew he had other intentions. I guided him into the living room and we sat on the couch. I placed a pillow between us in hopes that it would block the chemistry that was brewing. He asked for a kiss and I pecked him on the cheek. He clutched his heart and feigned a heart attack in the stylings of Red Foxx when he played the Fred Sanford character. "Ouch!" he laughed. Then he got serious, and a veil of lust clouded his eyes like a midnight storm. He hooked his forefinger and gently placed it on my chin, tilting and lifting my head towards his. When our noses touched, he whispered, "I love you."

My defenses broke and I let him kiss me. He eventually let go of my chin and eased his hand around my back, pulling me closer to him and pressing my chest against his. I followed suit and wrapped my hands around his neck, fully giving in to the power of the kiss. When our lips finally released their suction of each other, his tongue gave my bottom lip a final flicker. Through sex drugged eyes, he looked into mine and breathed, "I want you."

I threw the pillow on the floor that had been cock-blocking our groins and straddled his lap. He was rock hard. I unbuckled his jeans and slid down to my knees ready to taste the rod responsible for the bulge in his boxer briefs. He moaned as soon as he felt my breath get close. Just as I freed his penis and it sprang out like a Jack in the box, his cell phone vibrated and lit up. We both glanced at the same time as it buzzed away on the couch cushion next to us. The word "WIFEY" headlined followed by a preview of a photo text. It was Lisa laying spread eagle with her vajayjay front and center in the picture.

Another text immediately came through with "Starting without you. Hurry home, Hubby." His dick immediately retreated. There I was on my knees practically tongue on the head of it, but looking like I was holding a deflated balloon. I looked up at him and he was embarrassed. He covered his face with both hands and threw his head up towards the ceiling.

"Uuuggghhhh!" was all he could manage to say. I politely tucked his now flexible member back into its Hanes constructed home, re-buttoned and zipped his jeans, and then resumed my place on the couch next to him. I laid my head on his chest and gave him a hug to let him know that it was okay. After a quick squeeze, he wrapped his arms around me and returned the hug.

"Hey, you," I said to him, "no worries. One of us had to keep the both of us from going to hell." He chuckled and began to apologize.

"Let's just start over," he pleaded. He began to try to rub life back into his jones. When that didn't work, he took my hand and placed it on his softness in an attempt to resuscitate life back into what was now resting peacefully.
I quickly removed it now that I was fully sober and no longer intoxicated by desire.

"Awww, babe," I cooed to him. "I think it's cute that he only responds to her now. That's the way it should be and I'm proud of you." I kissed him on the cheek and went into the kitchen to get a glass of wine. I actually felt okay about what happened—or didn't happen. I was disappointed in myself for giving in so easily. I made a vow to never screw a married man, and yet there I was—dick in hand, and mouth in position. Where had my morals gone?

I felt Alex come behind me and wrap me up in a bear hug. "I do love you," he repeated. "I want us to be together. Just say you'll be mine."

Calm Sparkle

I was confused. How could he ask me something like that if he's married? Was he leaving her? "What are you talking about Alex?" I turned to face him so I could read his expressions. "Are you leaving? Don't leave for me. That's not what I want."

"No, nooo. I'm not leaving. You know I would never leave my son. I grew up without a dad and I would never do that to my son."

"Then what are you asking me?" Suddenly I felt like the wind had been knocked out of me as the reality of what he suggested started take shape. "You want me to be your mistress?" I spat out the word "mistress" as if it were poison to my lips.

"Yeah! I mean, NO! I mean—damn, Sparkle. You know I love you, and I want to be with you, and I don't want you with anyone else. Just be mine."

"What?" was all that I could muster up to say. I blinked furiously in disbelief. "Wait a minute. Let me digest this." I sipped my wine, and then took two gulps of it.

Alex took the time to offer up his plan. "Babe," he started, "we can see each other like every other weekend. We can take trips together—just until little man graduates high school, and then we can be together." I glanced up at him and he actually looked proud of his proposal.

I was disgusted. I was even more insulted. How dare he? Okay, so I had a moment of temporary insanity and we had sex well over a year before. Okay, so we almost— *almost*—had sex again. But I am *not* a mistress! I guffawed at him and shook my head. There were no words to describe the emotions that came crashing down on me. I finished the last bit of wine in my glass and took a deep breath, then I thanked God. Yes. I thanked God for answering my prayers. I prayed the Lord's Prayer every night and a part of that says to "lead me not into temptation." Sure enough, temptation was squashed that night.

And that is how we'd come to be where we were. Alex

no longer made my heart go pitter patter, and he no longer drenched my Vicky's, and he even helped to confirm that prayer definitely works! Last I heard, he was headed to a birthday vacation with Corey, and I wished him nothing but the best. I thought it best not to text and wish him a happy birthday knowing that Lisa was with him and my name was still forbidden to be spoken in their home. I don't blame her though, and I am sure there were absolutely no words that could make her believe that Alex and I were capable of being strictly platonic. My goal was to remain at a respectful distance and allow their union to blossom as it should.

I searched the crowd for Don. He was supposed to meet me in the reception area at six. I thought that I would be done with everything by then, but the Q & A session of my presentation on online dating ran longer than anticipated, and it threw me off schedule. It was 6:27 and I was frantically trying to make my way through the crowd. I truly adored my supporters, and normally I would welcome every hug, requests for selfies or book signature request, but I couldn't that day. I silently pleaded, "Ladies, puhleeeze don't stop me today. I have a date with an Adonis and I have been looking forward to it for weeks." I smiled politely and eased through the maze of people and tried to be as unnoticeable as possible while simultaneously scanning the crowd to see if he was anywhere within my line of vision.

I didn't see him right away, so I posted up at the reception desk. No one was there because the weekend-long event was over. The ones left in the building were shopping at the vending booths or just chatting and networking. With a moment to reflect, I started to think of how far Don and I had come from that chance meeting at the karaoke bar. Although we spoke and facetimed daily, we were unable to synchronize our schedules to physically meet in person.

I felt as if I'd known him my entire life, but I was a nervous wreck at the thought of seeing him. I had never felt that way about anyone before. With Arnold, I was married out of obligation. I stayed out of convenience.

With Alex, it was genuine. And we would always be friends, but he was my lust evoker. He was never much of an intellectual stimulator, but he indeed would awaken my loins. Don was different. He sparked my spirit. He challenged me and respected me, and most importantly, he adored my mind design. Whereas most men are threatened by it.

Before I could text Don to see where he was, he'd messaged me first. As I responded, a group of women that were leaving the venue spotted me and stopped to ask for a Facebook live post. We did a quick shout out to social media then began chatting about the conference. I was beyond relieved to see Don ease through the crowd and ask if he could interrupt the conversation. The ladies parted like the Red Sea after one good lookover of my golden Adonis. Several of them vocally stated their approval of my choice in dates; others just nodded in agreement. No one objected to me leaving mid-conversation.

As soon as Don and I locked eyes, I felt that same soul stirring. I knew immediately that we were lovers in a past life. We greeted each other with a hug. Much different than the hold he used to keep me from falling months before—tight, firm and secure. Home.

Dr. Adonis

That's her! I immediately recognized her face when I walked into the venue. There was a life-sized banner descending from the ceiling with her smile lighting up the canvas. After months of virtual conversation, I would finally get a chance to hold Sparkle—the woman that managed to capture the undivided attention of my wandering eyes.

We were set to meet at six, but I got there at five just so I could be a voyeur and watch her interact with others. I ordered a Long Island iced tea from the cash bar and found a seat in the last row of chairs that were directed at the stage. It was a nice set up. It was too much pink and glitter for my taste, but it was a women's event after all. There was a stage with a podium and drop down projector screen with about 300 chairs lined up in rows for those who wanted to hear the presentations. Forty-two vendors lined the outer walls. I knew it was exactly forty-two because Sparkle was very particular on that. "Forty-two vendors. No more, no less." When I asked her why she simply stated, "I just like that number." And that was that.

I loved watching her work the crowd. People admired her. And so did I. I had to check myself when I felt a tinge of jealousy as she coached the audience on how to date online. I knew that I didn't want her dating anyone else other than myself. I don't know what cupid had in that arrow the night he shot me, but it was potent.

I watched her search the crowd at the end of her closing remarks. I'm sure she was looking for me. She headed in the direction of where I was supposed to be waiting on her, but I needed a moment to collect myself. My soldier was at full attention just watching her in her element. I shot her a quick text so she wouldn't think that I stood her up.

"Hey, sexy. I love those white leather pants," I typed.

"Where are you?" she responded almost immediately.

"I'm here. Watching your adoring fans fawn over you. Lol."

"LOL. Ok, Handsome. Come rescue me."

I finished my drink and made my way to our designated meeting area. Sparkle was surrounded by a group of ladies who all seemed to be talking at the same time. Some were snapping pictures with cell phones, while others shoved a book and an ink pen towards her. In the midst of all the excited energy, Sparkle was poised, calm and smiling brightly. Giving everyone eye contact and hugs, she gave each woman individual attention and listened intently. I felt proud. Not sure why, but I did. She wasn't my wife or my woman, but I was proud that she would be leaving with me. I walked up to the group of ladies and interjected—politely of course. No man in their right mind would step to address a queen in the midst of her hive in the wrong disposition.

"Excuse me, ladies, may I steal her away? I've been waiting a long time to meet Coach Sparkle." I flashed a smile and winked in Sparkle's direction.

The ladies cleared a path and I could hear the mumbles of approval. "Wooooo! Yes, Coach Sparkle!" "Get it, girl." "Where did you meet someone like him?" "Does he have a brother? Uncle? Cousin? SON?"

I was used to women giving me attention, but in front of Sparkle, I was embarrassed and started to blush. It was definitely time to exit stage left and get some alone time with the woman that had stirred up an unknown chamber of emotions. I'd decided to take her to my favorite lounge. It was Venus vs Mars night. A perfect place to get an idea of how her mind worked.

Alex

How could she forget the meds? Corey was in the hall headed towards his room after his morning workout.

"What's wrong, bruh?"

"Man, Lisa forgot our meds! How could she be so careless?" Corey looked confused. Oh shit! Did I just let that out? Fuck it; he's my best friend, and Jr's godfather. I had planned to tell him anyway, so it was finally time. Besides, he ought to know.

"Meds?"

"Let's go somewhere and talk. I need to get this off my chest." Corey looked concerned, but he didn't say anything as we maneuvered through the corridors looking for a private place to chat. We decided to head out to the beach area. Once settled, I didn't waste time getting to the point. I had to tell him before I lost the nerve, or better yet, before Lisa had an opportunity to change my mind again—like she had months before.

"There's no easy way to say this, man, but—," I took a deep breath, "I have HIV." I blurted it out and held my breath to give the man I considered a brother from another mother the chance to digest this news. Corey had lost his father to AIDS four short years before and I hated putting his line dawg through it again.

"Just HIV, dawg?" Corey asked optimistically.

"Yeah. Lisa says we caught it early. It's not full blown AIDS."

"Lisa?"

I hung my head in shame and rubbed my bald head—reliving the moment she told me the life-altering news. I had always been so very careful. Always. I just don't know how. It had to be the oral I was getting and giving on the regular. "Yeah," I finally replied. I explained everything to Corey about how we found out and how Dori was helping to keep it under wraps with the prescriptions and such.

"What the hell?" Corey shook his head in disbelief. "You're telling me that you haven't been to a doctor?"

"Nah man. I told you; I'm trying to keep this on the low. If this gets out, it'll ruin my businesses."

"What? Are you living in the 90's? People don't trip out as bad on HIV anymore."

I just shrugged my shoulders. I don't know what world Corey was living in, but my world had people with a phobia of anything that even sounds close to AIDS.

Corey continued to talk, "Dude, this isn't adding up. You know I watched my dad go through this. How do you not have any follow-up doctor appointments? No follow-up blood test to make sure the drug regime is working?"

I didn't have a response for that. I had let my pride get in the way and just tried to keep things on the hush-hush. I read somewhere that if you missed a prescription dose, it's possible the body could build a resistance to the medication—or something like that. I gotta get back to my laptop and do some more research.

"And now you say that Lisa left your medications at home?" I hadn't realized that Corey was still talking. I nodded ashamedly.

"What are you taking?" Damn. I couldn't even answer

that.

"Just the usual, C-dawg. Look, let's head back up. I just wanted you to know. With you being Jr's godfather and all, I felt you had a right to know. That's all."

"You don't even know what you're taking do you? Damn, man! What the hell happened to you? Is Lisa's puss…"

"Hey! That's my wife!" I was up in Corey's face before I realized it, and before he could even finish the sentence. He broke the bro code. You don't talk about a man's wife in any way, shape or form when it comes to sex.

"My bad, bro," Corey put his hands up in a surrendering manner. He knew he had crossed the line. We both knew why. "My bad, Alex. You're right. You're my bro, man. I just want the best for you. As soon as we get back, you're coming to see Dr. Adonis. That's who kept Pops going as along as he did. I can't say enough about him. I'll set it up and you can see him first thing Monday morning."

I didn't want to agree, but I knew how persistent Corey could be. I really didn't have a choice. I guess it was time to start living in my truth.

"Alright, man," I conceded. "Go ahead and set it up." Corey whipped out his phone right then and there before I could change my mind or back out. After a brief conversation, he got news that Doc was booked up for at least four weeks, but would definitely fit us in on his first available opening. I was both frustrated and relieved. I needed every hour of those four weeks or so to sway Lisa to my side about leaving Dori and seeing a different specialist.

Chapter Six
Real Eyes Realize Real Lies

Lisa

It had been a month since Jamaica and Alex just wasn't himself. He'd planned a trip to Moonbow, but I wasn't worried about the homewrecker who shall remain nameless. After our last blowout, I warned Alex that if I ever heard her name again I'd cut his dick off. It had been a peaceful year, and I wanted to keep it that way. I still spot checked for any signs of funny business, but there hadn't been any activity at all—as if she never existed. And that is exactly how I wanted to keep it.

Alex

The sound of Usher Raymond's voice on the radio pulled me away from the spreadsheet that had my attention for over 10 minutes. "There's always that one person that will always have your heart—." I couldn't stop the smile from invading my face. Impulsively, I picked up the phone and sent Sparkle a text, "Love you. 'Til the end of time." A few seconds later she hit me back with "Heeeeey, boo! Right back at ya, kiddo ;-)." Her nonchalance stung a little, but any communication was better than none at all. I immediately deleted the conversation. From the past fiasco, I had since learned to reprogram her number under the name "Wifey" just in case I ever forgot to delete anything. The key to pulling this off was to never use names—always a pet name.

I know you're probably thinking of how wrong I was and that I was being the typical dog of a man that can't be satisfied with just one woman. The truth of the matter is that I just couldn't shake her, and I tried. Repeatedly! She was in my bones, and if I had to play the platonic role, then I was willing to do so. The hope was she'd eventually see things my way and come back to me. She belonged to me as much as I belonged to her. I thought back to our last encounter a couple of days after the trip to Kingston. Sparkle stopped through on her way to Orlando for a conference and we met up for lunch which led to dinner and a serious heart to heart.

"You know I love you, right?" I eased into the conversation after we had cocktails and a light lunch at my favorite oceanfront spot. I wasn't worried about being spotted because Lisa knew that I entertained clients here all the time. She wouldn't be suspicious if someone ran back to her and told her that they saw me having lunch with another female.

"Yeah—I know," was Sparkle's response, "but does Lisa know?" She had jokes, and apparently she thought she was funny because her laughter filled the air. I studied her for a moment before proceeding. I wanted to remember her as she was. Happy. Naïve. I knew that could all change once I let her know about my HIV status, but I needed her to hear it from me. Corey schooled me on the fact that she was kickin' it with the doctor that I'd see a few weeks later, and I didn't want to take any chances. Besides, she deserved that. I wasn't sure if she would cuss me out or get up and leave. Or even worse, be afraid to touch me, hold me, kiss me. I couldn't imagine going through the rest of my life without ever tasting those lips again. Granted, she hadn't kissed me in almost a year, but I was a patient man.

"Sparkle, I'm serious," I interrupted her fit of giggles and she took notice. "Let's take a walk," I suggested as I stood up and reached for her hand.

She took hold but quickly let go once she was on her feet. I led the way off of the deck of the restaurant where we ate before stepping out onto the bustling, bright walkways of Downtown Disney. Sparkle was silent the whole time—no corny jokes, no small talk, just patiently waited for me to say something. I struggled with the right words and finally just blurted out, "I tested positive for HIV."

I couldn't look at her. I stared past her until I felt her body against mine and a warm embrace that told me everything would be okay. I was stunned for a brief moment and stood frozen before returning the hug. I rested my head on top of hers, took a deep breath, and for the first time, I cried.

The phone rang jolting me out of my stage of reminiscing. The display lit up with the word "Wifey."

"Heeey, Boooo!" said the sing songy voice. It was Sparkle.

"Hey, beautiful! How are you?"

"I'm great! Just checking to make sure you are on schedule for your appointment on Tuesday."

"Yeah, babe. All is on schedule and the Weston's will be arriving in town on Thursday for blood work. Staying for a fun-filled weekend and then poked and prodded on Tuesday by your boy. You still seeing him?"

"Yep. He's still a solid contestant for this bachelorette." She laughed at her own jokes even when no one else did. "How did Lisa handle the news that you're coming to Moonbow to see a new doctor?"

"She doesn't know yet. I'll tell her tonight." I turned into the car dealer lot and parked. It was going to take a huge gift to break this news to Lisa. She was very particular about her doctor and adamant on not letting anyone else into our treatment. I quickly ended the call with Sparkle before she could begin to question me about why I waited so long to talk to Lisa about our new medical arrangements. I didn't want to be stressed out. I needed total Zen for what I had planned that evening.

Lisa

I was in the mirror putting the finishing touches on my hair for my date with my husband. He said he had a big surprise for me and I couldn't wait to see what it was. Dori was on speaker phone trying to help me guess what he could possibly have in store for the evening.

"Ohhhh! Maybe it's another trip to Jamaica since the last one was such a dud!" Dori chimed in.

I'd previously filled her in on the fact that the weekend was not the romantic, fun-filled adventure that I had hoped it would be. However, I did not tell her that it was because Alex was too worried about his blood count without having access to his daily dose of what he thought was lifesaving prescription therapy. I chalked it up to Corey's date being a bimbo.

"Naaah, I don't think that would be it." I halfway pondered the thought. Before I could make another attempt at guessing the surprise, I heard the garage opening announcing that Alex had made it home. "Girl, I gotta go! My bae is home!" I quickly wrapped up our phone call and adjusted my dress before stepping into the hallway and walking towards the door that Alex would come through. I made it just in time to see him step through the door wearing a humongous smile on his face. If I wasn't excited before, which I was, the joy on his face would certainly have set off bells.

"Hey you!" He swept me up and spun me around. Well, he was definitely in great mood. He placed me down gently and gave me a longing, passionate kiss. He hadn't kissed me like that since before the trip when he had his way with me by pinning up against the wall of his office.

"Well—" I exhaled, breathing heavily. He had literally

taken my breath away. What in the world could be up his sleeve? He smiled at me like he was ready to devour every inch of me right then and there. He took my hand and led me in a slow spin so that he could get a good look at my ensemble for the evening.

"Mmph, mmph, mmph!" was all he said. I accepted his approval and blushed a little. Were we finally *that* couple? The couple that is together forever but still act like they are teenagers. The couple that is so in love with each other that they feel like the dynamic duo and can crush any obstacle that comes their way. Had I finally gotten him to the point where I could put down my sword and stop being the only one in this relationship that was fighting with any means necessary to make us solid? My heart filled with joy. I'd finally won. Alex Weston was finally all mine.

Seeing the emotion in my eyes as I fought to keep a tear from falling, Alex said, "Hey, hey! None of that. The evening is just getting started." He kissed me again, running his hands down my back and onto my ass where they stopped and popped the string of my panties. He stopped the kiss and asked, "What's this?" He popped the elastic string again. "Take them off," he ordered before I had a chance to respond and tell them they were the sheer thongs he'd bought me on Valentine's Day.

He saw the quizzical look on my face and said, "Did I stutter? Take them off, wifey." Obviously amused with himself, he took a step back to watch my reaction. Not one to be outdone, I also took a step back to make sure he had an eye full as I obliged his request and slowly slid off the already barely-there material from around my hips, past my thighs and down my calves. As they fell to the floor around my ankles, it was my turn to surprise him. I dropped into a Chinese split to reclaim them from the floor and tossed them in his direction. His cat-like reflexes immediately kicked in. He caught them and brought them to his nose, inhaling my essence before tucking them into his pocket.

"Mmmm," he moaned then grabbed my hand and

ushered me out the door.

I was surprised to find a taxi at the end of our driveway and a little disappointed. I knew that Alex didn't want to drive because he wanted to be free to drink without the concern of getting us home safely, but I expected at the very least a town car, if not a limousine, for our night out. I guess he noticed the disappointment on my face because he laughed and said, "Stop being bourgeois." I just rolled my eyes and got into the car. I wasn't going to let my appreciation for the finer things get my attitude started and ruin the evening.

We pulled up to a cozy spot that was one of my favorites. It was a quaint spot in the heart of downtown that always featured a live band and the best cocktails in town. One of my favorite features were the light-up menus. And everything on it was spectacular. After we gave our drink and appetizer order, Alex handed me a box with black wrapping paper and a silver and white satin bow. Inside the box was a pair of red lace panties with a golden vibrating bullet tucked neatly away in the crotch. He leaned over and whispered for me to go put them on. I glanced around the restaurant, and everyone was privately absorbed in their own dinner and conversation and completely oblivious to anyone else outside of their bubble.

I took Alex's dare and I slid the panties over my feet and quickly up my legs, over my behind, and then sat up straight to look as if I was maintaining that same posture since we sat down. Alex scooted closer to me in the high-topped booth. One hand was thrown across the back of the seating behind my head, the other hand made its way onto the fresh lace that guarded my vagina. He spoke in my ear about the things that went on in the day—a new client he'd signed, and something about hiring a new admin assistant—hell, I don't know what he was saying. I just felt his fingers on my clit as he maneuvered the bullet into a position that placed it right up against my most sensitive hot spot. He slid back over to his original spot in the booth just in time for the waiter to bring our drinks. He licked his fingers while he watched me thank the waiter for the both of us.

I just wanted to throw everything off the table and ride him right then and there, and I didn't care who was looking.

"What are you up to, Mr. Weston?" I asked. "Why are you being so very attentive tonight?" I sipped my water before taking a huge gulp of my martini.

"I just want to apologize for my mood on the Jamaica trip," he answered. "I want tonight to be the night that you deserved while we were on the island. I know you wouldn't intentionally hurt me—hurt us. It was an honest mistake that you forgot the meds and I was being an ass. I'm sorry. I want to make it up to you." He raised his glass to me, and I reciprocated.

As I took a sip of my drink, the bullet inside my panties began to vibrate. "Ahh!" an involuntary groan escaped from my lips as I barely managed to place the glass back down on the table without spilling any of its contents. The vibrating stopped as quickly as it started, but the surprise of it all was enough to make me cream. Alex was all smiles. The vibrating started again—first quickly and then changed speeds, slowing to a gentle throbbing right up against my clit. I threw my head back in ecstasy as I tried my best not to moan. After about five seconds of bliss, it stopped.

Breathlessly, I asked Alex how to turn the panties off. He chuckled and said, "*You* can't." He held up a tiny remote control to show me that he literally had my pussy at his beck and call. Throughout dinner, I was hit with millisecond bursts of clitoral ecstasy and I was sure that my dress had a stain from all of the juices that were collecting in my sugar walls. My eyes filled with lust and I could barely make it through the meal. I quickly asked for a carry out box and Alex teased me about being ready to leave so soon. I just prayed that I could still stand up and walk out to the Uber.

Once outside, there was a diamond silver Maserati Quattro Porte sitting out front looking oh so pretty. Alex knew it was my dream car, so he allowed me to take a moment to admire it. Then I felt that vibrating again and my knees grew weak. He burst into laughter while managing to hold me up. He was so tickled with my reaction that he forgot to stop the vaginal massage that was going on under my dress.

"Please," I begged as I wrapped my arms around him to make it look like we were in a normal couple's embrace. I tried not to grind on him to match the rhythm of the bullet, so instead just stood as still as I could, barely breathing. It was embarrassing but so damn good at the same time. I clenched his shoulder blades and whispered, "Please, make it stop. I'm about to cum." And I buried my head in his chest while biting my lip to keep from screaming. He turned off the panties, but I needed a minute to regain my composure. My thighs were like a slip and slide. They were thoroughly lubricated and my vagina walls were opening and clenching as if it were ready to jump off my body and onto Alex's dick.

"Let's go home. Where's that Uber?" I asked. Alex held up a set of keys and said, "Who needs an Uber when you have a Maserati?"

I couldn't believe it! I looked at the car and back at him holding the keys, and just burst into tears. It was by far one of the best nights of my life. It's what I assumed love felt like.

Once we got home, I ripped off the panties that had been teasing and torturing me all night. I don't know what he paid for them, but they were reduced to a pile of shredded lace on the floor within a matter of seconds. I kicked off my shoes, and in one swift move, my dress was over my head and tossed in the air. I don't know where it landed. I didn't care. I just needed relief from the sexual tension that had built up all night. Damn the foreplay.

When I was completely naked, I turned my attention to Alex who was still unbuttoning his shirt. I went straight for the pants. Dropping to my knees, I undid his belt, pants button and zipper. The black slacks quickly fell with a thump to the floor as his pockets were loaded down with his wallet, phone and of course that remote control. I slid his boxers down to his knees and commenced to sucking his pipe as if it were the last cherry flavored lollipop left on earth—twirling my tongue around the base then licking up the shaft and landing on the tip of the head. I reached around and grabbed his ass cheeks, giving them a squeeze and slightly digging my nails into the skin while bobbing my head back and forth, allowing him to pump my mouth while my kitty throbbed in unison.

Just when he was about to crumble from weak knees, a sure sign that he was about to cum, he pulled away and laid me right there on the kitchen floor. We humped like high school teenagers on the bamboo flooring. Good old fashioned, missionary style with my legs wrapped around his waist, and him deep inside of me pumping away as if he only had 5 minutes to get it all in before our parents came home. The intensity and the urgency of it made me even more insatiable and we moaned, groaned and pumped like animals until we both exploded. I shook violently as I felt my juices release. He rammed hard into me in his final thrust and I felt him gush into me and joining the river that was already flowing. We both allowed our bodies to go limp and just laid there trying to catch our breaths. He slowly kissed me, and as he did, he began to rise again.

"Round two?" he whispered.

The next morning, we were sex funky and tangled in the sheets of our California King—exhausted and sore from the night before, but happy. Extremely happy! In fact, I was floating. I got up to shower and to make my king breakfast in bed. That was the plan anyway, but when I got out of the shower he was already in the kitchen making coffee. I kissed him good morning and started gathering ingredients for our meal.

"What time is your mom bringing Jr home?" Alex asked while taking a seat at the table.

"She said she'll be here around 1."

"Good. Gives me a minute to talk." He looked serious. I knew it was too good to last. "When I leave to go to 'Bow on Thursday, I want you to come with me." I let out a visible sigh of relief. I thought he was about to drop a bomb that would ruin my high.

"Really? Sure hun! I'd love to go see your mom." This confirmed everything for me. Him asking me to come to his hometown versus him running there without me proved that Sparkle was finally a very distant memory.

"Good," he responded with a smile. "I know mom will be glad to see us visiting as a family. "He took a sip of his coffee. "Also, I scheduled appointments for us with a really good hematologist for Thursday afternoon with follow up appointments on Tuesday."

I froze dead in my tracks. "You did what?" I asked.

"Look, babe, I know you trust Dori, and so do I, but it's time we go see the best that money can afford. No more creeping around. If we can be a testimony for other people, then let's do it! If we can get better medications, then why not? I'm sure Dori will understand."

My mind raced a mile a minute trying to find a way out of it. So, this was what all of the buttering up the previous night was about. He wanted us to get additional treatment. I had to figure a way out of it, which was a new experience for me. I was used to being the one in control. I controlled our relationship from the day I laid eyes on him. And there was no way that I was going to stop now. I still had five days to try to figure a way out of it. As soon as Alex would hear that we do not have HIV, the entire world that I'd built would come crashing down. I would *not* let that happen.

Dr. Adonis

"What do you mean you don't have any records available? There must be some mistake. Can you please verify the patient names and dates of birth?" Silence ensued as I watched Ms. Millie get annoyed with whomever she was speaking to on the phone. I assumed my secretary paused

Calm Sparkle

for a response from the other end. I continued to walk past her and into my office to review and sign the medical records for the day. Fully confident that whatever the mystery was, Ms. Millie would solve it. I had a date with Sparkle to prepare for; we were going zip lining and I was excited to see how athletic she would be.

I was signing charts when Ms. Millie interrupted, "Dr. A, we seem to have a bit of confusion regarding the Weston case." Ms. Millie was almost 70 but full of energy and southern charm with a deep North Carolinian accent to go along with it. She threatened to retire every year and leave me with nothing but a young, single, buxom bosomed, gold digger to replace her.

I looked up from the notations I was reviewing. "Weston case?" I questioned.

"Yes, hunnie, you know the one. That couple coming from Orlando. You said you would treat them as a favor to Mr. Thomas's son."

"Ohhhh! Yes! Ok, now I remember. What's the problem, Ms. Millie?"

"Well, I put in for the transfer of medical records like you asked me to, but the doctor listed here says they don't have any records to transfer. The last time they saw Mrs. Weston was two years ago. Mr. Weston is not listed in their records at all. They are sending me over what they have from her files, but so far nothing on the mister. I've called and left a message with the Westons to call me back so I can make sure that I have the right information. I just thought you should know what was going on."

"Hmmm, okay. Thank you, Millie. I'm about to duck out of here and start my weekend. Why don't you go on and do the same."

"You don't have to tell me twice! Woooweee!" She shut down her computer and grabbed her purse in what seemed like one swoop. She was definitely trying to leave before I changed my mind.

"Slow down, Ms. Millie before you break a hip!" I

laughed. She hobbled out of the office with one hand in the air. Did she chunk me the deuces? I couldn't help but laugh out loud.

As soon as I was sure Ms. Millie had cleared the building, I locked up the office and went to my locked cabinet where I kept my selection of "goodies" that helped me take the edge off after a long day. As a doctor, it's easy for me to get my hands on just about any drug on the market. Legal or illegal. I just wanted a small buzz until I got home. I pulled out a joint from a baggie I had sitting in front of my delectable options: ecstasy, white girl, and even that alligator shit that hit the market. I wasn't into gator bait; that shit was lethal. Good old Mary Jane would do. I poured a glass of Remy V.S.O.P to chase the smoke and resumed reviewing the charts. Just as I finished the last signature on the last patient chart, the office phone rang. Ms. Millie was in such a hurry, she forgot to forward the phones to the answering service.

"Good afternoon, you've reached Dr. Adonis."

"Hello, this is Mrs. Lisa Weston. I have a message to call your office."

"Ahhh, Mrs. Weston! There seems to have been some mix up; we just need to know who is currently treating you. The doctor we have on record is stating that they haven't seen you in two years."

"Ohhh, I'm sorry. Is this for the appointment on Thursday for me and my husband?"

"I believe so. I don't have the schedule in front of me. Hold on a second and I'll pull it up." I turned on the scheduling app to confirm it was indeed for that upcoming Thursday. It was.

"Well, I am so glad I caught you," Lisa said cheerily, "I'm afraid we will need to cancel that appointment. We won't be able to make it."

"Oh?" I was surprised. I'd shifted my other patients to accommodate them, but it was getting late and I needed to make a break for it if I wanted to be on time for my date with Sparkle. "Well, I don't handle the scheduling so please be sure to call back first thing Monday morning, and one of our schedulers will get that taken care of for you."

"Can't you just take the message?" I was starting to get irritated. She messed up my buzz with all the demanding, but I managed to smile through it.

"I will jot down the message, but again, please be sure to call back on Monday and confirm the cancellation with an actual scheduler." I scribbled the note on a sticky pad as I spoke to her.

"Okay. I sure will." The voice on the other end finally conceded and we ended the call. I placed the note on Ms. Millie's computer monitor so that she would see it as soon as she returns to work next week. *I'll let her handle that*, I thought to myself as I scurried out the door to try to beat the 4pm traffic. I got in the car just in time to hear the last 5 minutes of Sparkle's radio segment, "Ask Coach Sparkle."

"Sometimes life is like walking through a house of mirrors. Fun house or horror house all depends on perception. Either way, all mirrors reflect—," she paused for dramatic effect, I'm sure, "—you."

I pondered her statement. I was a bit high so I'm not sure if it really made any sense, but I envisioned fucking her in a funhouse of mirrors. Now *that* would be dope! No pun intended. Sparkle continued with the caller and told her to never be afraid to do a self-check.

"If things are getting crazy, seemingly out of the vision that you have for yourself and your purpose, always remember to go back to God and ask Him 'Lord, show me, *me*.' Less of you and more Him is always a journey, and it's okay to stumble. It's okay to see your reflection and laugh. It's ok to see your reflection and be afraid. Just remember to ask for help and guidance to stay on the right path to getting out of that house of mirrors."

She ended with her signature sign off, "Go forth and be productive, my angels. And as always, remember to live love!"

She didn't know that I listened to her faithfully. It started out as research. I wanted to know exactly what kind of lady I considered allowing into my world. Through Google I found her life coaching page, and from there I found her radio broadcast—three days a week from 3:45-4:00 pm.

At first I thought the public persona was all a cover-up. That was usually the case with a lot of locally famous people. But so far, Sparkle proved to be everything she projected. She was as real as they came. The only downside was that she made it very clear to me in one of our very first conversations that she was celibate, and would remain that way until she was in a committed, monogamous relationship. I asked her if that meant that she would remain celibate until marriage. Because if so, I would have been out the door before it was even opened.

"I would like to think so," she answered, "but I am not going to make that promise to myself or God. I promise that I will no longer give up the goods to what *I think* may be a relationship. If we have not verbally confirmed, and if I don't feel that this is a committed *and* monogamous relationship, then there will be no sex. Just saying we are boo'd up is not enough for me."

"When was the last time you had sex?" I had to ask. I just had to.

"Honestly," she answered without hesitation, "it's only been a year."

"A real year? Or some maintenance here and there?" Sparkle laughed. "It's been a solid year. I did have a maintenance man, but once I realized that my heart and my punani are a package deal, I had to let him go." We were silent for a moment. Then she continued, "I'm no angel. Far from it. I am human. I enjoy sex, but with the right person."

"Are you a prude? I cannot be with a sexual prude," I interjected half-jokingly but so serious.

"No, silly!" she giggled. "I am not a prude and will try

almost anything at least once, but not until I meet the right guy that is ready and committed to a long term relationship."

I felt disappointed and challenged at the same time. Time would tell if she was true to her word or just saying that because it was the politically correct thing to say. I just chose to enjoy her presence, and I was very much looking forward to our date that evening. Besides, a little ruffie could always speed things along if needed.

We met at the park where the zip lining trail was located. She said I hadn't earned the right to know where she lived yet. I was little offended at first, but remembered that she was a single mom and had only met me twice before, so I had to respect that.

Her ivory Volkswagen convertible Beetle was already in the parking lot when I pulled in. I parked beside her and was very pleased to see that she was appropriately dressed. She got out and met me in front of my car wearing yoga pants and an athletic tee. She wore her hair pulled back into a simple ponytail, no makeup, except for a bit of color on her lips, and no jewelry with exception of a pair of diamond studs. She looked as if she came to play and not to impress. And *that* impressed the hell out of me. I was really starting to like this woman.

We chose the difficult obstacle course, suited up and went to work. I was surprised at her courage and agility as we maneuvered through the challenges. Watching her perspiration glow against her cleavage did nothing to keep my mind on the safety procedures that we needed to follow. Once we made it through the course, we decided to go for celebratory drinks at a nearby restaurant that had an outdoor seating area. She agreed to ride with me, which was an absolute shock.

"What? Not Ms. I-N-D-E-P-E-N-D-E-N-T!" I joked.

"Whatever! Let's go!" she giggled.

Throughout drinks, which turned into dinner, conversation flowed easily as it always did with her. As we wrapped up the evening and I was taking Sparkle back to her car, I was silently planning our next date. She was no ordinary lady. I wanted to see where it would go, but she would have to come up off the cookies sooner rather than later.

Sparkle

I debated whether or not to invite Don up to my new condo following our zip lining date. I didn't want the night to end, but I didn't want to seem too easy either. Although we'd been talking for a couple of months, we'd only been on two official dates. I could hear Kat's voice in the back of my mind, like the little angel with the crooked halo on the left shoulder saying, "Go for it!"

He escorted me back to my car as the debate played out in my head like a presidential campaign. Don interrupted my thoughts when he gently placed his hand in the lower arch of my back as he guided me towards the driver's side of my beetle bug. He used his other hand to open the door for me then pulled me close and stared into my eyes. It was a deep look of studying, and not the lustful look that I was so used to seeing from men on the dating scene. The electricity between us was undeniable. It wasn't just sexual tension either. It was deeper—a soul connection. There was a comfort in his embrace. I felt safe and cared for. It didn't feel like Red Riding Hood preparing to be pounced upon by the big bad wolf; it felt more like when Superman saved Lois Lane from falling, and he just held her while reassuring her with his eyes that it was all going to be okay.

His look silently commanded me to look into the depths of his eyes and share what he was seeing, but it was all too intense for me. I wasn't ready for what I saw in his eyes. I saw the future, and I wasn't sure if I was ready to receive that kind of love. Giving is one thing, but to open myself to complete vulnerability and receive what his eyes offered, would take a whole new kind of bravery that I wasn't sure was within me. He finally released his hold and ushered me into the car, which gave me a few seconds to catch my breath while he watched me buckle my seat belt.

"Lead me not into temptation," I repeated over and over in my head. I decided *not* to invite him over.

Being a night owl, it was still early by my standards. It was only a little after 10. I remembered Alex and Lisa had an appointment with Don, so I shot him a quick text of encouragement. I took a nice, hot shower and then poured myself a glass of wine before making my way to the balcony. I turned on my Bluetooth speakers and started up a playlist on Tidal. As my favorite neo-soul sounds began to softly fill the air, I sat with my feet propped up along the railings and admired the glow of the moon on the Atlantic Ocean.

I smiled as I thought of how I failed to believe that I would ever afford such a place when they first started construction on the oceanfront condominium building. When they broke ground, I stopped by and got my hands on a presale pamphlet and put it smack dab in the middle of my vision board. It's amazing how much life had changed in such a short amount of time. It was as if being in the shadow of misery with Arnold was blocking all of the light that was trying to shine down on me. I used to wonder if I could make it on my own, but I later wondered what took me so long to get out and *try* to make it on my own.

Although I would usually only stay on the weekends that I didn't have Andre, he loved it there. I also bought a home in my parents' subdivision for the weekdays so that Andre would have a sense of neighborhood and a yard to play in. The condo was my sanctuary—my little slice of well-deserved heaven on earth. My phone rang at 11 pm on the dot as expected.

"Well, hello handsome," I answered.

"Hello to you, chocolate beauty." It was Aaron—my soldier boy, as I called him. He was a bit older than me—a retired army sergeant that I'd met at a speed dating event the day after meeting Don. It's funny how men seemed to fall out of the skies once I decided to give up sex and just date for fun. I wasn't looking for a relationship, just good conversation, fun experiences and great company. Unlike Don, Aaron and I had been on several dates over a few months. I avoided Don because I couldn't shake the feeling that once we connected, it would be forever. I wasn't ready for forever. I just wanted to enjoy the now.

"How was your date tonight?" he asked. I loved that about soldier boy. He was confident and not at all intimidated by openness and virtue of honesty.

"It was quite earthmoving," I said purposely to tease him.

"Earthmoving, huh?" he asked. "Not as earthmoving as our date; I'm sure of that," he referred to our date the previous weekend where he caught me in a moment of weakness. It started out innocently enough.

He took me to the skating rink. It was adult night for those 35 and up. The drinks were generously poured, and the DJ was on point with music from the 90s era. We all were having a great time trying to recreate our teen years. You couldn't tell us that we weren't as good as the kids from cult skate classic, *Roll Bounce*. Sure, some of us were shaky on wheels, but some of us old heads were still smooth dancing machines. All in all, it was an absolute blast!

Surprisingly, soldier boy was flawless on skates. His moves were rhythmic and silky. I enjoyed watching him glide around the rink incorporating wiggles, thrusts and kicks where appropriate. During "Butterflies" by Michael Jackson, Aaron took my hand and escorted me off the rink. He found a dark corner in the kiddie play area behind the rock climbing wall that was typically open during the day for family outings. However, for adult night, the entire area was closed and very dimly lit. He pinned me against the wall and asked if he could kiss me; to which I obliged. During the kiss, I felt his hands slide up my waist and rest on back. The kiss intensified and I could feel his thumb begin to rub the nipple of my breast. I let him. It was just a rub after all.

"Butterflies" ended and the super sultry "Nothing Has Ever

Felt Like This" by Rachelle Ferrell and Will Downing began to play. The DJ announced something about a couples' skate, but all I knew was that soldier boy was at full attention as he began to grind into me on the wall in the pretense of slow dancing, and breathing into my ear.

    I knew what he was doing and what was on his mind, but it felt so good to my sex-deprived body that I wrapped my arms around his neck and swayed with him, allowing myself to enjoy the grind. The next thing I knew, he lifted me up onto his shoulders. I grabbed the steps of the rock wall behind me that should have been used to help some toddler climb his way to the top. Both legs were on each of his shoulders, and his face was buried into my crotch. I felt his tongue lick me through the nylon sheath of my panties. My flimsy tennis skirt was over his head and hiding his face from me. He managed to slide my Vickie's to the side and his tongue did a nosedive deep into the abyss. Thank goodness the music was loud, because I know for sure that I screamed a little. His mouth was as poetic as his dance moves and it didn't take long for me to cum all over his face.

    He placed me down gently and I slid right down to the floor in a heap. I couldn't stand at all. I was breathless and speechless from the magnitude of the unexpected orgasm and from shock of what had just happened. He kneeled next to me with a big cheesy grin and said, "You're welcome!" All I could do was giggle. This solder was going to be something else indeed.

    Surprisingly, other than that incident, he was a perfect gentleman. He didn't try to get anything in return. He said he just wanted to make me feel good and that was enough for him. "Well, soldier, mission accomplished!" was my response. After he cleaned his face and I used a paper towel in the bathroom to blot the juice remnants that were making my thighs slide, we resumed a wonderful night of skating as if nothing sexually intense ever happened right under everyone's noses.

    I ended my nightly call with Aaron and I thought about

my current dating partners—Don and Aaron. They were as different as night and day. Both were very intriguing, but Don had something that I was still trying to figure out. Je ne sais quoi...

Lisa

I couldn't believe my luck! I was trying all week to find out what Doctor we were going to see in Moonbow, and boom! The information fell right into my lap! I was so giddy and proud of myself for cancelling the doomsday appointment that I went out and treated myself to a new wig. I pulled my sleek, new Maserati into the garage and grabbed "Sheena" from her place in the backseat where she sat neatly tucked away in fuchsia tissue paper, snuggled in a gold metallic paper bag. The hair boutiques were surely a far cry from the Asian hair markets that throw your wefts into a white plastic bag with "Thank You" stamped across the front in red ink.

As I made my way into the house, I could see Alex was on the phone in his office. I didn't disturb him; I wanted to tuck Sheena away before he could ask how much I had spent. He just didn't seem to understand paying top dollar for something that naturally grows on your own head. I noticed he had the suitcases laid out on the bed. I told him the appointments were cancelled, so I had no idea why he would still want to go to Moonbow.

After putting Sheena in the midst of my other glamourous hair pieces where she could no longer draw attention to herself, I headed back towards Alex's office. As I approached, I could hear him say, "Thank you for the call; we will definitely be there. See you tomorrow, Doc." My heart stopped. Did he just say...? I stepped into the office just as he hung up the phone. He looked pissed. I tried to play it cool.

"Hi, Hunnie." I tested the waters with a sweet, innocent tone before opening my arms to attempt a hug.

"Pack your shit and let's get ready to go." He barked, and walked right past me, managing only to give me a very grimacing look like he wanted to knock my teeth out. Thank God Alex is not a violent man. He would never physically hurt me, but I hate when he is angry nonetheless. I thought I'd push my limits a little further to see what all he knew. Time to play the dumb card.

"Babe, what's wrong?" I whined as I followed behind him down the hall and into our room where he resumed packing.

"You lied about cancelling the appointment, Lisa." I'm so tired of you sneaking around and trying to manipulate things to how *you* want them to go." He didn't stop packing while talking, and didn't give me a chance to interrupt either. "You think that I can't take care of my family? You think that because you're older that *you* should be the man of the house and make all the decisions? Enough, Lisa! Enough! We are going to see the doctor in Moonbow. We are going to get a stable drug regime, and we are going to tell our families so that we can start helping other people. Period. End of discussion. Now pack and be ready to leave in an hour." He didn't even yell. His voice was weary but final.

I realized that he wasn't pissed or angry. He was disappointed and hurt. In all my scheming and conniving, I forgot my mama's rule to always let a man be the man, or at least think he is. I began to throw some things in the suitcase while my mind worked overtime to figure out the next move. The packing ensued in silence and I tried to come up with scenarios to get out of taking the trip. Should I fake sick? Should I say mom is too sick to keep Jr? I was on the verge of a panic attack and felt the walls closing in on me, but there was nothing that I could do.

We dropped Jr off at my mom's and hit the highway—southward bound to Moonbow. "This is for the best," Alex said as he clasped my hand and kissed my knuckles while turning the steering wheel in the direction of I95 South in the process.

I smiled weakly and replied, "I know, Hun," before

pretending to sleep for the rest of the ride.

When we arrived in Moonbow, it was 2 am. Alex felt it was too late to call his mom, and she didn't expect us until morning anyway, so we checked into a hotel. Alex went to hit the showers, and it dawned on me. I could use Sparkle, just this one time, to distract Alex from going to the 11 am appointment.

While he showered, I grabbed his phone and tried to find her number. "Dammit!" I quickly covered my mouth after realizing that it was said aloud, and I peeked around to make sure Alex hadn't heard me. The shower water was still going so I was in the clear. I double-checked his contact list again, and nothing. There was no listing for Sparkle at all. My heart actually did a bit of a flutter with the thought that he had completely erased her. I checked the emails. Nothing. The one time I needed him to be creeping, I couldn't find any trace of her. Alex began to sing in the shower—horribly at that—but at least I still had some time. There was one last hope. I checked the text messages in hopes that there was a conversation with a random phone number that was not assigned to anyone. It didn't take long to see an unread message from—me?

"WIFEY: Safe travels! Let me know how things go after your appt. Prayers up for you and the Mrs." Time stamped at 10:15 pm. That most certainly wasn't from me! We were in the car at that time, and I was fake sleeping.

I quickly went to the contact information for "WIFEY" and there were four phone numbers listed— three of which were mine—home, mobile and my old work number from before we were married. Then there was a phone number listed next to the "pager" option. It was a 305-area code number, and I immediately recognized it once I saw it. A fiery anger arose inside of me that I have never experienced before, and I had no intention on putting out the flames. I'm pretty sure my eyes were bloodshot red from the sheer heat of my flaming emotions. I reread the text.

"WIFEY: Safe travels! Let me know how things go

after your appt. Prayers up for you and the Mrs."

Not only was he hiding her and calling her "wifey," she also knew! She *knew*! I could hear the pouring of water as Alex wrung out his towel, which signaled that he would be ending his shower soon. I had to think fast. I couldn't proceed with my plan to send Sparkle a text from Alex's phone asking her to meet for breakfast at the hotel. I was hoping a morning rendezvous with his so-called beloved would distract him enough to make him miss the doctor's appointment. However, knowing that Sparkle is aware that there is an appointment, and HIV is on the line, there is no way she would fall for that. I needed a plan B, and fast. Initially, I needed a plan to keep my marriage on track, and then I needed a plan to keep the heat off of me long enough to make his ass suffer for trying to play me for a fool. Payback is a bitch, Mr. Alex Weston.

By morning, I still had not come up with anything. And I was still pissed at the fact that Alex was indeed still talking to Sparkle. Not just talking to her, but was also sneaky about it. At least in the past he kept her name in the phone where I could see it. We went to the scheduled appointment, which was basically a bunch of lab work, and then a "hurry up and wait" to see the doctor. I tried to get Alex to eat breakfast before we left the hotel—toast, a cracker, a sip of coffee—anything that would ruin our compliance with the rules for a fasting lab test. He didn't fall for it. He pulled the apple away from my mouth so fast you would have thought it was poisoned by the evil queen herself.

Desperate for any way out, I popped a piece of gum in my mouth, hoping that the sugar from the gooey stick would be enough for a "get me out of labs free" pass. Alex stuck his hand out in front of my mouth for me to spit it out before I could get in two good chomps. Ugh! This was so frustrating! Finally feeling completely defeated, I behaved long enough for them to draw my blood. It was quick and painless. We were in and out within a matter of minutes.

After that, we went up a floor to await our preliminary appointment. While in the waiting area, I thumbed through an old magazine aptly titled Moonbow. Apparently, it was a local magazine that featured the hotspots, eateries, boutiques and such. I thumbed through it and admired a fashion feature from a boutique called The 'Tique when I turned the page and saw a featured story that stopped my world. There she was in a full-color page wearing a red pantsuit in the typical professional photoshoot pose—leaning back with her arms crossed and huge smile. She had Hershey chocolate skin as smooth as whipped butter, and mahogany stained lips. The title read: "Coach Sparkle, Empowering Moonbow's Divorcee's."

My eyes bulged and I tried not to rip the pages out of these people's magazine. I glanced over at Alex, and he was engrossed in the latest sports banter with a couple of other people in the waiting area. I tried to speed read the story. Something about a single ladies' expo being held—correction, it was already executed. I flipped to the front cover to see the date on the periodical, and it was dated two months prior. The story mentioned that she was divorced, hosted a well-known local radio blurb, had a weekly podcast and would be taking her expo nationwide on a fifteen city tour—including my city. She was coming to my turf. I read the caption under the photo: *Sparkle Timmons brings life coaching to the forefront of Moonbow's elite divorcee population.* I had seen enough. I slammed the magazine face down on the table, only to be met with a glossy full page ad of the expo. "Single! My status, my choice" was branded across the page along with the previous month's dates, times and location. As if I didn't have enough to worry about, knowing what she looked like, her occupation, and that she was damn near a local celebrity was just too much. No wonder Alex couldn't stay away from her. Hell, if I was a man, I would do her!

"Mr. and Mrs. Weston?" The medical assistant couldn't have called at a better time because I was seething.

We followed her into a room where she took our height, weight and vitals and then led us to what looked like a psychiatrist's office rather than an examination room. It was tastefully decorated with a nice maroon, leather couch that faced a maple desk. The walls were lined with what looked like boring health-related medical books. It was nothing special; just a typical library-looking conference room is the best way to describe it.

Not long after we were settled on the couch, I heard the door open behind me. I braced myself and began to mentally practice which facial expression to use when I appeared to be completely shocked at the doctor's report that we were both HIV-negative. The doctor came in and introduced himself as Dr. Don while taking a seat behind the desk. I didn't even bother to look up from my intense job of checking social media updates on my cell phone. I kept my purse close and my shades on so that I would be ready to bolt at any moment. I could tell by the trail of his voice that he was directing his attention towards Alex. Good; he could take a hint. I had no intention of offering him any information—no medical history, no "what brings you here"—nothing. I just wanted out of that office decorated cage so that I could run damage control before it was too late.

As he and Alex talked, I stole glances of him here and there—never lifting my head or making eye contact because I didn't want to engage him in any way. I knew I acted like a kindergartner in time out, but at the moment it was the best that my defense mode could come up with. From my stolen peeks, I could see that he didn't have any paperwork, not even a stethoscope. His lab coat was unbuttoned, revealing a pair of the pale blue medical scrubs. The only thing noticeable on him, other than his strikingly good looks, was the Breguet Classique watch on his wrist. The name plate on his desk said Dr. Donnie Adonis. Fate had kicked me in the ass yet again. I knew exactly who Donnie Adonis was. I hope that I appeared unmoved to the outward onlooker, because on the inside I was in a complete panic.

I glanced at the time and hoped that this would be over soon. I could literally feel the walls closing in on me. As I listened to the exchange between Don and Alex, I could hear them going through the usual background health-related questions. Don then began to explain to us that our visit was just a pre-treatment meet and greet that he likes to do with all his patients. He wanted to get to know each of us so that we were comfortable enough to disclose anything.

"When dealing with HIV, sometimes some very embarrassing life situations come up—past or present—and I expect you to trust me so that I can best treat you."

I'm sure he meant that "past or present." part for me. I didn't look up to acknowledge either way. He finally ended his spiel and then asked what questions either of us had before he proceeded with his plans for us. Alex and I both were question-free. Don then explained that lab results would be in by the following morning, and that he would review everything, including current treatment plan, with our doctor back home. My heart began to pick up a pace. He continued to say that he would meet with us again that following Monday for full results and a physical exam.

When he finally finished, and the formalities were all over, I grabbed my purse and scooted to the edge of the couch, poised to raise up and dart out. Alex, however, didn't move. I heard him say, "I just want to thank you, man. I know you took real good care of Mr. Thomas, and I know that you squeezed us in as a favor to Corey. I just wanted to let you know that I appreciate everything."

The doctor smiled and said, "Any friend of Corey's, is a friend of mine."

"Thanks. I really appreciate it," I heard Alex say again.

"I trust that everything we discuss will be kept within these four walls," Alex added.

"Rest assured, Mr. Weston. My doctor-patient confidentiality is bonded and sealed. Trust me; I do not want any lawsuits," the doctor laughed. Alex joined in.

"Good! Then I hope to see you at Corey's house on Saturday. I know he already told you about it."

The doctor replied, "I would never miss one of Corey's poker nights."

It was just my luck! The "good doctor" knew Corey? It was way too much. My body was on autopilot as I sucked my teeth, grabbed my purse and headed to the door. Behind me, I could hear them clasping hands in what was probably a handshake. Alex caught up with me just as I stepped out of the office door. I took a sigh of relief. I had until Monday to come up with a plan B.

"Oh! By the way, Mr. and Mrs. Weston—" the doctor called as we were almost home free and away from his earshot. I turned slightly and tried not to look him directly in the eyes. "Don't forget to leave your full medication history with Ms. Millie on your way out. We seem to still have trouble matching them up with what is currently on file at Dr. Tannen's office." At that point, I gave him the death glare. Did he just smirk at me? Ugh! The "embarrassing past" was really starting to get on my nerves!

As we headed towards the secretary's desk as instructed, I told Alex that I left my phone on the couch in the doctor office and I would meet him at the checkout window. My intent was to avoid talking about the medication and just usher out quietly until I could think of a long-term escape route. I'd let Alex handle the medication talk while I did a little phishing to see if Donnie Adonis remembered as much about me as I did him.

I knocked on the office door to which Dr. Adonis quickly replied that it was okay to come in. He looked up from his desk and smirked. Yep, it was definitely a smirk. I had to do a double-take to make sure I wasn't imagining.

"Well, well." The doctor leaned back in his chair and clasped his hands behind his head. "If it isn't ole sweet lips Lisa. Or as I recall, "Crystal Candy," the best stripper to ever come out of Sylvester, Georgia."

I stopped dead in my tracks. I glanced behind me to

make sure Alex was out of ear shot. I started squinting my eyes and leaning my head to the side as if I didn't remember him.

"You really don't recognize me, huh?" he chuckled and shook his head. "I'll refresh your memory: 1987. You were a sophomore at Georgia Tech but would go to Sylvester on the weekends to strip at Big Mama's Gentleman's Club. You were the premiere act at that hole-in-the-wall juke joint. Gave the best lap dances—the best head." His voice trailed off as he looked at me and licked his lips. It was obvious that he definitely remembered me, or should I say, *us*.

"Ohhhhhhh!" was all I could think to say. I decided to continue the charade. "Donnie! Donnie?" I feigned a struggle to recall his nickname while snapping my fingers and the whole nine.

Back then, he was one of my regular johns—my first john, actually. I had to pay my way through school and would drive out of Atlanta to a small town where no one knew me to make my money. He and his frat brothers stopped through—driving from Morehouse on their way to Albany State's homecoming weekend when he spotted me at work. He cornered me in the club before he left. We shared small talk, which is how we learned that we both lived in Atlanta.

Initially, I was flattered that he took notice because I was dumb enough to think that he was sincerely interested in dating me. It didn't take long for me to sober up and realize he was propositioning me for some head. I gave him a $50 rate, thinking that as a college kid he couldn't afford it. He reached in his pocket, pulled $50 and motioned for me to go for it right then and there at the table. I did. Before he left that night, he offered to pay me $300.00 a week if I broke him off on the regular once we were back in the 'A.' I took the deal--$300 was a lot of money to a starving college kid. I made decent money dancing, but by the time I paid for gas and hotel, it cut into my profit. This was easy additional income.

Calm Sparkle

I soon learned that angelic-looking Donnie was a freak with a capital F-R-E-A and K. It was a lot of fun though. Best *job* I ever had. He liked to experiment. I always felt that I was his test subject. He would do the craziest shit and study my reaction to everything—every stroke, every lick, every position shift. Anything he could come up with, he would try it with me first to make sure it guaranteed the results that he was looking for before using it on the women he considered worthy of actually dating in public. After the first couple of times, Donnie had me completely turned out, nose wide open, looking for him with a flashlight in the daytime. I was willing to start paying *him*, but I knew my place. Donnie was a rich kid from a wealthy family and I was just the hired help.

Donnie laughed, "Don't try to remember, sweet lips. I purposely never told you my last name. After all, it was just business, right? Mrs. Weston." He was obviously tickled with himself.

"I'm glad you find all of this amusing." I finally regained my composure

"On the contrary, I'm not at all amused considering the number of times that you and I have fucked."

I winced at that word, but he was right. It was just "fucking" to him anyway. He never knew how much I wanted to be one of the princess girls he would wine and dine and respect. "We always used a rubber, Don."

"True. But one can never be too sure. I've asked the lab to expedite your results, and I'll have them by the end of the day so that we will know what's what."

I suddenly saw a glimmer of hope. Donnie would most certainly play my accomplice in this. "Hmmm, okay, Donnie. Can I have your number so that I can call you later? For the results, that is."

"Mmmhmm," was all he said as he scribbled his private cell phone number on the back of one of his business cards and handed it to me. I quickly made my way back to Alex before he could have a chance to miss me. For the first time that day, I started to feel the weight lift. I smiled as I rejoined Alex, who was still talking to the secretary, and I could tell that he was not in a good mood. I was just glad to be out of that office with my marriage still intact.

Alex

I still felt like a fool leaving the doctor's office. How could I have been so prideful that I allowed Lisa to handle everything regarding our medical status. I didn't know the lab that had our results. I didn't know the date of our last blood tests. Hell, I didn't even know what medications I was popping every day! Or why they look different from one month to the next. Or if they were even working. The more I thought about it, the angrier I became at myself for not manning up and taking control. No wonder Lisa didn't respect me as the man of the house. I walked around like a damn baby and let her mother me for every little thing that I could damn sure do for myself.

I still felt the embarrassment when I had to give that lady my pill organizer box instead of actual prescription bottles.

"I'm sorry, Ms. Millie, but my wife forgot to bring the actual prescriptions. Here are the pills we take. Maybe the doctor can recognize them." I handed her my seven-day medication organizer. Each day held four pills. "We take one of each daily."

Ms. Millie raised an eyebrow and then peeked above the rim of her glasses. First, at the array of pills, and then up at me. Lisa was still in the doctor's office. How long does it take to grab a cell phone?

The elderly secretary finally spoke. She asked, "Just *one* of each per day?" Then there was that raised eyebrow again. Lisa emerged from the doctor's office and quickly cut in, saving me from the torturous embarrassment.

"Yes, one of each per day, but if you need us to bring in the actual prescription, or maybe the bottle from the pharmacy, we can just reschedule and make sure we have it on the next visit."

"Oh no. That won't be necessary, Mrs. Weston. We will just keep one day's worth of pills here and our lab can tell us what each one is for. Besides, once we get the detailed record of treatment from Dr. Tannen, I am sure everything will be listed there as well."

I couldn't get out of there fast enough. I hate feeling irresponsible. And all of this was happening in front of that dude—the one Sparkle was dating. I wondered if he knew that Sparkle was *my* girl. I knew she'd always be mine no matter who either one of us had in the picture. If it weren't for those life situations, we would be together. No doubt. I wondered if the good doctor knew that. If he didn't, he would by the end of Saturday night's poker game.

The rest of the day was uneventful. I hated the waiting part of the process. I wasn't anxious about awaiting test results for something I already knew the answer to. I was just ready to gain more knowledge about my condition and to let my friends and family know exactly what we were going through. Talking to Sparkle and seeing how she stood by me, albeit as a friend, it encouraged me to move forward in my truth. She was a real rider—her and Lisa both. I knew I should let Sparkle go to be happy with dude. He seemed like a nice enough guy, but I couldn't let go all the way. Call me selfish, doggish, no good—whatever. The heart wants what the heart wants. And if I only had a few years left, I would enjoy them with no regrets. I made sure to mention the boys' poker night in front of Lisa to remind her that she would be on her own that Saturday, and I wanted to avoid any drama.

As the boys' night rolled around, Lisa was surprisingly cool about the whole thing. She'd arranged for a spa day for herself, and then a relaxing evening in the hotel room. I took a chance and bounced out early that day. As soon as she left for her 3 o'clock massage, I was out the door. Within the hour, I was at Corey's house cracking open a beer and plopping down on the couch. I needed a night away from husband duties. Just freedom to be me.

"Al! If you don't get your big ass up off my couch and come out here and help me grill this food!" Corey yelled from the kitchen as he headed out the backdoor with a pan full of meat. I got up from my spot and went out to his deck where all the grilling went down. As soon as the sun hit my skin, the real "grilling" began—from Corey, that is.

"So, what happened with Don today?"

"Man, looka here. It was cool but I was so damn embarrassed. You know, Lisa didn't bring the prescription bottles again, and I felt like a fool because I have to admit that I have no idea what shit I'm popping every day." My phone sounded off signaling a text message. It was Sparkle checking to see how the appointment went. I told Corey that I'd be back and went into the house to call her.

"Hey, you," my standard greeting when she answered the phone.

"Hi! Just wanted to know how the appointment went today. You didn't have to call. A text response would have been okay."

"Yeah, I know. But I just wanted to hear your voice."

"Boy, whatever! Lisa is going to cut your balls off if she catches you talking like that. So, what's the deal? How did it go?" I hated that she no longer flirted back with me. Ever since the night Lisa sent that text and interrupted what would have been a great night, Sparkle became steadfast when it came to maintaining a strictly platonic relationship. I didn't understand why she didn't agree to be my girl back then. I could understand with the whole HIV news but she didn't even know about my status when I asked her. We could have been traveling the world together and living our own secret life.

"It was good, babe. We will know more at the follow-up appointment in a couple days. Today it was just blood work and consultation. You know I'll keep you posted."

"Good. I know you two will be fine. I just want you to keep your spirits up, my friend." Damn, she used the 'F' word. That stung. I had to get some time alone with her and turn this thing around.

"Can I see you tonight?"

"Naaah, I have a date tonight. Why? What's wrong?"

"I just want to see you. Just to talk."

"Okay. Let's meet for lunch before you go back home." Lunch? Lunch? That's definitely an "F" word kind of meet up.

"Why? Are you going out with Don tonight??"

"How did you know about Don?"

"You know I keep up with everything you do. You can't keep anything from me."

She laughed at my response. It was a good time to remind her of how I felt, "Sparkle! You know that I still love you. You know if things were different—." She quickly interrupted me.

"Look, Alex, we go way back, and I appreciate our history. I am grateful to have you as one of my best friends. Bottom line, it is what it is. Don't ruin a friendship by trying to get more out of me than you're allowed to receive. Respect your vows so that I can continue to respect you."

"You didn't respect any vows when we made love in that hotel room." I knew that I shouldn't have said it. I wished I could have taken it back as soon as the words left my lips, but I was pissed and hurt. She talked to me like I was just some average Joe. I was better than that. *We* were better than that.

"Really, Al? Really? You want to bring that up? Okay, let's go there! Yes, we fucked back at a time when I was vulnerable. Not making any excuses for the part that I played, but we were both dead ass wrong for what we did. And truth is, Alex, reality hit like a brick when your dick went on hiatus as soon as your *wife* called when we almost did a round two the last time I saw you. I was grateful to God because that was the kick in the ass that *I* needed to remind myself to stay true to my morals. Then for you— *you* of all people—to ask me to be your damn mistress—.

What the fuck was that?"

Damn, I really pushed a button. Sparkle rarely ever cussed, and I think she used all the words she knew in just the ten seconds. "Babe, I'm sorry," I tried to back pedal. It was too late. She hung up the phone. I tried to call her back but she sent me straight to voicemail. I threw my phone across the room in frustration and just leaned back on the couch. I was too exhausted to deal with that shit.

Lisa

So, while Alex planned to escape for his boys' night, I was busy scheming my own plans. I had to make sure that my hard work was not about to come crashing down on me. Don and I planned to meet at 4 o'clock in the hotel's lounge. As promised, he was able to get our lab results and identify the pills we were popping that same evening we left his office. He knew that I was up to something and wanted to know details. Once that was taken care of, I would return my focus to finding out the motives behind him still texting Sparkle on the low.

I told Al that I was going to a 3 o'clock spa appointment, but instead I headed out to the hotel's business center to do some research on my nemesis. I purchased some airtime as a guest user so to not have the internet usage show up on our hotel bill at check out. It was practically empty, with the exception of an elderly couple desperately trying to figure out how to print their boarding passes for their flight home. I was not in the mood to give grandma and grandpa a tutorial, so I kept my head down, avoided eye contact and grabbed a semi-private cubicle in a far back corner. I fired up the desktop, keyed in the code that I was given and went directly to Google. I typed in "Sparkle Timmons" and a bunch of stuff about an interior designer filled the page.

"Can you make it bigger? I can't read that!" I heard the old man say. I peeked up from where I sat. The senior citizens were both squinting at the computer screen a couple of PC's ahead of me. I quickly put my head back down before they could notice that I was halfway listening and went back to my research. That was definitely not the Sparkle Timmons I was looking for. I searched for the Single Ladies Expo, and had no luck with that either. She was definitely nothing more than a hometown hero.

Tap. Tap. Tap. Tap. TAP. TAP. TAP. TAP. A continuous clicking noise came from the direction of the technology-misguided duo. It kept getting louder. They were obviously tapping on the keyboard in an attempt to make it do their command. I heard the old lady say, "You're doing it wrong, Walter!"

"How can I be doing it wrong, Amelia? It says *central*, plus sign, and the *P* to print!" The tapping, which was near banging level, continued.

"Well, maybe you have to punch the *P* and then the *central* button! You're doing it backwards!" I heard a pause in the clicking and then three very deliberate single tap.

"See, like this." Mildred reached over her husband's hand and tap, tap, tapped, which I assumed was her pressing the "ctrl," the plus sign, and then the "P." I almost choked trying to contain my laughter at these two. A hotel housekeeper came in to empty the trash and refill the printers with paper. The poor, unsuspecting gentleman walked in and made direct eye contact with the confused couple. They immediately bombarded him with pleas for help. I silently giggled and returned to the task at hand.

I had to think on a more local level. I went to Facebook and ran a search for Single Ladies Expo in Moonbow, FL. Finally, I got a few hits. Who needed Neve and Max from *Catfish*? I could track down annnnnnybody.

Calm Sparkle Discussion Questions:

Chapters 5-6

1. Given what you've learned about Alex so far, how would you describe his character? Do you consider him to be a good husband? Why or why not?
2. Lisa says she could tell that the lovemaking has changed yet she is determined to hold on to her marriage. Do you agree or disagree with Lisa's tenacity to her husband?
3. Why do you think Sparkle turned down Alex's proposed solution for them?
4. What do you do when faced with your greatest temptation(s)? Does temptation win?
5. At this point, what do you think will happen with Sparkle and Dr. Adonis?
6. Do you think Alex really loves Sparkle or does he just want a side chick?
7. In Chapter 6, we begin to see Lisa allowing her wall to come down. Are you Team Lisa or Team Sparkle?
8. Have you ever had steamy night like the one Alex created for his wife?
9. Dr. Adonis seems to be feeling Sparkle out. Do you think he will be disappointed as he gets to know her better or will she be "the one"?
10. Sparkle appears to finally be living her dream life. Are you? If so, how? If not, why not?

Calm Sparkle

Chapter Seven
When the Funk Hits the Fan

Sparkle

Oh, how I loved Saturdays! I arrived home from Andre's soccer game, and even though it was Arnold's weekend with our son, I never missed a game or a practice. It was noon and I had an hour to kill before my lunch date with Don. Later that evening, I'd planned for a date with Soldier Boy, and I needed to see if anyone sold chastity belts to make sure what happened two weeks prior didn't happen again. If Don, or anyone for that matter, asked me the last time I'd had sex, I wondered if I'd have to disclose the rock wall rendezvous. Besides, didn't most guys say that only penetration counts as sex? Who was I kidding? A sin is a sin is a sin. I decided to update the Coach Sparkle social media pages. I had an hour to be productive, so I made the best of it.

"What is meant for you has no sense of deviation. It is your destiny, so it will be on a collision course to you and for you," a Claude Jenkins quote.

I pecked away at the keyboard and entered the quote for the day. I switched over to the email account and began to look for inspiration for Sunday night's podcast. I longed for the day that I would learn to stop procrastinating and stop pulling all of my shows together at the last minute. My intended guest speaker backed out days before, citing a family emergency, but said that she would "love to reschedule for the following week." I needed to fill the time with another topic of discussion for my listeners. As I scanned news articles, nothing popped out at me right away, and I lost focus thinking about my dates.

There was a time when I would have thought that going on two dates on the same day with two different men was whore-ish. That all changed when I had an epiphany during one of my group sessions with pastors' wives. It was called "The First Ladies," and it was an anonymous group. Every third Saturday, I would host a conference call to maintain anonymity, and the call would offer a safe haven for prominent deacons' and pastors' wives from all over the country to discuss private life matters, gain encouragement and get advice from each other—a teleconferenced support group for those who were always supporting others. I was the only person who knew the members and the churches they led. They didn't even know each other. The non-disclosure agreement required that they use code names, or as we called it back in college, a *club* name, and could not use the real names of anyone that they discussed. Surprisingly, this group was my rowdiest list of clients with the most amazing stories and needs for advice on the most incredulous situations.

One particular Saturday, one of the ladies had her church hat in a tiff because her youngest son wanted to marry his high school sweetheart. Her argument was that she wanted him to be like Hakeem from the Eddie Murphy movie *Coming to America*. She wanted him to go out and sow his oats, so to speak.

"I'm serious, Coach," the conversation flowed, "I don't want him settling down with the first girl he meets! He needs to get out and explore what's out there!"

"Really, Sister Anastasia?" I questioned. "Is it possible

that this is his God-given mate and he knows that this is the woman he wants to spend the rest of his life with?"

"Of course, it's possible!" She didn't sound convinced as she blurted this out. "I'm sure right now that he is very sure of himself."

"Well, what is it about the young lady that you don't like?" I asked.

"It's not that I don't like her. She's a lovely girl and from a good family. I just don't want to see him make the same mistake that I did. I have only been with one man my entire life and I often wonder what it would have been like to go out and date. To have *something* to compare things to. To not feel like I've missed an important part of growing and learning."

"Ooooooooo, Sister Anastasia!" one of the group members interrupted, "you want to know how it is to sow *your* wild oats!"

The group cackled and "yes chile'd" in agreement.

"Laugh all you want!" Anastasia chuckled. "You know exactly what I'm talking about. Better for him to get it all out of his system now than to be a scandal in the making twenty years down the line."

"I agree with you, Sister Girl," another group participant chimed in. "He's only eighteen. That is way too young, and there is too much world to see. At that age, we all think we know what we want until we get to twenty-five or thirty. It's not like it was back in our grandparents' day. They were expected to marry straight out of school. Things have changed even in our own generation! Now our kids have access to more and can experience more than we ever did. What do you think, Coach?"

As a coach and not a counselor, it's not typical to give advice. My job was just to facilitate the conference call and ask thought-provoking questions that ignite deeper conversations. Somehow, this particular group always had a way of pulling me into their debates.

"Well, in my honestly candid opinion," I answered, "I

know for sure that God gave us life to enjoy the freedom of choice. With that, I truly believe that God puts our soulmates in our paths at an early age. I believe that ninety-five percent of us make the choice to not be with the one that He chose for us. Much love to the five percent that actually get it right."

Sister Anastasia was the first to jump in, "So what I hear you saying is that I need to just let him do whatever he's going to do because this girl just might be his God-mate?"

"I'm not saying anything, Sister Anastasia—at least not anything on what you should do. I am just simply giving my opinion. But let me ask you something else: do you think that the young lady's parents have the same hesitation on her behalf as you have for your son?"

Most of the ladies threw in their two cents in favor of the damsel's parents whom they believed would not have reservations because the woman should remain pure. All of this led to a discussion on society's double standards of men versus women in the world of dating, and whom is considered appropriate. Slut shaming was inevitable with this group—even with some of them who had a past that could put Kendra Wilkinson to shame. That's what led me to believe that I needed to sow my royal oats—not so much in sexual sense, but in the world of dating. What was wrong with dating around? You don't have to have sex with a man just because you go out with him. Dating around was completely different than sleeping around. Of course, I kept my thoughts to myself during the group session. After all, the call wasn't about me. Thus, I began my embracement of dating a variety of suitors while maintaining a vow of chastity.

Adonis

Ole sweet lips Lisa! Wow! As soon as she walked in the office I got an erection. She used to let me do any and everything to her and seemed to enjoy every minute of it. She was the best employee I ever hired. She was actually pretty smart too from what I could remember. She always made the Dean's List at Emory. I couldn't remember what her major was though. It's good to see she made something of herself. I think, at the very least, she married well.

I put a rush on those lab results once I realized it was her. We used to be hot, heavy and consistent back in the day. Last thing I needed was for a whore to be the literal death of me. Thankfully, everything came back negative. And the so-called meds that her husband gave Ms. Millie were nothing more than over-the-counter vitamins. Lisa asked for the opportunity to explain it to me in person. I planned to meet up with her so we could talk over a few drinks. I can't lie, I was also hoping to get some head while she was in town. It could help alleviate some of the tension that built since Sparkle was playing the celibate card. She better be glad that I was feeling her, or it would have been a wrap.

Lisa sat at a table furthest away from the door and foot traffic when I arrived. Wearing a soft white, off-the-shoulder, silk top she almost looked angelic. My muscle memory kicked in again and little Don started to twitch.

"Down boy, Not yet."

"Hey, sweet lips! You look beautiful today," I greeted her with the warmest smile I could muster, trying not to look like a wolf ready to pounce. I slid into the seat at the table and we sat across from each other looking eye to eye. She gave me a closed mouth smile and a nod of the head before taking a sip of her Long Island iced tea. Before I could get settled and look around for a waiter, one appeared and placed a matching tea in front of me and then hurried away.

"Well, I see you remember what I drink."

"Of course. I remember everything about you. Dr. Adonis." She still didn't smile. Instead she got right to the point. "Look, let's cut the shit. No need for small talk; let's just get to it. I need your help. And yes, I'll do *anything* you want." Lisa took an ice cube from her drink, put it to her lips, sucked it in and swallowed it whole.

"Ok, Lisa. What's going on? Tell me everything." She went on to tell me about the mouse trap she laid for this multi-millionaire air mechanics mogul over in central Florida that was 10 years her junior—how she tricked him into marrying her impulsively and without a prenuptial agreement by staging false HIV positive test results and then giving him vitamins as a placebo treatment plan. Man! The girl was a piece of work. If she could tell me that, I could only imagine the things that she's done that will go with her to the grave. But it was beginning to work in my favor. Initially, I was going to ask her for some head to top me off before my date with Sparkle, but I was starting to see her as a potential business partner.

"So, you want me to do what exactly? Go along with your lie and tell your husband that you are both HIV positive? I can't do that!"

"Nooo! No! I wouldn't ask you to do that—risk your license and all. I need you to tell Alex that the tests are now reporting as negative. A mix up at the lab, or a miracle of God. I don't care what you tell him, but I have the kid now and some years behind us, so I'm not worried about him leaving. I'm in the safe zone as far as that's concerned."

I just shook my head and finished off the last sip of my tea. "Why are you telling me all of this, Lisa? What is it that you need from me?"

"I just need you to be honest about our current test results, but withhold the information that you have about the previous tests and the medications that I've been giving him. That's all."

"Medications?" I had to laugh at that. "Your husband should be the healthiest man in all of the East coast with those supplements you've been feeding him!"

We both laughed and I reached for my phone which was in my pocket. Sparkle had just sent a text thanking me for lunch, and to let me know that she enjoyed our time together. I shot her a quick text back: "The pleasure was all mine, beautiful. Offer still stands if you'd like to catch that midnight movie tonight." I placed the phone on the table and returned my focus to Lisa.

"Okay. I will give your husband the truth as far as his health since he came into my care—which is HIV-negative, and as far as any past test results or treatments, I'll be honest about that as well and let him know that we never received the medical records so I couldn't confirm his past results. I won't lie for you, but I won't throw you under the bus either."

Lisa let out a sigh of relief and finally smiled. "Thank you, Donnie."

"Don't thank me yet. What's in it for me?" Her smile disappeared again. Her serious, all about business look returned.

"What exactly is it that you want? I'm not a young, broke, college kid anymore."

"Oh, come on. You know we had some good times. I bet the tricks you use on your husband now are things you learned from me."

She blushed before saying, "Ok, you got me. We did have some extraordinary sessions. But I won't be bought that easily. Let's just say that you owe me this favor."

"Naw, sweet lips. Let's just say that *you* owe *me* a favor if I do this for you."

"Well what exactly is it that I can do for you? The man who has everything."

"Ok. I'll be perfectly honest with you since you've been honest with me." I leaned forward and propped my arm up on the table, tapping my fingers in rhythm to the light jazz that was coming from the lounge speaker system. "'I want you to use your nosey investigative skills to tell me all you can on this new hunnie that I'm seeing. I'm seriously thinking about settling down with her, but I want to make sure she doesn't come with any hidden drama. You know the Adonis name can't have any blemishes."

"Ok. Why me? Why not just hire a private investigator or look her up on Google?"

"I've run Google already. And you are now my P.I. It'll be easy. She's a life coach. Just act like you need help with your marriage or some shit. Get close to her for about a month. See what you can find out, and let me know if she is as clean as she presents herself to be and we'll both go on with our lives."

"Life Coach?"

I pulled out my phone and pulled up Sparkle's website and sent it via text to Lisa. "I just sent you her link. Do what you do. I'll do what I do and we'll call it even." Lisa pulled up the text that I sent.

"Sparkle? This Sparkle?" Lisa exclaimed pointing at Sparkle's image on the phone.

"Yeah. Why? You know something?"

"Nah, but I know *of* her; she used to date my husband."

My eyebrows raised at that statement. I sat back in my chair to process the new information. Corey told me that she used to date one of his buddies, but I never bothered to follow up and ask which one.

"Really now?" was about all that I could intelligently say in the moment.

"Yep! Supposedly way back in the day. College sweethearts or some shit."

"Supposedly?"

"Well, a year or so ago, she and my husband reconnected. The only evidence I have are some texts and emails. Nothing concrete, but I keep my eye on this chick."

"Sparkle? Well, I know *my* Sparkle wouldn't be hitting it with anyone—and especially not a married man. I'm sure she'll come up clean in that aspect. I'm just looking for any past dirt that could ruin my shot at becoming Surgeon General in the next ten years."

"Say what you want. I know the smell of my husband, and one night he came home with a different scent after a visit to this Hoboken town of yours."

"Really now?" I was starting to sound like a broken record. "When was this, you say?"

"It's been about a year now."

My wheels started turning. Sparkle said the last time she had sex was about a year before. Could it have been with Lisa's husband? Did she really let a married man hit it? Adultery? Does Sparkle think she has HIV? Maybe *that* could explain why she was so stern on the celibacy rule. It was definitely an interesting turn of events.

Lisa

Sparkle, again? What the hell did she have that I didn't? I thought it was just Alex, but to find out that she had Don too was annoying. Arrrrggghhhh!

On the other hand, how marvelous of an opportunity to meet her to just land in my lap. I couldn't believe my luck when I checked the text from Don and Sparkle's face popped up. I was very familiar with the site since I literally had just finished stalking it before Don met with me. I had a reason to call her up and sit face to face with her. Oh yes! I was happily ready to accept the challenge. I could get to the bottom of the recent text messages, clear up the whole HIV fake routine and still keep my man. All in all, I'd say it was definitely a successful day.

Alex

It was around 10:30 and poker night was well under way. Corey had hired some aspiring models to dress in bikinis and stilettos while serving food and keeping our glasses filled. No one would have to leave the table except to take a piss.

Drinks were flowing, poker chips were being tossed, cards were being shuffled and trash talk was at an all-time high. On the flip side, as much as I hated to admit it, Don turned out to be a pretty cool cat. He put me in mind of Terrence Howard's character in *The Best Man*—very low key, laid back with an air of not giving a damn. He definitely had a privileged upbringing. There was nothing he bragged about but just his air.

I was surprised to see him show up. I thought he would be out with Sparkle. I guess her date was with someone else, or she just lied as a way to let me down easy. Don was definitely in his comfort zone by the way he eyed the bunnies and openly flirted with one in particular. Seeing that he was still open to other women let me know that thing he and Sparkle had going must not have been too serious. That was a huge relief. At the end of the night, when everyone was headed out, I pulled Don aside.

"Look man, I can't thank you enough for what you're doing for me and the wife. And I appreciate your confidentiality tonight."

"Dude, I am a professional. You don't have to thank me for doing my job. But I know you didn't follow me out here for that. Wassup man?"

I threw my hands up. "Aight, man. You got me." I lowered my voice to make sure no one else could hear. "Look, I hear that you're dating a really good friend of mine. Man to man, I care a lot about her. Just be real with her is all I'm asking."

"So, you know about Sparkle?"

"Yeah. I heard a little something."

Don slowly nodded. "I got you, dude. But I don't think Sparkle is any of your concern anymore. Or was that not your wife with you at my office?" I wanted to knock that smug smile off of his face.

"She's *always* my concern—dude."

"Whatever, man." Don laughed it off and we did the bro shake before he left. Don may have laughed, but I was dead ass serious.

Adonis

"Be single. I dare you!" Sparkle's voice rang in my ears. I listened to a replay of the previous night's podcast. Trying to stay on top of everything she did was like having a second job, but I admired her energy and her ambition. She definitely was not one to sit around and wait for a man to pay her bills—yet another gold star for Sparkle. I hoped Lisa's research turned up clean.

"As Beyonce' said, 'When life gives you lemons, make lemonade!'" Beyonce? Come on now, Sparkle. I know damn well she was not going to credit Bey with that old ass infamous quote.

"Okay, okay," the podcast continued, "so maybe Beyonce' did not actually come up with that coined phrase. However, you must admit she sure brought it back to life with the 2016 release of her *Lemonade* album. She gave voice to all of the feelings of frustration that any woman that has been involved in a passionate relationship gone sour has ever felt, but couldn't express."

"Mrs. Carter completely transformed the illusion that a heartbroken woman will sit in a corner and obey like a sad little puppy when their man has been caught cheating. She made it okay for a lady to throw up the middle finger, cuss his ass out, and say 'Boy, Bye.' Women, who are often tagged as jealous or crazy when extreme retaliation seemed the only source of revenge are now liberated and allowed to—well—heal. That's right, ladies. It's okay to wade in lemon water before finally finding that right mix of sugar. On tonight's show, we will focus on healing, and for laughs, our question of the day is: What is the craziest thing you've ever done in a relationship? But first, let's hear a little something from Queen Bey herself. Our first song of the evening will be 'Sorry'" The music began to play and Ms. Millie signaled that the Westons had arrived.

I was still a little pissed at this Alex dude trying to step to me about Sparkle. If only he knew what kind of ho he had for a wife. And what the fuck did he care for anyway? Did he and Sparkle really have something going on? I would find out in due time. Until then, he just needed to stay in his lane.

When the two walked into the office, Lisa looked a lot

happier than she did the first time she graced the doorway. On that first visit, she was quiet and somber. Of course, I know why. She thought I was about to blow her well thought out plan. She smiled big when she came in.

"Good afternoon, Dr. Adonis! How was your weekend?"

I wanted to say, "Dial it back a notch, girl. You're over-doing it." Instead I joined her in a smiling competition and played along. "It was great, Mrs. Weston! I saw my girl on Saturday. I always enjoy spending time with my lady."

Okay, so that wasn't very professional. I just did it to mess with them both. Funny how one couple could have so many secrets between them. Whomever I decided to move forward with could have no secrets from me. I didn't play that. I turned my attention to the sucker of the hour, "Hello, Mr. Weston. Good to see you again." I reached out my hand and we did a quick professional shake. He looked nervous. Poor guy. Let me take him out of his misery. "Mr. and Mrs. Weston, please have a seat. I have some very exciting news for you!" I figured there was no need to drag it out; just cut to the chase and get them out of the office. I turned off the podcast and pulled up the Weston's medical file. When they were both seated, I gave them the news.

"Mr. and Mrs. Weston, I'm not exactly sure why you are here. We ran your blood samples five—yes, I said five—times, and each time they came back negative for the HIV virus."

"What? Are you serious? Oh, my Lord it's a miracle!" Lisa was overdoing it again.

It took all I had not to roll my eyes. Instead, I just plastered on a smile and said, "Well, yes. I guess it could be interpreted as a miracle."

Alex seemed to be in a state of shock. Lisa hugged and kissed all over him as if she'd just won the lottery. I guess in a sense, she did. When Alex did finally find the words, his tone was the complete opposite of Lisa's.

"Stop bullshitting me, Doc," he spat out angrily.

"You're just trying to tell me this so that I'll stop taking the necessary treatment. You *want* me to get worse and die!" Lisa and I both looked at him confused.

"What the hell?" I stepped out of professional character for a moment, but then immediately composed myself and rephrased my response. "Mr. Weston, I am not quite sure why you would make such an accusation, but I assure you that I am being completely open and honest with you. You nor your wife have the human immunodeficiency virus. I'll be sure that you get a copy of all of the results from the tests that we ran when you check out today."

"You're going to sit there and tell me that all of a sudden I am cured?"

"Mr. Weston, I can't speak for your previous doctor, but from the information that I have from my pathology teams, there is no trace of any viruses in your blood stream. At worse, your potassium is low and Mrs. Weston is slightly anemic. Otherwise, you're both very healthy individuals."

"Don't 'Mr. Weston' me!" Alex exploded, jumping up from his seat. He leaned over my desk, knocking over my pen holder and all the contents spilled out and rolled sporadically across the desktop. Some crashed to the floor.

He came close to my face and breathed, "We *both* know what this is really about!"

He turned and headed towards the door. "Lisa! Let's go!" Lisa looked startled and quietly followed behind her husband as they headed to check out. Ms. Millie came in as soon as they cleared the door.

"Are you okay in here, Donnie?" She called me Donnie when her mothering instincts came out and she was concerned about me.

"I'm fine," I lied. I was ready to punch a hole in the wall. Who did Alex Weston think he was? First, the confrontation about Sparkle and then an explosion in my office? I could feel my cheeks heating up and I was sure that the anger had my face flaming red. "I'm fine," I repeated to Ms. Millie. "Can you go make sure they get checked out okay. And make sure the girls give them complete copies of all the tests we ran. Then dismiss their patient file."

Ms. Millie didn't say a word; she just scurried out of the office, closing the door behind her. I poured a shot of scotch and knocked it back. I needed something a little stronger if I was going to make it through the day without cussing someone out. I went to my private stash and pulled out a little powder. I sprinkled some out on the desk in a neat little line and chopped it up a little finer with the razor I kept under my nameplate. Lisa came flying through the door just as I sniffed up the row and damn near caught me.

"Damn, Lisa! Don't you knock?" I wiped the debris from the table while acting like I was picking up the pens and pencils from her husband's earlier tantrum.

"I just wanted to come in and apologize. I've never seen him like that, and it surely wasn't the reaction that I was expecting."

"Just do your part of this deal and let's be done with it." I waved her out of the office and she complied.

I pulled up the schedule to see if I could leave. Damn, I still had four more patients.

Alex

"Corey! Your boy is a flake!" I called Corey as soon as I got to the car. Lisa insisted on going back into that fake ass doctor's office to get a copy of those fake ass medical records.

"Woah! Calm down, man. Don? Man, Don is the truth! I told you he took care of pops when—." I didn't want to hear about pops. This was different. I cut Corey off before he could say another word in defense of this quack of a doctor.

"I don't care what he did for your pops! I'm telling you man, he just played me! And I know it was because I stepped to him about Sparkle."

"Wait! You did what? Man, get a grip! Whatchu steppin' to him about Sparkle for? You are a married man.

You have no say so in what goes on in Sparkle's life. You need to chill with that shit, bro."

"Fuck outta here with that, Corey. Bottom line is your boy sat in that office and said that me and Lisa came up negative. You believe that shit! All these years now, and all of a sudden, after I step to him about Sparkle, he comes back with that bull shit!"

"Why, Al? Why would he lie about the tests being negative? If anything, he would tell your dumb ass that you was dying and put you on all kinds of dope and shit. You ain't making a bit of sense man. And where is Lisa?"

"She's in his office getting the so-called lab results. I don't even want to see it. I'm headed to the free clinic and getting my own testing done. Won't nobody know me down there."

"Do what you do, man. While you at it, take a home HIV test, home pregnancy test, DNA and anything else you need to calm your damn nerves. You know how many people are waiting to get into Don's office, and he pulled you in as a favor to *me?*"

"Aight, bet. If the other tests come out negative, I'll apologize to your friend and even buy him a vanity plate for his Bentley. But right now, he better stay the hell away from me. And Sparkle too!"

"Sparkle?" Lisa's voice rang in my ears. I didn't even see her coming to the car until she was sliding into the passenger seat.

"Look, Corey, I gotta go. Lisa is back with those fake ass results. We're headed to the clinic. I'll hit you up later." I started to pull out of the parking lot. I wanted to get as far away as possible.

"So, what was all that about Alex? Is this what you meant about letting you be the man?"

And there she goes. I was not in the mood, but she heard me say Sparkle's name, so I had to humor her before it really blew up into something huge.

"Look, Lisa. I just want us to be extra sure before we

start celebrating. We have one doctor saying we have HIV, and another doctor saying that we don't. Let's just go for the tie breaker before we get too happy. And that's all I have to say right now."

She gave me the side eye with an "mmm-hmmm." I knew that it meant that she would want further explanations but at least she was willing to wait, which was fine with me. I needed time to explain all that I was feeling. When D said that we were negative, of course I was elated. But damn! It changed everything! If Lisa and I were really HIV-negative, I would divorce her and go after Sparkle with all that I had. I needed to be absolutely sure that we were indeed one thousand percent negative.

Chapter Eight
Siri, Call Mom

Sparkle

I couldn't believe my eyes. Donnie had made a beautiful, home-cooked candlelight dinner. He served lamb chops, broccoli and candied carrots. As he poured me a glass of wine, he leaned over and whispered, "Happy six month anniversary." I giggled like a school girl.

"It's only been three months, Don."

"Yes, but we were dating for 3 months before we went exclusive, and don't make me count the 2 months we just chatted on the phone before actually having that first official date. We're damn near at 25 years if you look at it that way!" he laughed, and I laughed along with him.

Things were so easy with him. He had a fresh perspective on things and never seemed to be judgmental, even when I told him about my one slip up with Alex, a married man. He understood and reminded me that God forgives. It's not like I took him up on his mistress offer. I actually turned away from temptation when I could've been caught up as a side chick in a weaker spiritual place. I felt safe with him. I shared everything with him. Everything except sex, but I felt that it was finally our night. He was such a patient man. He never pushed the issue, and never crossed the line. I knew we weren't married, but I never promised that I would wait until the "I do's" were said and done.

As Don sat down at the table, I got up and turned off the television. He would always play CNN whenever I came to visit to help keep our minds off of sex. He said nothing killed a boner like seeing a Black Lives Matter protest or Anderson Cooper moderating a debate between his guests. On that night, I needed the boner. I turned on his stereo and the sounds of Jill Scott filled the airwaves. Don looked up from his plate and his eyes got as wide as saucers when he saw me starting to untie my wrap dress. He quickly put his fork down and a smile as big as Texas began to slowly invade his cheeks.

I swayed in rhythm to the music, doing my strip tease that I'd practiced all week. In the end, I stood right in front of him wearing crotch-less cage panties and a matching bra. I straddled him and gave him a lap dance before making him stand and removing his pants. I licked his male g-spot, as they call it, and his knees buckled. I took his balls into my mouth and gently sucked and tugged on them. He groaned. I kissed the tip of his penis, and he grabbed me by the arms and pulled me up to a standing position. He stared into my eyes. I could see the love. Ever look into a man's eyes and see the love he has for you? It's a look that melts your heart. And he had that look.

He kissed me. It was deeper than any kiss we had ever shared. When he pulled back, he looked into my eyes again and said, "Are you sure?"

I pulled his head down towards me and kissed him gently before answering, "Yes. I'm sure."

He pulled me close and hugged me. Then very softly, he said, "No." He pulled his pants back into place.

I took a step back. "No?" Surely, I didn't hear him right.

He closed the gap between us and very firmly said, "No." I tried to read his face for a sign that he was joking.

There was no smile. The love was still there. His face was still soft and kind and he mouthed the word again. "No." Then kissed me as if to seal the word from his lips to mine. He stepped back and looked me up and down. He walked around to the back of me and placed his hands on my shoulders, kissed the back of my neck allowed his bulge to caress into my backside. He wrapped his arms around me in tight hug and then I heard him walk across the room. When I turned around he was bringing me the dress that I'd let crumple into a pile on the floor in front of his theatre sound system. I am so freaking confused. I didn't say anything, I just put on my dress and started to grab my keys.

"Where are you going?" he asked. "Just because we're not having sex you want to leave me?" Now the smile was back. He guided me back to my chair and pulled it out for me to sit. "Sit down, love. Finish your dinner. We have all night."

He returned to his seat at the table, "Sparkle, we aren't going to rush this, but it is good to know that you are true to your word. You, my dear, are certainly *not* a prude." He raised his glass to me in a toast. I had to laugh at that.

"Cheers to being an undercover freak," I chimed in.

Lisa

Alex had changed since our Florida visit. It had been three and a half months and he was still incredibly distant. He was still an absolutely perfect father, but he definitely changed tunes when it came to us. He hadn't talked to Sparkle. I know because I downloaded a call recording device on his phone, and each night when he showered, I listened to all his calls from the day and then deleted them. He didn't even notice the extra app on his phone. I did all the research I could on the internet on Sparkle and she came up clean—much to Donnie's delight. I still wasn't convinced. I just knew I would find out something. I'd tried reaching out to her as a new client, but I was told that she was not accepting any new applicants by a very cordial and professionally written automated email response to her web form.

After my third denial response, I had to wait until Alex left the house before could try to call the office. There must have been some sort of mistake. I was not an applicant. I was not looking for a job. It was as good a time as any to schedule my appointment with the fantabulous (insert sarcasm) Sparkle. The phone was answered on the first ring and the gentleman sounded very cheerful—as if he already had twelve cups of coffee.

"Good morning, and thank you for calling Sparkle's Moonbow Coaching Facility! My name is Todrick! How may help you?"

I wanted to gag. It was way too early. Instead, I plastered on a smile to try to trick myself into matching his enthusiasm. "Well good morning, Todrick! This is Penelope Williams. I was trying to schedule an appointment with Coach Sparkle, but the automated response says she's not accepting any new applicants. I think I hit the wrong web form. I'm not applying for a position, just looking for a life coach." I added on my fake laugh to add emphasis to my feigned cheeriness.

"Ohhhh, Ms. Williams," said Todrick in an overly exaggerated sad tone of voice, "I'm sooooo verrrrry sorry, but Coach Sparkle has closed registration for new one-on-one coaching clients. The deadline was two weeks ago. But you are welcome to try again next year! Just be sure to get your request in early; Coach starts her interview consultations promptly the day after registration closes."

That was incredulous. I obviously didn't hear him right. "I'm sorry, Todrick. Am I missing something? I want a life coach, so I request to make an appointment, and then I get a confirmation. Isn't that how this works?"

Todrick was tickled. Obviously, I must have said something extremely funny. "No ma'am!" He finally said, "Coach Sparkle likes to give the most unique experience possible to ensure a full life transition—to guarantee the clients get the vibrant life they desire and deserve. She only accepts four one-on-one clients per year. Every three months, a client graduates, so to speak. And that is when there is an opening for someone new."

"Ohhh, I see." I had to admit, I was slightly impressed. Out of sheer nosiness, I asked the follow-up question, "So how exactly do I get to benefit from Coach Sparkle if I'm not one of the chosen four?" This seemed to set off a flurry of marketing scripts, which Todrick was happy to rattle off.

"Of course, Ms. Williams! We have community courses, group sessions, as well as a myriad of virtual groups and conference calls! Would you like for me to get you registered for something today?"

"No, thank you, Todrick. I'll go back to the website and see what will work best for me."

"Ok, well don't hesitate to call me back if you need any help navigating. There's also online chat available. Oh! And if you really need to see a coach in a one-on-one setting, we have some other coaches that we highly recommend that we can refer you out to!"

"Really, Todrick, thank you, but that will be okay. I'll find something on the website."

"Well alrighty then, Ms. Williams! Thank you so much for calling, and may the rest of your day be as rare and beautiful as the Moonbow!"

And that is pretty much how my first attempt to meet with her went. I hung up from that call thinking, "Moonbow? What the hell is a moonbow?" I thought it was just the name of their island. I took a moment to actually look up the term on the internet and learned that it was a real thing. Who knew? I went back to the website, and of course, the option to "click here" for a one-on-one consultation was no longer there. Options for public group sessions, virtual classes and life skill courses were all available just as Todrick promised. I opted to sign up for the virtual group called "Boss Wife." The description said something about balancing life between being the H.B.I.C.

in the boardroom to being the W.I.F.E. in the bedroom. It sounded interesting enough.

My goal was to buddy up to her as "Penelope Williams" and get all the dirt I could. My phone rang and it was Dori. I really wasn't in the mood to talk. It was too freaking early in the morning, and my bestie knew it. I silenced the ringer and said out loud to the air as if she could hear me, "I'll call you back, sis."

I ran a bubble bath to get some relaxation in before I went to mom's house for lunch. I didn't know who the women were that complained that they needed more out of life. I loved being a housewife! I hadn't worked since Jr was born and I didn't plan on ever working again. I struggled so much with Marvin, my first born. I found out the month after my college graduation that I was pregnant. The so-called wonderful Dr. Donnie Adonis was the father that I'd always kept hidden. I always wanted to be his main woman, and not just his side chick hook up for $300 a week. That money paid my tuition, my rent, everything. I used to pretend that he was my boyfriend, and he was making sure that my bills were paid. He was the only one that I was sexing during the last three months of our arrangement. I tried to prove to him that I was wifey material, but it all fell on deaf ears.

On our college graduation night, he had his way with me one last time, and left me a $500 tip on the table with a note that read, "It was nice doing business with you. All the best, Future Dr. D." I knew that was my sign that it was over. I would never see him again. When I found out that I was pregnant, I called him three times before he finally answered. He sounded aggravated that I dared to call him.

"What do you want, Lisa?" he growled into the phone.

"I just wanted to see how you were doing. I miss you." I didn't mean to say that I missed him. It just slipped out before I could stop it. I wish I could have swallowed it back because his next words cut like glass.

"A whore misses her John? That's funny. What? You

ran out of money?" At that point I just hung up the phone. If I didn't know it before, I knew it at that moment. To Donnie, I was just the hired help. That's when I vowed that I would always control anything that had to do with me and mine. Starting with the tiny human that was planted in my uterus. The baby would grow up to do great things, and Donnie would never be allowed to be in Marvin's presence—ever. The only other people who know who Marvin's real father is are Dori, my mom and Jesse, my ex who died in the car crash.

Just as I stepped into my bubble bath, the house phone rang. The caller ID announced, "Call from Dorothy Hutchison." It rang again. "Call from Dorothy Hutchison."

"Dori, I said I'll call you back!" I yelled out towards the phone and slipped into my warm, bubbly, liquid abyss.

Alex

I raced home screaming, "WHAT THE FUCK?" at the top of my lungs as I imagined my hands around my wife's throat. I have never been a violent man, and Lord knows my mama would've kicked my ass if she knew what I was thinking. Mama! That's who I needed to calm me down.

"Siri, call mom."

Siri quickly replied, "Calling mom mobile."

I spotted a cop, so I eased my foot off the gas to allow my 2015 shark silver BMW 750Li to slowly decrease in speed until it reached the legal limit of 55 mph. No answer. An immediate auto-response text came through stating: "In a meeting. I'll call you back." Mom was always up to something. I was about fifteen minutes away from pulling into my driveway. I just needed to be sure that I got there before Dori had a chance to open her big mouth and give Lisa warning that I was headed that way, and that I was armed with the truth. Speaking of truth, I owed Dr. Adonis an apology.

"Siri, call Dr. Adonis"

"Calling Dr. Adonis work."

Ms. Millie picked up on the second ring and placed me on hold before Don picked up the phone.

"Good morning, Dr. Adonis speaking."

Was it me or did his voice sound slurred? He couldn't be drunk that early in the morning. It was only 10:30. I shrugged it off. I must have heard him wrong. "Hey, doc. It's Alex Weston"

"Alex! Hey man, you ready to come clean up these pens you knocked off my desk?" Doc laughed.

"Ha! Yeah man. Actually, that's why I'm calling. I just wanted to apologize for going off like that."

"It's cool, dude. This is a sensitive subject and I don't let my job affect personal life. So, what can I do for you?"

"Well, like I said, I just want to apologize. I had myself tested three times, and they all came back negative. You were right, and I'm sorry that I jumped to conclusions. As a man, I wanted to make sure you heard that from my mouth to your ears. I appreciate all that you've done for me and my—for Lisa and I." I just couldn't bring myself to call her my wife.

"No worries, dude. We're good. Really. I'm glad you can get some peace about it."

"Thanks, man. I'll holler at you next time I'm in town." We hung up from my truce call. The only thing I didn't tell him was that the next time I came to town, Sparkle would be coming back with me.

I pulled up in our driveway. I knew I'd better calm down before I went into the house. I turned off the engine and closed my eyes while leaning my head back. I took a couple of deep breaths and started to count to ten. I didn't know if it would work, but I'd heard about it a few times over the years. As I tried to relax, I thought back to what I had just learned. After getting the third negative result for the HIV virus, I drove over to Dori's office. Dori was the practitioner that had been treating us on the down low, supplying the meds, tracking our progress, and saving me the embarrassment of having to actually go in to see a doctor.

I arrived at the clinic just as Dori was walking from her car into the building. I caught up with her and we went into her office.

"Dori," I started after we had our casual greetings and she could no longer handle not asking me why was I there. "Thank you for all that you've been doing for us, but I just thought you should know that I don't blame you for giving us false information. Just wanted you—."

She quickly interrupted me, "False information? Alex what the hell are you talking about?"

"The HIV results."

She looked baffled, and then she slowly muttered "HIV?" She dragged out the "v" and her voice went up an octave, changing the statement into a question.

"Yes, Dori. The HIV that you have been treating Lisa and I for over the past three years."

Dori spit out her coffee and choked on the words as if she was the one that birthed them from her vocal chords. And that is when the unthinkable began to dawn on me.

"Dori, for the past three years, your best friend—*my* wife—has been feeding me medication that she says she is getting from you. She came home with papers with your office letterhead and your head doctor's signature on it stating that our HIV tests came back positive. That was three years ago." I spoke slowly and deliberately. I needed Dori to hear everything, and to agree with everything that I said. Anything less than her agreeance was incomprehensible. I studied her face, and for the first time since I've known her, she was quiet. She had a look of utter shock, as if she had just seen a ghost. Her eyes were wide with confusion and her head very meticulously turning to the side as if she wanted to shake her head to signal a "no."

My heart dropped. Her expression said it all. Dori had no clue as to what I was talking about. I grabbed my keys off her desk and was out the door before she could wipe that stunned look off her face. I caught a glimpse of her in my rearview mirror as I peeled out of the parking lot. She was poking at her cell phone. I assumed she was probably trying to call Lisa and give her a heads up that the gig was up. It was obvious that Dori was innocent in all of this—as innocent as I was.

"FUUUUUUUUCK!" I screamed at the top of my lungs and banged my fist on the steering wheel. It was all so clear to me. There was never any HIV threat. Lisa made all that shit up. Why was I too stupid? How could I not go get it checked for myself? I banged the steering wheel a few more times. I yanked the keys out of the ignition and opened the door. My phone rang just as I was about to get out the car. It was mom calling me back. It was not the time. I sent her to voicemail and left the phone in the car. No interruptions were needed.

I walked into the house and I could hear Lisa talking on the phone. She had the speaker phone on and was trying to explain herself to Dori.

"Girl, I'm sorry!" Lisa said.

"Sorry, hell! Lisa what were you thinking? You told that man he had HIV? What the fuck, girl? And then you go and drag *my* name into this? What were you thinking?"

"I know! I know! Dori! Just listen!"

"Girl, I can't deal with you right now! You have done some crazy shit in the past, and you know I've had your back, but you just risked my license! My LICENSE! Do you get that? Everything you did had *my* name on it! You don't care about anyone except yourself!"

"Dori! Dori!"

All I heard was dial tone, and then Lisa let out an angry scream and the sound of what could have been the phone hitting the wall then crashing to the floor. Before Lisa could have a chance to catch her breath, I walked up on her. She was wrapped in a bath sheet, hair up in a shower cap with traces of bubble suds on her shoulders and legs. When she saw me, there was an immediate look of fear in her eyes.

Surprisingly, I was calm. I envisioned myself storming into the house, yelling, and immediately throwing things, but when I looked at her, all I felt was disgust. I had all the confirmation that I needed when I heard the conversation between Lisa and her best friend. She couldn't deny anything, and she couldn't explain it away.

"You have fifteen minutes to pack your shit and get out of my house," was all that I said. I calmly turned and walked away. I went into my office and closed and locked the door behind me. It wasn't to hide from her; it was to keep myself from trying to kill her.

Adonis

It was a long, rough day. Two of my long-term patients had died. One of them as expected from complications due to AIDS, and the other was totally unexpected. He was healthy, strong and vigorously living his life. He had just turned 19 two days before. He first came to me at age fifteen as a pro-bono case. Each year, Big Brothers Big Sisters of America allowed me to host ten at-risk youth. I'd talk to them about safe sex, of course. I'd show them the effect that AIDS has on the human body, clear up any myths they may have, and educate them on how it is contracted. I'd take them out for lunch on my yacht and that is where the second half of the day is spent. Volunteers would give them job aptitude and behavioral tests so that they could get an idea for what they may want to do when they graduated high school. We would research the different salaries and coach them on the importance of keeping a good credit score all while watching the dolphins play and sipping cool beverages under the Florida sun.

The kids would really enjoy it, and so did I. It gave me an opportunity to give back. Usually, I didn't see any of them after the course was over, but Tony called up my office the very next day. He asked if I could speak with him privately. I was in between patients so I had a few minutes to kill. I thought he was either going to ask if I would be his big brother or ask for some money. I made a small wager with myself: if he asks me to be his big brother, I would take a shot before the next patient, but if he asked me for money, then I would take a snort. It was a win-win as far as I was concerned. Instead, Tony asked if I could spare a few minutes to talk to him privately, and in person. Guiltily, I must admit, I thought he wanted to get me alone and rob me. You just never know with these "at-risk" youth. One of my colleagues had his wallet lifted while he was doing a free clinic at a homeless shelter.

With that in mind, I set up a meeting with my young thug for that afternoon at my office. When he arrived, he was wearing the same clothes from the day before on the yacht. I remembered because while the other kids wore their best name brand outfits, Tony had on a plain white tee with a knock-off Lakers jersey, pants that were 3 sizes too big in an era when the kids are wearing skinny jeans, a pair of Jordan's that had to be released at least five seasons prior and had seen better days, but he was neat and clean.

He had a great sense of humor and tried to act like he wasn't paying attention so as not to get teased, but I could tell that he was absorbing everything around him. Tony was on time and sat quietly in the lobby until I called for him. He walked into the office with his head hung low and took slow deliberate steps. He looked as if he were a kid marching to his doom rather than a thug on a stealing spree. Once he sat down, he explained that he didn't know who else to talk to but he needed help. I thought it was the intro to the big shake down and he was going to say his mom was dying and he needed an exorbitant amount of money for the surgery or some shit like that. Instead, he began a different story.

He explained that his stepdad was sleeping with other men without his mother's knowledge. Worst of all, the stepdad was sexually abusing him—forcing him to perform oral sex as foreplay before he would go in and screw Tony's mom. He told his mom, but she didn't believe him. She called him a liar, and then told the stepdad who, of course, denied everything. Ever since Tony told his mom, the stepdad began raping him whenever his mom left the house. He tried telling his guidance counselor at school, but because he stayed in trouble with fighting and failing grades, the school just swept it under the rug saying that he was trying to deflect from his own behavior, and that he needed to be accountable for his actions.

I couldn't believe what I heard. It was such a far cry from the way that I was brought up. Tony continued, and he told me that he overheard his mom and stepdad talking and learned that one of their friends had died from AIDS three weeks before. Tony knew for sure that the stepdad was sleeping with the man who died, and he wanted to be tested. He explained that he didn't have any money to pay for it, and he didn't want to go to a free clinic thinking that he wouldn't get the best of care.

After hearing Tony's story, I explained to him that as a medical professional, I was required to report it to the state and that he could be placed in temporary foster care. Tony said he didn't care. He said if he didn't get out of that house, he was going to kill his stepfather and his mom; and if that didn't work, he would kill himself. That was enough for me to implement the Baker Act which would buy him some time away from the house. I called my friend LaToya who works for the Department of Children and Family services and asked her what to do as far as getting the kid some help. At fifteen, I was still a virgin. Tony had experienced more than I could ever imagine.

Over the years, Tony and I kept in touch. He would frequently drop by the office to shoot the breeze and tell me his latest plans. He wasn't surprised to find out he tested positive for HIV, yet he wasn't scared either. He said, "If Magic Johnson can make it, so can I!"

Once the state took custody of him the day he left my office, the rape kits corroborated his story. He spent three days under psychiatric evaluation with the Baker Act requirements and then was sent to a group home. At fifteen,

Calm Sparkle

it was hard to get a foster family, especially one that had a sexual past inflicted upon him. Tony didn't care. He was just glad to be out of that house and away from his parents. He seemed to blossom in his new school, stayed out of trouble, made some friends in the group home. I would buy him some new threads from time to time, and he loved going to the Miami Heat games with me.

On his 18th birthday, he aged out of the system and was left to fend for himself. I offered to pay for his college but he declined. He said he wanted to make it on his own, so he began working a paid apprenticeship at an auto shop while attending night classes at the community college. That wasn't bad for a kid whom life had given such a rough start, which is why I was completely heartbroken to learn that Tony was in a motorcycle accident that took his life. I didn't expect that for him. His life was just getting started.

The entire office was somber at hearing the news. Ms. Millie had to take the day off. She considered Tony her adopted grandson, and she just couldn't handle hearing the news. I somehow managed to make it through the day and then it was time to unwind. I took a shot of bourbon before heading out to my car. I needed to take the edge off. By the time I got to the car, I was catching the tail end of Sparkle's fifteen minute segment.

"Remember, there's a fine line between self-preservation and self-sabotage. Don't be so guarded that you miss out on love because you keep slamming the door in its face. Have a great afternoon, loves!"

Just hearing her voice made me feel at ease, but it didn't take away the ache in my heart. It just hit me that Tony was gone. I dealt with death all the time, but I'd been lucky enough to not have anyone close to me die. Sparkle kept talking about a "God" but I didn't see any proof of Him anywhere. I didn't tell her I didn't believe in her god; I didn't think she needed to know. Some things a man should just keep to himself to eliminate arguments, like drugs and religion. I definitely wasn't going to risk losing Sparkle over some mythical man in the sky. I would support whatever she believed if that's what it took to keep her with me.

Sparkle

It was six o'clock on a Wednesday evening and I was at home helping Andre with his homework when I heard the doorbell ring. I was surprised to see Don standing on the other side of the door. I don't welcome pop up visits and I don't allow my suitors to meet my son, so his visit was a double whammy for me. I stepped out onto the porch to see what was so important that Don would stop by unannounced while I had Andre. His face was flushed and his eyes were red, yet he was trying his best to smile. I gave him a quick hug, but he wouldn't let go. The way he held me told me that he needed something to hold on to so I let him wrap me up in his arms for as long as he needed. When he finally released, he said, "Tony died today. Motorcycle accident."

I gasped. I couldn't believe it. I had never met Tony personally, but Don spoke of him often, and I'd seen enough pictures to feel as if I had known him as well. I invited Don in. He definitely had a reason to bypass the "call before you come" rule. Andre' peeked from the kitchen table with curiosity. When Don saw him, he quickly straightened up.

"I'm sorry! I—I didn't think."

"It's okay." I replied, "Come on in and meet my son. When he is done with his homework, you and I can talk."

After introductions, Don asked what we were working on. I tried to remain positive and just say "math" but Andre answered before I could and said, "My teacher says it's math, but mom says it's 'common core crap!'" I was so embarrassed. I really needed to watch what I'd say around him. Don found the comment hilarious and gave me a kiss on the cheek.

"Well, do you mind if I take a look at it? Maybe I can help." Don took a seat with Andre's permission and, surprisingly, the two of them hit off. I didn't expect it considering Don didn't have any children of his own, nor siblings either. He was an only child that grew up the son of a prominent corporate real estate attorney, Donnie Adonis II, and the only grandson of the multi-millionaire hotel resort mogul, Donnie Adonis, Sr. Don's grandfather started the family business with just a bed and breakfast. The family would later own 214 luxury resorts across the globe, including five private islands. Don's father went into law and opened a law firm that handled all the hotel's legal affairs. Don, not wanting anything to do with the family business, went into medicine much to the disapproval of his predecessors.

When he described his background, I couldn't help but laugh. "When you come from a family where being a doctor is considered rebellion, you must have some really deep pockets!" I joked. Don didn't find it amusing.

While he took over helping Andre with his homework, I decided I would take the opportunity to start dinner. I glanced over at the two of them from time to time and it would melt my heart seeing how well they hit it off. Usually, Andre is very reserved and protective of me, but he seemed to be relaxed and attentive to everything Don was saying. It definitely gave me the warm fuzzies seeing it.

Once homework was done, Andre asked Don if he would stay for dinner. Don looked at me, and I signaled that it was okay. Dinner was wonderful. Laughter flowed as Andre told us recess adventures for the day, and how he nailed it when it came to the classroom spelling bee which earned him a trip to the treasure box for a new eraser. It felt very natural, and I began to feel heart flutters when I watched Don and Andre interact. After dinner, Andre and I walked Don to his car. Andre ran off doing somersaults in the yard while I stood at the car with Don.

"I'm so sorry that we didn't get to talk, but thank you for helping Andre with his homework."

"No, thank *you*, and Andre' for allowing me to intrude.

This definitely beats going home to an empty house." The sadness returned to his eyes.

"Are you going to be okay tonight?" I asked. Don wasn't looking at me. He watched Andre play in the moonlight. I could practically see his emotion on his face.

"I never had that," he said. I turned to look at Andre'. Confused, I had to ask, "Had what? A soccer ball?"

Don cracked a weak smile then finally looked at me. "No, silly," he answered brushing away some hair from my face and tucking it behind my ear. I wondered if he noticed my tracks. He continued, "I never had that free-spirited childhood. I always had to present myself as polished and polite, well-behaved, speak when spoken to, couldn't get dirty—." His voice trailed off. "I was allowed to do clean sports like swimming and water polo. Bowling and archery. Nothing that required sweat or getting dirty. Look how free Andre is. Not caring about what anyone else thinks. Not caring if his ball makes the goal, or even if his socks match."

I had to giggle; Andre was wearing one purple sock and one green sock thanks to "Crazy Sock Day" at his school. Although, for Andre, he truly didn't care if his socks matched on a daily basis. Don then said, "I wonder what it feels like to just live." Suddenly, he got down on one knee and my heart stopped. He looked up at me and said, "Sparkle, I want to ask you to marry me, but I will wait and do it right. I don't have a ring just yet but I will go buy one tomorrow. So, for tonight, I promise you my heart for the rest of our lives. I promise that I will be the husband that you deserve and a great bonus dad to Andre if you will have me. I don't want to play around anymore. I'm ready to live life according to my rules, *our* rules."

I was in a state of shock. The last thing I expected when I awoke that morning was a—what would you call this? A "pre-proposal." My heart said "yes." From the moment we locked eyes at that karaoke bar, I knew there was something there, but my mind was telling me "not yet."

I pulled Don up to meet me face to face again. And I

answered, "I'm not saying 'yes', but I'm not saying 'no.' I'm just saying, 'not yet.' I need Andre to really get to know you. I need to see if we really do fit and it's not just the hormones, or the loneliness, or even Tony's death talking. Let's just keep on the path we're on and in a year, we can revisit this."

Don kissed me gently and hugged me while whispering, "We may not have a year to wait." He pulled away and said, "I respect you and all that you are saying. I respect Andre and look forward to getting to know him. I can't agree that I will wait a year to become your fiancé', but I will wait for as long as you like to become your husband officially. If that means a five-year engagement, so be it. But I know in my heart that you, and now, after meeting him, Andre, are meant to be in my life." He kissed me on the forehead and got in his car and drove away. My heart fluttered, my vagina tingled, and my mouth was frozen into an eternal smile that lit up the night's sky.

Later, after Andre was asleep and I was settled, Don called and we were able to talk about Tony. It was hard to hear him so heartbroken. I reminded him that although Tony started off with a difficult childhood, God allowed his latter years to be full of hope and joy. Don didn't seem to have much to say about it. We ended our call with a prayer and he told me that he loved me, and thanked me for allowing him to meet Andre.

And that is when it started—that moment when the wall that I spent years building around my heart began to crumble. If I let it collapse into a pile of rubble so deep that it buries my running shoes, will Don still be there when the dust settled? Was I ready to be truly vulnerable and find out?

Lisa

So, it had been a while since Alex found out about the HIV sham. I thought he was just playing when he told me to get out. I thought he would calm down and then we could talk it out and I would be able to convince him that I was also a victim of false test results. After telling me to leave, he locked himself in his office for two hours—the same office where he made love to me up against the wall. I knew not to knock or disturb him at that moment, so I just quietly waited. I packed a bag with a few things to make it look like I planned to leave. When he finally came out, it was only because it was time to pick up Jr from daycare. Usually, I would pick him up, but Alex was determined to do it himself. He seemed shock to still see me there in the house.

"I'll get Jr," I said to Alex. "No need to disrupt his schedule. I'll go get him then fix dinner like always, and once Jr is asleep, we will leave so he won't ask a bunch of questions." I lied way too easily to my husband. I had no intentions to going anyplace. I pointed to my bags over by the door, "See, I've already packed our things."

I noticed Alex would wince whenever I said "we" and "our." Did he really think that I would leave without Jr? Al looked down at his watch then shrugged and said, "Whatever." He turned to walk towards the bedroom. I went to get Jr and came right back home with every intention of acting as innocent as the virgin Mary, but to my surprise, I turned into the driveway only to be greeted by the sight of a locksmith crew. Alex had already ordered changes on the locks. Tuh, he could change them all he wanted. I wasn't going anywhere.

Things proceeded to move a lot faster than I anticipated. As if the change of locks weren't enough, Alex gave me an ultimatum. I could either leave and agree to a divorce granting Alex full custody of Jr and monthly alimony of $5k per month. Or, I could stay as long as I agreed to a legal separation with a co-parenting roommate agreement, and waive all alimony rights until Jr went off to college and we both were free to see whomever we pleased. I would take the guest house out back and he would stay in the main house with Jr. I accepted option two. It gave me time to figure out my next move.

The following week, I returned home from an

embarrassing shopping spree in which my card was declined while trying to purchase a pair of gloves from the clearance rack. They were cashmere lined and only $59.99. I thought the sales lady was playing a joke on me when she swiped and it still declined. I initially blamed it on the chip reader and insisted that the clerk run it the traditional way. Of course, the machine wouldn't allow a swipe due to the detection of the chip, so she had to key it in by hand only to get the same declined message.

    I went home prepared to cuss Alex out for not paying the bills, which further proved that he needed me and couldn't keep up the charade of no longer being man and wife. Al wasn't home. And he never gave me a key since the locks changed, so I didn't have access to the house. I went around back to my dungeon as I liked to call it. Although the guest house was far from a dungeon with the spa-like bathroom, fireplace in the cozy living area, and sky light in the master bedroom, it was more like a 1-bedroom apartment. When I walked up to the entry door, there was an envelope on the tiny porch. I could tell from the return address that it was from the attorney's office. I was in no mood to open it, so I tossed it on the kitchen counter.

    I logged into my laptop and pulled up my GPS tracker to see where Alex was. I used to have him on the "Find My Friends" app but he'd since deleted me. The joke was on him because I had a tracker in all his vehicles so I could always find him if I needed to. I had it placed right after the trip when he came back smelling like another woman. How did I lose control?

    My phone alarm went off. It was time for my first virtual group consultation with Sparkle's Moonbow Coaching. I hated the name, but whatever. I logged into the webinar and was prepared for an hour of surveillance mode. I pretended to be attentive and asked questions every chance that I could so that my name would stand out from the others. About halfway through, I realized that she was wearing what appeared to be an engagement ring. You couldn't miss it from a mile away. It had to be at least a four or five carat solitaire. Since she was always supporting the single ladies, I didn't think anything of it until she used the phrase "my fiancé," which made me sit up and pay attention. Well, this was definitely a new development. I grabbed my phone and sent Donnie a text.

"Hey, stranger! How's it going?" It was short, simple, and not too probing.

It took fifteen minutes for him to respond, "Hey, Lisa. What's up?"

I quickly responded while I still had his attention and while I knew exactly where Sparkle was. "Not much. Just thought I'd check on an old friend. How are you?"

"I'm happy, and I'm engaged, so don't text me again. Lose my number, *friend*."

Well damn. He shut me off like he did right after college graduation, but I wasn't the same naïve girl that I was back then. I spat back, "Look prick, I just thought you should know that Sparkle and Alex plan on meeting up this weekend. He leaves tomorrow and is headed your way. I am assuming that Sparkle is your intended bride."

A good ten minutes passed and Sparkle began to wrap up the webinar. Don never responded, but I knew that his radar was up. Alex was bolder when he felt that he didn't have to hide and sneak. I would go to the main house when he got home in the evenings and spend time with Jr. I would feed, bathe, and put him to bed as if nothing had changed. As soon as Jr fell asleep, Al would quickly banish me to my quarters. However, he never missed an opportunity to express his newfound freedom while I was there. He openly spoke to Sparkle on his phone and in my presence. He would leave his Facebook page up on his computer in the office with the door that was once always shut now kept wide open. He even texted openly and left his phone laying around. That is how I heard his cozy conversation with Sparkle confirming dinner plans for Saturday. I just busied myself and pretended to be getting more of my things out of the closet or drawers and tried to stall to get as much information as I could. When he hung up the phone, I didn't shy away from asking him anything.

"So, you're meeting up with Sparkle this weekend, huh?"

He didn't answer, but I knew he heard me. I kept talking anyway, "I also heard you say you were taking Jr with you. Just leave him here with me. No sense in dragging him up there only to leave him with your mom while you enjoy your newfound single life." He must have been bat shit crazy if he thought I was going to let him take my baby anywhere near that trick.

"Cool," was all he said. I gathered my things and headed back to my sleeping suite and immediately called my mom. I told her that Alex and I were going away for the weekend and asked if she could keep Jr. She agreed. My next move was to reserve a rental car and a hotel room. My plan was to go Moonbow, catch them in the act, and then file for divorce claiming infidelity. Alex only filed for separation, which left the door open for me to file for a full divorce. The State of Florida does not require a minimum separation period, and with no prenuptial agreement, I would get the house, full custody, and half of everything. My plan was set and I was good to go until my card got declined. I heard Alex pulling up in the driveway. He always blasted his music as if he wanted to provide a concert for the entire neighborhood. I wondered why he was at home so early. I hadn't even picked up Jr yet. I met him outside.

"Alex, my card was declined today."

"You don't say." He didn't look at me but got out of the car and started to walk towards the house.

"Well, did you pay the bills? Do you need me to handle that for you?

"Yep. I paid them. And nope, don't need you." That last part stung. As he walked into the house he said, "I cancelled your cards and removed you from all my bank accounts. Get a job if you want to shop." Then he slammed the door in my face. Anger began to simmer within me; it started with a tingle in my toes and worked its way through my body. I was sure steam was coming from my ears. I clenched and unclenched my fist. If any neighbors were to jog by, they would think I was Drew Barrymore's *Firestarter* character. My phone alarm sounded off again. It was time to pick up Jr.

That was my answer! When I returned from picking up Jr, Alex warmly welcomed us. Well, warmly welcomed his son, but allowed me to come in the house. We went through our unusually usual routine until Jr was asleep. I used the baby to my advantage.

"Alex, hun, you're right. I will get a job."

No response. It was like talking to a brick wall.

"Alex, why don't you talk to me?" He glared at me with hate. I couldn't believe it. The man that made love to me so intently that I shed tears of joy on the very floor where I stood just a few short months before, looked at me as if I disgusted him. "Alex, please." I couldn't believe that I begged. But there I was—begging.

"You want to talk, Lisa? Now you want to talk? After leading me on for all these years with that lie? What the fuck do you want me to say? It takes every fiber of my being to tolerate being this close to you. The only reason you are right now, the *only* reason, is to be a mother to Jr. That's it. Period. Point blank." He stared me down as if he dared me to say something.

"How can we make this work? What can I do? I did all of this because I love you! I wanted to be with you. I just wanted you to love me back." I let the tears flow.

In response to my vulnerability, he laughed in my face and walked off. I followed behind him with a different mission in mind. I had to get some money to sponsor my private eye trip. I didn't count on him cancelling my cards or removing me from the accounts. I had about $265K stashed away in an account that I'd had since college, but I didn't want to touch *my* money if I didn't have to.

"Alex, I'm going to need some money if I'm going to keep Jr this weekend." There was silence for a moment then he came back into the kitchen and dropped his black AMEX card on the table. I could see that it was a new card. It still had the gummy tape on the back of it. He must have opened all new accounts rather than just removing me. The hurt was real. The anger was blinding.

I remembered Sparkle saying that hurt was the root of all anger during the webinar, which pissed me off even more that I actually retained some of what she said. I snatched up the credit card and went back to my exile suite. I fired up the laptop and prepaid for the rental car and the hotel room so there wouldn't be any issues at check in. Then I went online to the credit card account, and just as I thought, he may have changed the locks and taken me off of the information, but he didn't change his online account passwords. I easily obtained access and added myself as an authorized user and ordered a duplicate card be sent to my mom's address. It wouldn't be back in time for the trip, but at least I would have it for the months ahead. If Alex wanted to end the marriage, he could go right ahead, but I wasn't going down without a fight.

Kimberly D.L. Pittman

Calm Sparkle Discussion Questions:

Chapters 7 & 8

1. What are your thoughts on the "Dating around" philosophy?
2. Do you agree with Sister Anastasia that a young man should sow his wild oats before settling down?
3. Were you surprised to learn of Lisa and Don's connection?
4. We learned a bit more about Dr. Adonis in these chapters. Do you think he is a good fit for Sparkle? Why or Why not?
5. Alex's response to finding out his blood test results caught Lisa & Don off guard. At that point did you think Lisa would ever be revealed?
6. Put yourself in Dori's shoes the day that all was revealed. How would you have reacted if you were Dori?
7. Do you think Lisa will maneuver her way out of this sticky situation and win Alex's trust back?
8. Lisa once again manages to keep composure and control when finding out that Alex is still talking to Sparkle. What do you think this says about her character? How would you describe Lisa?

Chapter Nine
Sunset Wishes

Dr. Adonis

I didn't want to believe Lisa when she said that Sparkle was going out to dinner with Alex, so I asked her. She and I had a relationship where we promised each other complete honesty. I kept my end of the deal, and I trusted Sparkle to keep hers. She didn't know about all my habits, but she never asked, therefore I never had to lie.

I called her up immediately after speaking with Lisa and asked if she wanted to fly over to California and take Andre to Disney Land for the weekend. She agreed that it would be a nice break. I felt a sense of relief. I'm not sure why. Alex was definitely no threat to me, but I guess I couldn't bear the thought of Sparkle keeping a secret from me. Hypocritical, I know, but it is what it is. My relief was immediately taken from me as quickly as it was given when she followed up with "Can we leave Saturday morning rather than Friday? I'm meeting an old friend for dinner." My heart flinched. Lisa was right after all.

"Really?" I casually asked, "with who?"

"My buddy, Alex. I think he's one of your patients. He told me he and his wife went to see you a few months ago."

All I could manage to get out was "Hmmm. Is that so?"

Sparkle continued talking, "No worries, love! I know better than to ask you anything about him or the visit or anything of that nature."

"Oh, I know, babe. So, how do you know this Alex, did you say?"

"We went to school together. We dated back in college. He's actually good friends with Corey as well. I'm sure you know who he is."

"Hmmm. Is it that tall, dark super rich, but not as rich as me, guy?" I joked with her. She caught it and giggled.

"Yes! That's the one," she confirmed.

"Well, isn't that the same guy that caused you a moment of weakness? The married guy?"

"Yes, hun. That was him. That was a looooong time ago, hun. Nothing at all for you to be concerned about. Besides, he has HIV and he is very much married. Absolutely no reason for you to be concerned, my love."

I admired her trying to instill a sense of comfort at the thought of her going to dinner with an ex-boyfriend, but it was absolutely no help in hearing that "he's married and has HIV" when I knew for a fact that he's as clean as a whistle and married to a whore whom he was probably about to drop like a hot potato for tricking him into marriage.

"I'm good, babe. I trust you. I know you can conduct yourself as the future Mrs. Adonis." I had no choice. Any other response would drive her to him and away from me. I would just have to move up my plans a little to ensure that she didn't slip through my fingers.

Sparkle

I cleared my entire calendar for Friday through Tuesday. I needed a few days to regroup. Don's suggestion to go to California was just what we needed. I could just taste that giant, smoked turkey leg that was always the highlight of my Disney visits. Thursday after Andre's soccer practice, Don met us at my place, and we had another great evening laughing at Andre's recess recap. Once Andre was fed, bathed and in the bed, Don and I snuggled on the couch in the den and watched television. He sat on the end and I laid with my head in his lap while he twirled his fingers around my hair. We loved to watch *The Big Bang Theory* together, and usually Don left once the episode was over. That night was different. As the credits rolled, he looked down at me; it was the soul stare that I had seen earlier in our relationship—the one that told me we were kindred spirits from another lifetime.

"You know I love you and Andre more than anything."

"I know, hun. We love you too." He began to stroke my face, and then he bent down to give me a luxuriously passionate kiss. It was filled with all the love his heart couldn't find the words to speak. I felt the bulge in his pants beginning to grow underneath my head, and his hands moved from my stomach to my breast. When he parted ways with my mouth he said, "Let's become one tonight."

I smiled. I felt that we were already one mentally and spiritually, but to hear that he wanted to combine physically made me warm all over. We had spoken of it before, especially the night that I gave him the lap dance, and we decided that if we had come that far, we may as well wait for marriage. "Are you sure, hun?" I asked myself as well as him.

"I'm sure," he answered.

We got up from the sofa and turned out the lights, secured all the house locks and peeked in on Andre who was sound asleep. We headed to my bedroom and I tingled with excitement. When we got to my room, Don went straight to the bathroom and began to fill the tub with water. He added my lavender bath salts and the matching bubble bath. Then he lit the candles that were placed around my spa-style tub. He returned to the bed where I sat on the edge thinking that he was going to ravish me, and not simply bathe me and kissed my forehead. He told me not to move and that he would be right back. When he returned to the bedroom, he had his gym bag. He opened it and pulled out more candles, a set of red satin sheets and some massage oils.

The tub was filled, and he shut down the waterfall that was creating an ocean of bubbles and turned on some music. "Can I move now?" I asked playfully.

He turned off all the lights, came over to where I was sitting, and offered both hands to help me up. He unbuttoned my blouse, removed it from my shoulders and allowed it to fall listlessly to the floor. He did the same for my bra, and then my skirt, but I wasn't wearing any panties. He rolled down my jet black, lace-topped thigh highs and peeled them from each foot very carefully. Once I was completely naked, he pulled my hair up, doing his best to wrap it into a ponytail, and then led me to the bath and helped me in.

"Relax. I'll be right back." That was all he said before disappearing back into the bedroom. I heard him rustling around and shaking sheets. He'd made up the bed. I leaned my head back and enjoyed the soothing water and the intoxicating scent of vanilla lavender. I can't remember the last time that I'd ever felt so relaxed. The instrumental jazz version of Janet Jackson's "Anytime, Anyplace" came through the Bluetooth speaker and lulled me into a state of lazy sensuality.

I heard Don's footsteps coming towards me. When I opened my eyes, he stood beside the tub completely bare. His golden bronze skin glowed against the candlelight. His eyes smiled at my chocolate clashing against the pure white of the bubbles. I reached out my hand to him to invite him to join me. Instead, he kneeled, took my sponge, added some body wash, and he bathed me gingerly, as if I would break under the pressure of his hands. When it was time to rinse my body, he asked me to stand, and then he finally joined me in the tub. It was my turn to pamper him. I returned the favor by bathing him from head to toe. I could tell by his deliberate movements that he intended to make this night last as long as humanely possible. That was just fine with me! He towel-dried me and paid special attention to my vaginal area with a few extra pats; he then dried himself, blew out the bathroom candles and led me to the bed. The light jazz continued to fill the room at a low volume. It was barely audible, but enough to keep the relaxed mood intact.

"Tonight, we will become one in the most spiritual way possible. Tonight, is all about the senses. I want to feel you, not just your body, but your essence." He spoke softly as he continued, "a few rules for tonight."

"Rules?" I interjected and he quickly put his fingers to my lips, which I licked to his surprise and he chuckled.

"Patience is the lesson tonight, Sparkle. Rule number one—no talking. Rule number 2: follow my instructions. Rule number 3: no inhibitions or insecurities. Final rule—expect to experience love."

He gave me a glass of wine, which I finished in a few gulps. "Patience, Sparkle! Slow down!" he laughed.

He sipped his Remy then led me to lay down on the fresh, deep red wine satin sheets. He rolled me onto my belly and drizzled warm massage oil on my back. He proceeded to massage the nape of my neck. My shoulders, each arm, my back, my entire body began to feel like Gumby. Just when I thought he was done, he moved down to my hips and thighs and continued to massage all the way down to my toes. It was heaven feeling his hands hit just the right pressure points. My body felt like limber and fluid and completely stress free.

He rolled me onto my back and pulled me into a sitting position. He positioned himself in the bed with his back against the headboard and instructed me to straddle him. I did as I was asked, and once we were in our lotus position he brought his forehead to mine and asked me to focus on his breathing. "In" he inhaled. "Out." He exhaled. Slowly and rhythmically, we breathed in. We breathed out, and consumed each other's life force with each breath. I exhaled me and inhaled him. He lifted his head and looked into my eyes again. As we stared into each other's eyes, breathing in the essence of each other, he told me to explore his body with my hands without breaking the breathing or the eye contact. And I did; I glided my hands across his shoulders and biceps. I cupped his face and massaged his temples with my thumbs; I ran my fingers up and down his spine. It was a hypnotic experience to gaze into his soul and see his love for me. I breathed him in and felt his groin come to life between my legs.

Having his hands graze all over my body, he slowly pulled me to him and asked to kiss me. He told me not to kiss back and to just let him give, and I should just receive. As he kissed me, he pulled me into a hug then gently flipped me from the straddle position into a laying position on my back. We were missionary style and the weight of his body melded with mine. He resumed the soul gaze and gently placed the tip of his penis at my vaginal entrance.

He watched my expression as I automatically closed my eyes in anticipation. "No," he whispered. "See me, feel the experience. Eyes open, babe."

I groggily opened my eyes as he allowed his mouth to worship my body with warm, soft kisses on my chest and neck before we locked eyes once again. So torturously slowly, he continued to enter me. Interlocking his fingers with my hands, he slid as slow as the second hand on a watch until he was fully within me. And he held it there. My body was on fire. From the bath to the massage to the kiss to the breathing to having him in me and not moving—just holding still, breathing each other and feeling the unity of being one.

"Don't move, my love," he whispered as he kissed my lips. My hands held his; my mouth held his. My vagina held him. And I clenched repeatedly, squeezing his cock and eager for a thrust. The music played, the candles glowed, the scent of the massage oils filled the room. Feeling his love for me, breathing his love for me, was all too much. I was overwhelmed.

He said, "I love you. Can you feel it?" I couldn't speak. He gently kissed my forehead, the tip of my nose, my lips. Then he says, huskily, "On the count of three, we become one." His eyes found mine once again as he whispered his count, "One." I began to thrust my hips and he stopped me. "No babe, silence. Stillness. Just feel me inside of you. Focus on the love as I transfer it from my body to yours."

I slid my hands down his back and gripped his buttocks, trying to plunge him deeper inside me. He was so poised and relax. "Let's start again," he said. "One. I love you. Two. I love you. Three. I love all of you."

Then his mouth enveloped mine. I felt his body clench up and he gave one strong pump deep inside me and let out a primal moan. Suddenly, I felt a rush of his warm liquid gold entering me and filling my walls. My body instinctually responded to the receipt of his love as it flowed into me. My kitty clenched tighter and faster, repeatedly trying pull out every ounce of his life source. The trembling started from my womb and spread throughout every inch of me as I joined his primal ecstasy scream and flooded his juices with mine. Shaking violently with pleasure, we created our own earthquake, which produced its own floods and soaked everything within the area of our mating.

As our bodies calmed down, we were both limp with exotic exhaustion. He remained inside me although he was limp. Tears began to trickle from my eyes. He truly loved me—adored me. He created the night to worship me as his future wife. That was true love-making. It wasn't the humping, or the positions, or who would cum first. It was about the spiritual joining of two souls that only want to adore and appreciate each other in every sense. Where had he been all my life?

Alex

It was finally Friday. I'd been planning the night for two weeks. I finally got Sparkle to agree to meet me for dinner. I never told her about what Lisa had done, or that I had a clean bill of health. I wanted to tell her in person. Corey told me that she and ole boy got engaged, but I wasn't hearing any of that. Engaged is not married. Hell, I was married. With all the shit Lisa put me through, she should just be glad that I was giving her the arrangement I'd provided for legal separation.

For our dinner plans, I would have one of my private jets fly us over to Nassau for a private oceanfront dinner for two. I didn't want anyone else around while we talked it out. I was sure I could get her to come back to me. She just needed to remember how much we were meant to be together, and it was time to stop letting life get in the way, and time for us to live as we should have all along.

It was 4:30 pm on the dot and the limo was right on time. We arrived at Sparkle's at 5 o'clock. I was all smiles until I rang the doorbell and Donnie answered the door.

"Hey, Alex! Wassup?" The good doctor reached for my hand in the customary hand greeting that all brothers give, ending with a chest bump. "Come on in, Sparkle will be right out. You know how women are—never ready on time."

I was confused. Did he not realize that this was a date? I was there to take his woman out on a date, and he was trying to be best bros. Then it dawned on me, he didn't think that I was any competition. We would see about that when Sparkle wouldn't come home that night. Just then, Sparkle came into the living room. She looked beautiful wearing a pair of jet black jeans and a royal blue sheer cowl necked blouse with a black camisole underneath. Her hair was up in a loose ponytail with bangs lightly grazing her eyelashes and framing the sides of her cheeks; she wore simple gold hoops and classic black Louboutin's.

Donnie beat me to the punch and said, "Wow, love! You are stunning as always." They hugged and kissed and Sparkle giggled as if I weren't even there.

"Ahem," I cleared my throat to remind them that I was

in the room. My temperature was slowly rising, but I kept my cool because I knew that once Sparkle heard what I had to say, it would be her last kiss with the good doc.

"Sparkle, I hate to break up this love fest, but we really need to get going. Oh, and grab your passport." That caught both of their attention.

"Passport?" they both asked in unison.

"Yes. Passport. You're going to need it."

"Alex, I can't go away on a trip; I only have the sitter until 11 and we have plans in the morning."

"Don't worry. I'll have you back in time."

Don said, "Where are you taking her, homie?"

"Just a quick flight over to Nassau for some ocean fresh conch. You don't mind do you, bruh? Just a couple of friends catching up. That's all."

"Nah, bruh, I'm good. I trust Sparkle, and I know she will come home to me in the same way that she is leaving."

"Cut out all this passive-aggressive bullshit, you two. Alex, stop trying to antagonize, Don," Sparkle chimed in.

"Don, don't forget to stop by the sitter's and give Andre his tablet. He's waiting for it. I'll see you in the morning, hun," she said as she kissed him goodbye.

Although I knew the docs days were numbered, it still killed me to see her show him so much affection.

En route to the airport, Sparkle asked, "Bahamas, huh? Fancy!"

"Whatever." I did a horrible job at hiding my pisstivity at her kissing on Don.

"Whatever? What's that all about? What's wrong with you?" she inquired.

"Nothing."

"Driver, can you please stop and take me back home?"

"Woah! What? Wait! What are you doing?" Was she crazy? I'd just paid all that money and she said to take her home before we even got two blocks from the house?

"Look, Alex, if you are going to be a sourpuss and in a foul mood, I'm not wasting my Friday night on your bad energy. So, take me home and we can do this on another day when you're not so in your feelings."

I looked at her and she was dead serious. She pulled out her cell phone as the limo came to a stop and prepared to make a U-turn. "Driver, I'm sorry. Please keep going as planned." The driver rolled down the partition and asked Sparkle if she was okay and if she wanted to return home. Sparkle looked at me and I managed to crack a smile.

"I'm fine," she replied, "yes, please, let's continue. Thank you for asking." The driver merged back into traffic and resumed our route towards the air hangar. Sparkle returned to face me. There was something different about her. She was always confident, always beautiful, but there was a presence about her that I couldn't put my finger on. I liked it. It was sexy and intriguing. "Ok, Alex, let's have some fun!" She put on the latest Bruno Mars playlist and poured herself a glass of wine. Watching her make the best of the moment brought a genuine smile to my face, which replaced the fake one that I'd had just moments before. And to think, in just a few short hours, she would be mine again—for good.

Lisa

I made it safely to Moonbow without any issues. I had a honey blonde wig and an overnight bag filled with nothing but sweat suits—something that I would never wear. I was in full incognito mode. I had a hotel room directly across from Alex, and he had absolutely no idea that I was there. As far as he was concerned, I was back at the house with Jr being the perfect mother. Thank goodness, he still had no clue that I purposely got pregnant. That was one secret that would go with me to my grave. As long as Dori didn't completely turn on me, that is.

Thursday night turned out to be uneventful. I followed him all day and night. He went to see his mom, went to Corey's karaoke spot and sat at the bar shooting the breeze. Around midnight, he left and I followed him to a house. Not sure who's, but I assumed it was Sparkle's. The two-car garage was closed, but Don's car sat in the driveway outside of the enclosure. Alex sat in the driveway for a while. I saw the glow of his cellphone emit from his hands in the darkness. I snapped a few photos using my night vision camera to begin my photo journal so that I could prove that he was cheating and get half of his shit. He waited about five minutes and then backed out and drove back to the hotel where he stayed for the rest of the night.

On Friday, he started out the day early. He went to see his mom at her job for lunch then back to the hotel. That was it! Just when I started to get bored, I heard him leaving his hotel room. I grabbed my keys and stepped into the hallway to follow when I noticed that he made an abrupt U-turn and was heading back towards the room. I jumped back into my room and closed the door. Peeking through the peephole, I saw him disappear into the room and then hurry back out, but with his cell phone in hand. I peeked my head out the door in time to catch him turn the corner towards the elevator. I put my shades on and followed suit.

I was disguised in my pixie cut blonde wig, giant gold hooped earrings, a gray velour sweat suit with a plain white tee underneath and plain navy blue Keds—none of which I would ever have in my wardrobe. I bought everything from the thrift store—except the wig, hazel contacts, and a fake gold tooth cap.

As I turned the corner, Alex was stepping onto the elevator. "Perfect timing," I thought as I rushed to push the button to call for the next elevator. Alex's foot stepped into the doorway preventing it from closing. The one time I didn't want him to be a gentleman.

"Join me," he smiled and held back the automatic doors to allow me to step inside. I smiled and nodded, being sure to only give a top teeth only smile like Denzel, which showed my gold tooth. I kept my head down and looked at my Keds as the elevator began to descend. I could feel Alex looking at me, but I didn't dare lift my face to meet his. Finally, he said, "How are you enjoying Florida?"

Calm Sparkle

I tried to disguise my voice and sound Jamaican—no, Spanish—no, Jamaican. In my confusion over what accent to choose, I just blurted out, "Tis fine. Tis fine. I enjoy." So, in the push and pull between a Jamaican or Spanish accent, my conversation came out like the Korean lady that did my nails. I was so relieved when the elevator opened. I ran off and headed to my car.

I heard Alex shout from behind me, "Have a great evening, Lisa," and then he laughed loudly and heartily. I just kept moving. I was not going to let it intervene with my plans. He had no proof that it was me. "Lisa" could have been anybody. If I stopped and turned around, the game would be over, but if I kept moving then I could continue as planned. Then it dawned on me. He wasn't headed towards the parking garage to get his car. Did he valet? I rushed over to my rented Nissan Sentra and peeled out of the garage in an attempt to catch up to him leaving the hotel entrance. As I pulled up to the front of the hotel, I saw him getting into a stretch black Cadillac limousine.

"What the fart!" I snapped a couple of photos for my records. I followed the limousine back to the same house that he parked in front of the previous evening. Donnie's car was there again. This time, Sparkle's garage was open showcasing a black Chevy Suburban and a white convertible Volkswagen Beetle. There were toys and bicycles in the garage as well. The limousine parked horizontally and blocked the driveway, and the chauffer proceeded to let Alex out of the car. I sat three houses down and watched through my zoom lens. Trying to control my anger to just a simmer, I couldn't help but think "What would Beyonce' do?" About twenty minutes later, Alex and Sparkle emerged from the house. There was no sign of Don. I sent him a quick text, "WYD?" just to get a gauge on where he was with all of it. I snapped a picture of Sparkle's driveway with the happy couple getting into the limo and added it to the text. That ought to get his attention.

The limo began to pull away once the two were secured

inside, and I began to follow suit. A few blocks later, the car pulled into a small shopping center. I didn't expect that to happen, so I ended up driving right past them. As I prepared to make a U-turn, they were back on the road and passed me by catching the yellow light while I got stuck at red. Don text me back as I awaited the green signal and kept an eye on the direction the limousine was headed.

The car's SYNC system read the text to me: "Go home, Lisa. Nothing to worry about. In fact, come party at my crib tonight." What the hell was he talking about? There was no time to think about it; I'd finally caught up to the limousine.

A good ten minutes later and we were at the beach at his mother's boat dock. I watched as they boarded onto his mom's boat and the two of them literally sailed off into the sunset like a damn romance novel. I was completely pissed. He *never* put that much care and thought into anything he did for me. In fact, I was always the one doing the planning and the dating and the wooing. What the fuck did she have that I didn't? I sat and watched until the boat was out of sight. Tears began to stream down my face—hot, angry tears as I felt my blood boil. I could hear Queen Bey in my head singing "RING THE ALARM! I BEEN THROUGH THIS TOO LONG! BUT I'LL BE DAMNED IF I SEE ANOTHER CHICK ON YOUR ARM!" I called Don back and told him to text me his address, and I was on my way.

Dr. Adonis

Lisa came over and I poured her a drink. It was only fair that if Alex and Sparkle were out on a so-called date that Lisa and I should kick it for the evening.

"Bahamas?" Lisa shrieked and fell down onto the couch when I told her the plans for the evening.

"Yep." I was already on my second glass of Hennessey Black. "Hop a boat over to the main island where one of your husband's private jets would fly them to Nassau for dinner and then back home." I fed Lisa the itinerary. I was

Calm Sparkle

a bit ticked-off that Alex would have the nerve to take my fiancée' on a date, let alone out of the country, but after Sparkle and I had the tantric experience, I knew I had nothing to worry about. She would come home to me, and once we were married, she would cut off all communication with Alex. That night, I was going to finish off the last of my stash and say goodbye to drugs forever. I was ready to start my life as a responsible husband to Sparkle and bonus father to Andre. But first, I wanted one more night of fun.

I had enough weed for two more joints. I rolled them and gave one to Lisa who had just finished a double shot of tequila.

"No worries my friend," I said as I handed her the blunt. "Alex will be back home to you tonight, and Sparkle will be back in my arms by 11."

"How can you be so calm about this?" she inhaled her first puff and held it like a pro.

"Remember when you let me keep practicing tantric on you back in college?" She nodded as she exhaled slowly and leaned back into the couch, allowing the hemp to travel through her blood stream. She asked for another drink to chase the smoke. I mixed the tequila with pineapple juice on the rocks and told her to sip it.

I puffed my hand-rolled cigarette as Lisa burst into laughter. "That shit was so funny the first couple of times!" she spat out in a fit of giggles. "You trying to talk like you were hypnotizing me. 'Lay still and don't move.'" She mocked my amateurish attempts at the tantric from our explorative years. I laughed along with her. It had to be a sight to behold back then.

"But, damn, D," she inhaled deeply on the lit rolled grass between her fingers and threw her head back before releasing the smoke back into the room through her nose. "When you finally did get it right, that was some pure ecstasy. Best orgasm ever."

"Yep." I agreed with her. I began to chop my last four lines of the white lady on my glass coffee table while holding the joint in my mouth and allowing it's scent to fill the air. "That tantric is some pretty dope shit. But you know, practice makes perfect, right?" Lisa nodded in agreement. "Well, after all these years, I've trained my body to cum on command." Lisa's eyes widened in disbelief.

"What?"

"Yep." I sucked up a line of coke through my right nostril and then took a hit of my joint. "I have learned complete control of my body right down to taming my sexual instincts. Sparkle isn't going to leave me—especially not for your husband."

"Well dayum," was all Lisa could say. Then she quickly followed up with, "Can you teach that to me?"

I laughed. "Lisa, you don't have enough self-control to keep a lie going, let alone complete harmony of your body!" I snorted up the second line of coke in my left nostril.

"Fuck you, Donnie!" she kneeled down and took my third and fourth line, clearing the table.

"Damn, Lisa! That was my last bit of coke!"

"So! Buy some more!" she quipped back.

"I'm not touching this stuff anymore. I'm clearing out my stash. Time to be marriage material and not a junkie doctor."

For the next hour, Lisa and I laughed it up and reminisced on the good times. High as kites, the both of us were without a care in the world. By 8 o'clock we were beyond ripe. The only thing left in my stash were two mollies and a sample of heroine. I'd never tried smack so I figured I would use it up to see what all of the hoopla was about.

"Here," I said to Lisa as I handed her the mollies. "Save these for a rainy day. I'm going to take this hit and see what all the hype is about before I give up drugs for good."

"Don't do that, D. I hear that shit is addictive. Sparkle will leave your ass if you spend up all of your millions on some crack."

"It's not crack. Crack is whack." We both rolled over in laughter at my Whitney Houston impersonation. It wasn't so much that it was funny, but we were high as all get out. I went into the bathroom and grabbed a syringe, a tie from my bedroom, and a spoon and candle from my kitchen—all the things that I had seen in an old Richard Pryor movie. I Googled how to shoot heroine and got the directions on what to do next.

Lisa went over to the corner, turned up the music and danced by herself to "Tootsie Roll." She said she didn't want to watch me take the first hit that was about to turn me into a toothless, homeless, broken-down drug fiend. I laughed, but she was serious. I prepared my arm at the injection site and followed the directions to a tee. I filled the syringe with a small amount of heroine the rock produced once melted down.

"Here goes nothing!" I raised the needle to Lisa in a celebratory toast of sorts. She rolled her eyes at me, turned her back, and kept dancing while cranking up the volume.

"Cotton candy, sweetie go! Let me see that tootsie roll!" blared from the speakers as I shot the needle into my vein and slowly pushed the forbidden liquid into my arm and forcing the foreign stream to mix with my native blood flow. The rush I felt was completely unexpected. It was like a burst of tingling euphoria. It started in my chest and radiated throughout my entire body. It was better than any orgasm or high that I had ever experienced.

I sat back in the chair and allowed the needle to fall to the floor and refused to care about the mess or the evidence that sat before me. I'd clean it up later. All I felt was a sense of total peace. I couldn't even tell if I was conscious. Lisa appeared to be dancing in slow motion. I no longer heard the music. Bliss took over my consciousness and I couldn't wipe the smile off my face. I focused on the burning candle that was still on the coffee table in front of me as scenes from my childhood began to play like a movie. "Hi mom," I mumbled to the candle. I saw my high school years playing in the candle flame movie before me. I was homecoming king. What a great night. College years. What fun. Lisa was so green to all the sexual lessons that I taught her. I laughed hysterically at seeing her dance on the pole for the first time. Med school. I'd fucked all my female professors and earned a 3.7 GPA. It was nothing to be proud of, but I was still a great physician nonetheless. Sparkle. I saw the night we first met at the karaoke bar. I saw Andre. I reached out to him, but my hand wouldn't move. The light of the candle was fading. It became dimmer. The bliss took over. Was I still breathing? I heard Lisa screaming my name. What was she so upset about? My eyes rolled up and I could see the clock hanging above my fireplace. 8:33. And then, blackness.

Alex

The yacht ride from Moonbow to Key West was picture perfect. We had cocktails and danced to go-go music the entire thirty-minute ride. From the boat dock in Key West, a chauffeured Rolls Royce shuttled us to airstrip where we boarded one of my jets. Sparkle was blown away by all of the amenities. I felt proud that I was able to impress her. By the time we landed in Nassau, I felt better and less possessive because of what I had seen earlier. Sparkle always had a way to brighten up my mood. We talked and played Gin Rummy on the flight over. I let her have her little platonic façade for the moment. Things would soon change. I noticed her engagement ring, but I didn't say anything about it. No point in that. A white town car picked us up from the airport and took us to our private beach location where a decorated gazebo awaited with candles and roses. A server stood at attention and held a bottle of champagne as if he'd been there all night just for us. Once seated and the drinks were poured, it was the moment that I had been waiting for. It was time for the truth to come out.

"Sparkle, you know how grateful I am for your friendship. We've known each other since we were kids.

Hell, I damn near raised you!"

She laughed, which was a good sign that she was relaxed and comfortable. "Alex, I appreciate all of this, but why did you bring me all the way to Nassau for what appears to be a romantic dinner. You're married. Need I remind you again that I am not, and will never be, your mistress. I never was one to share my belongings."

"I know, I know. You made that quite clear last year. I really just wanted to tell you what was up since seeing your boyfriend in his office."

"My *fiancé*," she corrected me while waving her left hand as if I needed proof.

"Yeah, whatever. But look, long story short, I don't have HIV. I tested negative three times."

Sparkle practically choked on her sip of champagne. "What do you mean?"

"Turns out that Lisa, my wife, faked the whole thing. We never had HIV. What I thought was a drug regime to keep HIV from growing into AIDS was just a bunch of over the counter vitamins that she would put into a pill box. The whole thing was a sham. The marriage was a lie."

"Wow," was all that came from her lips as a look of disbelief rested on her face. "That is bat shit crazy, Al."

"Tell me about it. I mean, I always knew that she was a bit insecure about our age difference. She always worried about some younger chick sidelining her, but damn!"

"Well, she shouldn't be concerned over the age difference. It's the fact that she got you on a technicality that should have her worried."

The waiter delivered our main course as we finished up the appetizers. "Well, none of that matters now," I continued once we were alone again. "I put her out the house and we are filing for legal separation until we can work out the divorce terms."

"Are you serious, Alex?"

"Hell yeah! She went too far, Sparkle. Just too damn far." I looked across the table at her, and she had barely touched her food as she watched me intently as I talked. I reached out my hand to cover hers. "Baby, this means that we can finally right all of our wrongs, and we can now be together. The way it's supposed to be." I watched her facial expression change from sympathy to curiosity as the gravity of what I'd just said began to sink in. I walked around to her side of the table and kneeled down next to her. "Sweetie, did you hear me? We can finally be together—me, you, Andre, Nicole, Jr.—the way it was meant to be from day one before we let life get in the way and screw up our destiny."

"Life, Alex? Go back and have a seat, hun. Let's talk about this for a minute." I did as she asked and resumed my place at the table. "Alex, life didn't get in the way of our destiny. Your dick did. You wanted to explore your options. You felt you were too young to be tied down. Remember? And then you pushed me away after your football accident. You wouldn't talk to me for years—YEARS, Alex. Life didn't get in the way. You did."

"Sweetie, we were just kids. You were the one who up and got married after college." I knew I sounded childish, but us not being together wasn't all my fault. Sparkle played a role in that as well.

"True enough. I did indeed. However, I wasn't going to sit around and wait for you. I had to go on with my life. That's neither here nor there. Let's fast forward to when we first reconnected. We were both still legally married. We both committed adultery. I think that is strike two for us."

"Strike two? What are you talking about, woman?" She ignored me and continued.

"But then, after I got my divorce, you asked me to be your mistress. *Me!* You wanted me to be the mistress. For me that showed that you had no respect for me other than someone that you wanted to screw. You obviously had no respect for your marriage since you were still trying to get into my pants, and God knows who's else's. Alex, if we were to run off into the sunset together, I would never be able to trust you because I know firsthand that you're a cheater."

I couldn't believe what I was hearing. It wasn't at all how it played out in my head. I guess she saw the hurt on my face because it was her turn to reach out and place her hand on top of mine. Her voice was gentle when she spoke.

"Look, Alex, I'm not pretending to be the virgin Mary in all of this. I played my part as well. But I'm trying to grow from my mistakes. We had a nice run romantically, but that phase of our relationship is over. Let's just be grateful that we are able to remain very good friends. I'll always be here for you in that capacity."

"I understand" was my response. Damn. Was I too late? The waiter brought our desserts and took away our dinner plates, of which neither of us had eaten enough. Sparkle turned toward the ocean and took a deep inhale as if trying to breathe it all in. She closed her eyes and a faint smile invaded her lips. I heard her say, "Donnie?" as if she was calling out to him. She opened her eyes and looked around.

"Do you smell that? Is that you?" She sniffed deeply again. "Smells like Donnie is here."

"You really do love him, huh?"

She smiled so genuinely that it broke my heart. She didn't have to answer. Her body said it all. "What time is it?" she asked.

I glanced at my watch and replied, "8:33."

Lisa

"Oh shit! Don! DONNIE! WAKE UP GOT DAMMIT!" I shook him, slapped his face, pulled his eyelids open, and all he did was slump down even further until he was a lifeless body on the floor. I tried to find a pulse and there was nothing. "SHIIIIT!" I placed my head on his chest to listen for a heartbeat. I couldn't hear anything and he wasn't breathing. I broke out into a sweat as panic consumed me. If I called 911, Alex would want to know why I was there. He may even accuse me of being irresponsible. I was already guilty of tampering with medical information. And how would I explain all the drugs? I had to get out of there.

While grabbing my things and trying to remove any trace that I was there, I had an epiphany. Marvin, my son, was the only child of an only child of a multi-millionaire. Maybe it was time to cash in on that. I thought if there was some way to prove that Don knew about Marvin, which he didn't. It was a longshot, but I was going for it.

I snuck out to the car, careful not to be seen, and grabbed my purse. Going through my wallet, I took out Marvin's third grade picture. It was old and a little tattered, but it served its purpose. On the back, which was still blank after all of those years, I wrote, "Marvin Blakely Adonis," and placed it on his dresser mirror—someplace it would be sure to be seen by whomever came to collect his belongings. Hopefully, it would be his mother. Moms always get nosey. It was all I had on me, but in a couple of weeks, I would call Adonis Jr, Don's father, to express my shock and condolences, and then introduce myself as the mourning baby mama. Surely, they would welcome me and Marvin with open arms—and wallets. Who needed Alex after all? I resumed cleaning up evidence that Don wasn't alone in his indulgence party by wiping off my glass, and placing it in the dishwasher. I flushed the remaining roach of my blunt and fixed the couch pillows. It was as if I was never there. I used the jacket of my sweat suit to wipe off the door knobs and left the house, heading straight out of Moonbow and back home to Whitfield. I made a quick stop to grab my things from the hotel room, and I was highway bound. Rest in peace, Donnie. It's been real. My future was set.

Sparkle

I thought it was odd that Don didn't respond to any of my texts or answer my calls, but I brushed it off and assumed that he was just tired. When he didn't show up the following morning for our trip to Disney, I began to worry.

Calm Sparkle

He was supposed to meet us at 6:30 for an 8 am flight. It was 6:45 and there was no sign of him. His phone went straight to voicemail and I hadn't received a text from him since the previous afternoon.

"Andre! Sweetie! Come on, let's go!"

"Is Mr. Donnie here?" he yelled out from his room as he trotted towards me.

"No, not yet. Let's go get him and wake him up," I said in attempt to remain calm. I had a sick feeling in my stomach, and my heart felt an ache that wouldn't go away. "Lord," I prayed silently, "please let Don be alright. Please, God." Just as we were heading out the door, my phone rang. "Donnie?"

"Sparkle, it's Mrs. Adonis." I stopped in my tracks. It was Donnie's mother. She and I hadn't met in person but we would chat from time to time, and Donnie and I would facetime with her on occasion. She lived in Hampton, so for her to call me could only mean bad news. "Sparkle," she repeated and started to sob. Tears automatically began streaming down my face.

"No," I whispered into the phone, "don't you tell me anything bad about Donnie. Don't do it, Mrs. A, please, please," I pleaded. I leaned against the door for support for what I knew from the sound of her voice would soon come. "No, Mrs. A, please."

I heard sobs on the other end of the phone and tussling. Then Mr. Adonis got on the phone. "Sparkle, honey, Donnie's gone."

"Nooooooo!" I slid down to the ground and the phone slipped away from my hands. My heart was ripped from my body and my eyes produced their own Niagara Falls. "NOOOOOO!" I screamed to the heavens. "God! Nooooo! Whyyy?" I couldn't control the emotions that flooded through me.

Andre, not knowing what was wrong, ran over and clung to me and repeatedly asked, "Mommy! Mommy! What's wrong? Mommy! Don't cry!" Andre began to cry at the sight of seeing his mother so torn, and I was too broken to comfort him. All I could do was hold him as tight as I could and rock him in my arms as I did when he was a baby.

"Why, Lord?" The pain was too great to bear. It paralyzed me. I couldn't talk. I could barely breathe between the sobbing. I finally managed to whisper my beloved's name, "Donnie…why did you leave me?"

Chapter Ten
Better to Have Loved

Sparkle

Three months passed since Donnie's death. I kept telling myself, "It was better to have loved and lost than to never have loved at all," but I couldn't lie; it was hard. I mean—hard to even pull myself out of bed each day. If it weren't for Andre, I would lay in the bed all day until my sun shined again. I handed over my coaching clients to one of my colleagues and I assumed a behind the scenes position. I only hosted group sessions for the bereaved.

It was all that I could push myself to do because everything still reminded me of Don. I was still so very angry with him for taking his own life. The coroner said it was suicide. They found lots of drugs in his system. So much so that his death had to be intentional. His parents blamed me, and when they found out that I had been in the Bahamas with an ex-boyfriend the night that Donnie died, they wanted nothing to do with me. They didn't even tell me where the funeral services were, or where he was buried. I had no closure. I had no answers. I had no Donnie. Andre was all that I had and I poured every waking moment into my precious little boy.

Nights were the hardest, and the loneliest. I couldn't bring myself to change the pillow case that Donnie slept on the night we made love—the night before he died. His scent was long gone, but I still clung to it and I added to its tearstain collection each and every night.

However, one day I awoke feeling a little bit lighter. It was a Saturday, and it was the day that Andre and I were moving to Key West. I had been collaborating with some other coaches and we'd joined forces to open a second Sparkle Moonbow's Coaching Facility. It would be full life coaching community complete with certification classes as well as CEU credits. Basically, a college campus for life coaches that would serve the surrounding community in various ways. It kept me out of the spotlight of dealing one-on-one with clients, and kept my focus on cultivating new coaches. I felt excited about the change, and I was ready.

Corey expanded his karaoke bar and took over the city's old skating rink where Soldier Boy and I had our rendezvous. Last I checked, he was doing well and seemed to be happy with his love of the week.

And Alex and Lisa? Alex and I still talked from time to time. He remained respectful of my wishes to keep things platonic. He said he would wait for me as long as it took. I told him to go find another woman to stalk and we both laughed. Alex did move forward with the divorce. He was tired of fighting with Lisa, so he agreed to shared custody of Jr and to pay Lisa $8 grand each month in alimony and child support. It wouldn't be long before the papers were finalized. And then, my phone rang.

"Heeeey, Al!"

"Hey you! You ready for the big move?"

"Ohhh yes, I can't get out of here fast enough. I need some new scenery, ya know?"

"Yeah, sweetie. I can't even imagine what you've had to go through."

"Well, such is life, right? How is Lisa? What shenanigans is she up to now?"

"I don't know. She packed her shit, and she and Marvin went to the Hamptons yesterday. Said she would be gone for a couple of weeks. Wanted to spend some quality time with Marvin. When I talked to Marvin, he said something about meeting his real bio dad. I didn't have the energy to entertain whatever it is that Lisa is up to. I just wished him blessings and told them to have a good trip."

Insert comfortable silence. We did that a lot. When he mentioned the Hamptons, I immediately thought of Don since that's where he was from. It was time to change the subject, "Sooooo, guess what?"

"Hmmmm, you realize in the midst of all of this drama that you really are still truly, madly, deeply in love with me?" he joked in response. Wait! Was he joking??

"No, silly! Well, you know I'll always have love for you. You're my boo! But no, that is not what I want to tell you."

"Ok, what?"

"I'm pregnant"

"Whoa! What? Pregnant?"

"Yep. Pregnant. And yes! It is Don's! God left me a little ray of sunshine after all."

"Wow, babe! I can't say that I'm happy because it's not *my* baby. But you are a great mom and I'm happy for you."

"Thank you, Alex. That means a lot. It really does. In fact, you're the first person that I've told."

"Really? So, you *do* love me? I knew it!"

"Soo silly, boy! Whatever!"

"Seriously though, babe, I'm happy for you. If there is anything you need, don't hesitate to ask."

"Thank you, hun. I appreciate you and your friendship." I made sure to put emphasis on friendship. "Alex, seriously, thank you, but now it's time for Andre and I to hit the road and head south."

"Are you absolutely sure you want to do this?" he asked for the millionth time.

I laughed, "Yes! Alex, I am sure! Just don't forget to check on Kat from time to time when you are in town."

"Now, *that* you don't have to worry your pretty little head about. Who knows? Maybe you'll see my U-Haul pulling up in the house right next to yours one day." I wasn't

Calm Sparkle

sure if he was joking or not, but I laughed nonetheless. "Alright, well take care sweetie. Stay in touch."
"Always."

~~The End~~
New Beginnings.

Calm Sparkle Discussion Questions:
Chapters 9 & 10

1. Did the book end the way you thought?
2. Was any of the story predictable? If so which parts?
3. Which parts of the book did you find to be the most shocking?
4. What was your favorite part overall?
5. What was your least favorite part?
6. Who is your favorite character and more?
7. If there is a sequel, who would you like to read more about?
8. Don and Sparkle had a tantric night. Have you ever indulged in the tantra? Do you believe an "on demand" orgasm is possible?
9. We've reached the end of the book, are you Team Lisa or Team Sparkle?
10. Team Alex or Team Don?

About the Author

Coach Kimberly D. L. Pittman is a Certified Christian Life Coach specializing in relationships and date coaching. Her target audience is divorcee's that are striving to leap into the next chapter of their lives. She chose this particular niche' based on experiences within her own personal life as well as those around her.

Prior to turning her focus solely on coaching, Kim successfully owned and operated KDLP Enterprises. KDLP Enterprises is a business consulting firm which started in 2002 as a pro-bono service to local entrepreneurs in the Duval County area. Through her services with business consulting and training, many professional relationships were formed and cultivated as well as personal friendships. It is through these relationships that Kim was able to recognize the need within herself (and others that were "saving the world") to receive as much as is given. And thus, began the making of Kim, the Life Coach.

Coach Kim began coaching privately in 2010 for a group of hand selected individuals across the state of Florida. Looking to expand her brand, Coach Kim became certified in 2016 through The League of Visionary

Excellence under the direct supervision of internationally known, highly respected, Coach D. Nicole Williams CPCLCT. With this new accolade, Coach Kim diligently began growing her private selection of clientele. She currently coaches women nationally via teleconferences and emails from Florida to Minnesota to Nevada and beyond.

With 2017 came a new year and a new directive. "For each blessing, be a blessing." With this new impartation upon her heart, Coach Kim prepares to broaden her audience from private clients to helping the masses. Her new community-focused awareness led her to Coach D. Nicole once again where she was awarded the opportunity to partner with The League of Visionary Excellence as co-director. Joining forces with The L.O.V.E. will allow the privilege of coaching a wider sector of women within group settings. Coach Kim now offers a variety of confidence building, coaching, virtual classes as well as community-based, in-person training group sessions. To receive updates on Coach Kim's training schedule, visit her website at www.coachkim.net.

Note from the author:

Thank you so much for your outpouring of support! As a token of my appreciation, here is a sneak peek into the upcoming sequel, "Calm Sparkle II: Mama Issues". This is taken directly from my laptop without any polishing or editing. I present to you raw and uncut:

Calm Sparkle II *Mama Issues*

Enjoy!
-Kimberly D.L. Pittman

Prelude

As cliché as it may sound, the gray skies and consistent drizzle of rain seemed fitting for today. I sat in the back seat of my parents Coupe DeVille as we rode from my grandmother's gravesite. I looked down at my mud covered red patent leather mary janes that protected the dove white bobby socks with the ruffle lace trim. My father sat on the passenger side in the front staring out the window watching the city scenery as my mother drove us towards home. She seemed completely unbothered by the event that seemed to rip my and daddy's souls into pieces.

Mom turned down the radio and smacked my daddy on the back of the head in what seemed to be all in one swift motion. Daddy's head jerked forward then back making contact with the rolled up window and leaving a greasy smudge where his forehead kissed the glass.
Mom…shifting from unbothered to annoyed began ranting,

"Simon. I know got dern well you ain't over there crying!! Sniffling like a punk ass, Man up dammit!"

Daddy didn't move. He didn't speak. He didn't respond or show any acknowledgment towards her. Instead, he inhaled deeply and wiped away the tear that rested on his cheek. But he never took his eyes off the passing scenery in the window. Mama seemed more aggravated with his silence and continued her belittling.

"Bad enough you had to embarrass me at the service. Throwing yourself on your mama's casket like that. What

the hell is wrong with you?? You're so damn weak! I
don't know why I even married you. Crying and carrying
on like a bitch. Your damn sister had to come hold you
like the tittie fed baby you are. How the hell a grown man
gonna cry like that all up in church. Makes no damn sense
with yo' weak ass. Acting like you ain't never seen nobody
die before"

I couldn't take it any longer. I loved my daddy more than
almost anything. The only thing I loved more than him
was my granny. His momma. The queen that we just saw
buried. My little hands were balled into fists on the seat at
my sides and I did something that I knew I should never
dare to do ... I spoke when I wasn't spoken to.

"His momma died! Can't you understand that!? Do you
want me to care about you when YOU die??"

Mama adjusted the rear view mirror to get a good look at
me. Her glare said it all. I was going to get the switch
when we got home. But I didn't care. My granny's honor
was worth every forthcoming lick. Surprisingly , instead of
scolding me, mama seemed amused. She snorted a laugh
then returned the verbal abuse to my dad.

"Ha! Look at that, Simon, you even got your 10 year old
little girl taking up for you. That's how weak and pathetic
you are as a man." She sucked her teeth to emphasize her
disgust. We pulled into the driveway that leads up to our
ranch style, red brick home sprawled on two acres of land
and decorated with a white picket fence. I didn't dare
move until told to do so. Especially after that momentary
show of bravery against my mother. Mama put car in

'park', turned off the engine and turned around in her seat to fully face me.

"Lil girl , I'm going to let that little remark slide on account of I know you love your granny and you're not yourself right now. But don't you ever get in your head to speak to me that way again. When we get in the house, you go straight to your room and don't you dare come out until time for school tomorrow morning, otherwise, I might forget that I gave you a pass."

"Yes ma'am" I mumbled. I was hungry, I was grief stricken and I was told that I better not shed a tear. Death is a part of life and if I really wanted to cry then I would be given something to cry about. I looked over at daddy who still sat motionless in that passenger side front seat. Mom got out of the car and "Naomi walked" her way up to the front door and let herself in. Once she was out of sight, I spoke to him.

"Daddy ….. are you going to be okay?"

For the first time since we got in the car, he moved his eyes away from the window and turned to look at me. He reached for my hand and I scooted up in the seat so that my fingertips could touch his.

"Yes, lovebug. I'll be just fine. And so will you. "He raised my tiny hand to his face and pecked my fingertips. We got out of the car. I went to my room as instructed. If only I had known that would be the last time that I would ever see my father…

Chapter One The Great Escape

July 4th. My Independence Day in more ways than one. It is my 18th birthday and I can finally get out of my mama's house. The only happy memories I have from this house are from when my daddy was here. The thought of him used to fill my heart with what little I knew about joy. Now as I think of him, an all encompassing anger consumes every fiber of my being. He left me with this woman that calls herself my mother. If a mother is a person that births you for the purpose of having a free slavehand then she deserves the Mother of The Century Award.

I can hear her footsteps coming towards my room and I quickly grab my generic brand, oversized headphones and cover my ears. Pretending to be rocking out to noise drowning music, I bop my head in time to the imaginary beat as she flings open my bedroom door almost knocking a doorknob sized hole into the wall as it slams against the plaster. I have been ignoring her screeches demanding that I come to her in the kitchen for the past five minutes and now she was here to impart her fury. I pretended not to notice and kept dancing around the room with my back to her in hopes of avoiding the inevitable blow to the back of my head. No such luck, the corner of her three inch wedge sandal managed to catch the back of my skull right below the band of the earphones. The brunt of the hit pushed my head forward and knocked me off balance causing me to fall face forward on my bed. Before I could get my bearings, I heard the crack of the whip and felt the sting of leather slicing into the skin on the back of my thighs. Two more lashes dug into my back. My plain white tee was defenseless as the thin material tried it's best to protect my flesh. The attack stopped as suddenly as it started. I curled into the fetal position and mentally braced myself for another round of lashings, instead I heard her hobbling in the one shoe on, one shoe off fashion over to where her first shoe landed after knocking the sense out of me. "Sit up!" she barked. "Yes ma'am." I spoke lightly as I immediately obeyed and assumed the position I knew she wanted. Sitting straight up on the edge of my bed, proper posture, feet together, head bowed and hands folded neatly on my lap. This is the way that she taught me.

"Take those headphones off!"

"Yes ma'am." Keeping my eyes down, I used my right hand to swiftly remove the headsets.

She paused for a minute but I could feel her next to me looking through my open suitcases that sat on the floor. I had already packed my closet and was in the middle of emptying my dresser drawers when she started yelling for me to come to her in the kitchen. I knew that ignoring her would have consequences, but I didn't care. I just needed to make it out of the house on my own two feet before the end of the day. If she put me in the hospital again, I would be stuck here at least another thirty days. I just need to stay strong a little longer.

"So you call yourself leaving today?" Her voice grew closer and then I could feel her standing directly in front of me.

"Yes ma'am." I spoke barely above a whisper. I could not take the risk of pushing her beyond her current mood. The last time I angered her she attacked me from behind with the mop handle. Once I fell to the ground, she pulled me by my hair and dragged me into the bathroom where she took a razor blade and sliced my wrists. I passed out from the sight of the gushing blood. I thought my life had finally come to an end. I was tired of living and death was welcomed. Instead, I awoke in a hospital. Mama sat next to my bed holding hand and appearing to be the perfect picture of a heartbroken mother. As my eyes fluttered open, I could see the nurse or doctor or whomever it was standing over me and shining a light into my eyes to check for pupil dilation. She had me Baker Acted that day. Telling the EMR team that I tried to kill myself. I couldn't risk that happening again. Not today.

"Ohhhh. That's right." She said as if she was just remembering something. "You turned 18 today." I could hear take a few steps back. I am sure she is probably in the mirror now to readjust her clothes and hair.

"Yes, ma'am." I answered.

"Well whoopty-doo!" She came back towards me, cupping my chin with her hand and jolting my head to meet her at eye level, she shoved her face directly in front of mine. She was so close I could feel her breath as she spoke. My chameleon-hazel eyes locked with her ice blues and she said "I'm glad you're leaving. But you ain't taking shit out of my house. You leave this place the same way you came into this world, butt ass naked with not even a pot to piss in." She shoved my face backwards and my neck jerked painfully, but I quickly recovered and assumed the bowed head position. I can hear her zipping my suitcases closed and she takes them with her as she exits the room. I sit silently holding my breath, listening to see if she would return. As soon I hear her banging dishes again in the kitchen and chatting on the phone with one of her friends. I ease up off the bed and softly close my bedroom door. Heading straight to my dresser, I open the bottom left drawer. Thankful that she hasn't touched anything in there, I reach below all of the folded undergarments and find my pre-paid cell phone. Mama has no idea that I have it. My best friend, Tiffany, gave it to me for Christmas so that we could text at night and I could keep up with the drama of my classmates at school. It was a great escape from my life in this palatial dungeon. I quickly send Tiff a text asking how much longer before she would be ready to pick me up. She responds right away that she is twenty minutes away. Relieved that things were still on schedule, I turn and face the mirror. My wild, sandy brown, curly hair and golden-wheat colored skin is a far contrast from my mother's vibrant red hair and ivory white complexion. Maybe this is why she hates me so much.

Watching the hands on the clock felt like watching a pot waiting for it to boil. I took one last glance around the room. Mama said that I couldn't take anything, but I grabbed a couple pair of clean underwear, my cell phone and the eight year old program from my grandmother's funeral. Stuffing the items in my purse, I checked the clock one last time. Tiffany should be here any minute now. I thought it only appropriate to tell my mother 'goodbye'. It was my way of gaining control of my life. I headed to the kitchen where she was still gabbing away on the phone and stood silently in the doorway awaiting her permission to enter the room as I had done so many times before. She waved me into the room as she asked the caller on the other end to hold on.

"I thought I told you not to take anything from my house. Leave those clothes here. I'll let you keep the flip flops and that cheap ass bag you call a purse." I was confused. Does she really want me to walk out of here naked? As if reading my mind, she yells "You heard me! Take off those clothes and get out of my house!" She turned her attention back to the telephone and the skillet she was tending to on the stove. I did as asked and removed my tee shirt and shorts. Folding them neatly, I placed them on the table next to a pile of mail. Normally I don't pay attention to such things but an envelope on the top was addressed to me. I glanced up and mama was busy chopping up onions into the skillet while holding the phone with her ear pinned against her shoulder. I quickly grabbed the letter and stuffed it into my purse. I made my way towards the front door. Towards freedom. Mama's voice called out from behind me.

"I said leave my house the same way you came into this world! I mean butt ass naked! You lucky I let you keep your flip-flops!" I stop dead in my tracks and take off my panties and bra. Leaving them in a heap on the floor in front of the door, I walk out with my head up. All of my life she made me bow my head in her presence. I was never allowed to look at the world in front or around me. If she is making me re-enter the world butt ass naked then with this rebirth, I am facing the world head on. Eyes wide open and no looking back. I walked to the edge of the driveway in nothing but my flip flops and a purse over my shoulder just as Tiffany's car was turning into the driveway. She put the car in park and stood with her arm draped over the driver's side door.

"Damn, boo! What the hell your mama done did this time?!?!?" Tiffany was a straight A student but she insisted on breaking every grammar rule ever written as her way of self-expression.

"You know how she is, Tee." I started making my way to the passenger side.

"Ahh hell naw, Bee!! You ain't about to get your vajayjay juice all over the seat of my car! Where yo damn clothes at, chica?"

Just then mama appeared through the front door with her rifle and began yelling, "You got five seconds to get your sorry ass off my property!!" She cocks the gun and aims it in our direction as she starts counting backwards from five.

"Get in!! Get IN!!" Tiffany screams. She slid into driving position slamming the car door closed. I dive into what is now literally the shot-gun seat as she peels backwards out of the driveway. My left flip-flop was sacrificed in the process but there was no way I was going back for it. As Tiffany punches the gas pedal and floors it, we lurch forward and her little Ford Escape earned it's name by getting us safely out of range and rocketing down the street just as mama fires a shot blowing the brick dome shaped mailbox to pieces.

About a mile down the road, Tiffany pulls over. She's

crying and trembling so I know she needs a moment to calm down. I reached into my purse to put on the clean undies that I had previously stashed. "What the hell was that??" she yelled at me as if I were the one that pulled a gun and aimed it at us. I fished around her back seat, found her gym bag and took the liberty of wearing her tee and shorts that she kept for the day she actually decides to use her annual gym membership. "That's just mama." I finally answered when I saw that she was intently looking for me to make sense of what happened.

"That's just mama??!?!" She mimicked. I don't like being mimicked. She knew this.

Unable to hide my irritability, I gave her the blank stare. "Look, do you want me to drive or what?"

She looked at me in disbelief. "How can you sit over there so calm?? We just got shot at!!"

Her words registered with me, but I just don't understand why she is so upset. What mama did back there was nothing compared to what I've endured over the last 8 years. I needed Tiff to get it together and get this car moving as far away from Robeson County, North Carolina as possible.

Chapter Two: Eleven Eleven
MARVIN

I lay in my bed thinking of how much my life changed within a thirty day time frame. Just a few short weeks ago, I was a new college grad with a bachelors in education from Florida A & M. My summer plans were to meet up with my frat brothers in Jamaica and rent a house for the summer months to wild out before we all did the grown up thing and got jobs. However, my mom had an abrupt change of plans. Out of the blue, seemingly anyways, she tells me that my paternal grandparents want to meet me. She dropped this pod of news as casually as if she were announcing that she purchased a new wig. I'm 24. I was raised my entire life believing that I didn't have any paternal relatives. My mom's first husband, whom I always believed to be my father, was raised in the foster care system. We are the only family he has to my knowledge. Then "bam!", mom tells me that I have grandparents.

I roll over and glance at the clock, 11:11 pm. Only six hours until I leave and head back to Florida. I've been in VA for three days now. Mom seems to love it here, but I just don't think this place is cut out for me. My so called grandparents seem nice and all, but I can tell they are as skeptic of my biological connection to them as I am. I can find no resemblance of myself to them or their dead son that mom recently reveals to me as my father. She says we have to look beyond the drastic complexion difference and see the similarity in the features. I reach over and grab my ipad to google "Dr. Donnie Adonis". Apparently this is my bio dad's name and this is the ritual that I assume every night since the day I found out about him. I summon up images on Google from the ipad then grab my cell phone, turn the camera on selfie mode and I study the features as mom instructed. My smooth dark ebony skin and full lips are a direct inherited trait from my maternal grandmother and her father before her. I have my mother's nose and dimples. I did always wonder where I got my soft curly hair and hazel green eyes. Odd traits for such a dark skinned, black man from Florida raised by his Nigerian grandparents. Turning my direction to the smiling image of Dr. Adonis, I see a very fair skinned man. So light that he appears to be interracial. His hair is cut low to the scalp so I can't tell if it has a curl pattern. His eyes are dark brown with long lashes like his mother's. He looks nothing like me and I look nothing like him. We don't even look to be distant cousins, let alone father and son.

I'm not sure what game my mother is playing and up until we arrived in VA, I wasn't sure as to why she is dragging me down this rabbit hole. Upon first meeting, It is very obvious the Adonis' are loaded. Not just average new money, millionaire loaded like mom's last husband, Alex. No, this family is on another level of wealth. That generational shit. So much so that my new found "grandfather" is rumored to be in negotiations to buy out a portion of Hilton Head, South Carolina to build his 215th resort. Learning this tidbit of information made playing along with mom a bit more entertaining.

Satisfied that there is no way in hell that the man smiling back at me could be my dad in way, shape of form, I clicked on the search result from Moonbow Times obituary section.

Dr. Donnie Adonis, 37, died at 8:33 pm on May 19, 2017 due to sudden cardiac arrest

> *Dr. Adonis was born on November 5, 1980 in Hampton, VA and made Moonbow, FL his home upon completion of his medical residency at Moonbow Regional Hospital. He was a well-respected youth volunteer with Big Brothers Big Sisters of America, an active Morehouse alum and President of Moonbow's 100 Black Men - Moonbow Chapter.*
>
> *He is survived by his mother and father, Donnie and Alexis Adonis; paternal grandparents Arsia and Donnie Adonis Sr; maternal grandparents Rosie and Herman Maxwell and numerous aunts, uncles and cousins....*

I close out the screen without reading any further. No point in continuing. I know the write up by heart. I've been reading it at least five times per day for the past three days since I first heard the Adonis name. I find it very odd that a man so young would pass away from a heart attack, especially a physician, but this is what all of the news outlets are showing.

I turn off the Ipad and decide to send my stepdad, Alex a text. "*Hey, Pops. Mom says we will be in going to Moonbow in the morning. Just thought you should know in case you're visiting Grams.*"

He quickly responded, "*Thx, son. Safe travels. Let me know if you need anything.*"

"Can I come home, Pops?" I don't know why asked, I already knew the answer. I guess in the midst of all of this

Calm Sparkle

paternal uncertainty, I just need some reassuring. Alex has no idea about Donnie Adonis. I will have to tell him in person.

"Of course! I'm divorcing your mama. Not you. You are still my son. You will always be my son. See you soon."

Alex and mom are in the process of divorcing, but he and I are still cool. I have nothing but respect for the man that helped raise me, paid my way through college and is holding a position for me to work by his side in his aviation leasing company. He never told me why he put mom out of the main house and filed for divorce but on the same token, he never speaks ill of her, at least not in my presence or my younger siblings. I respect him all the more for that. The clock blares 12:11. Damn! An hour has passed already? Let me take my ass to sleep. I have a long day ahead of me.

To be continued ...

Made in the USA
Columbia, SC
21 September 2023